THE COMPLETE ADVENTURES OF

ERIC TRENT

VOLUME 1

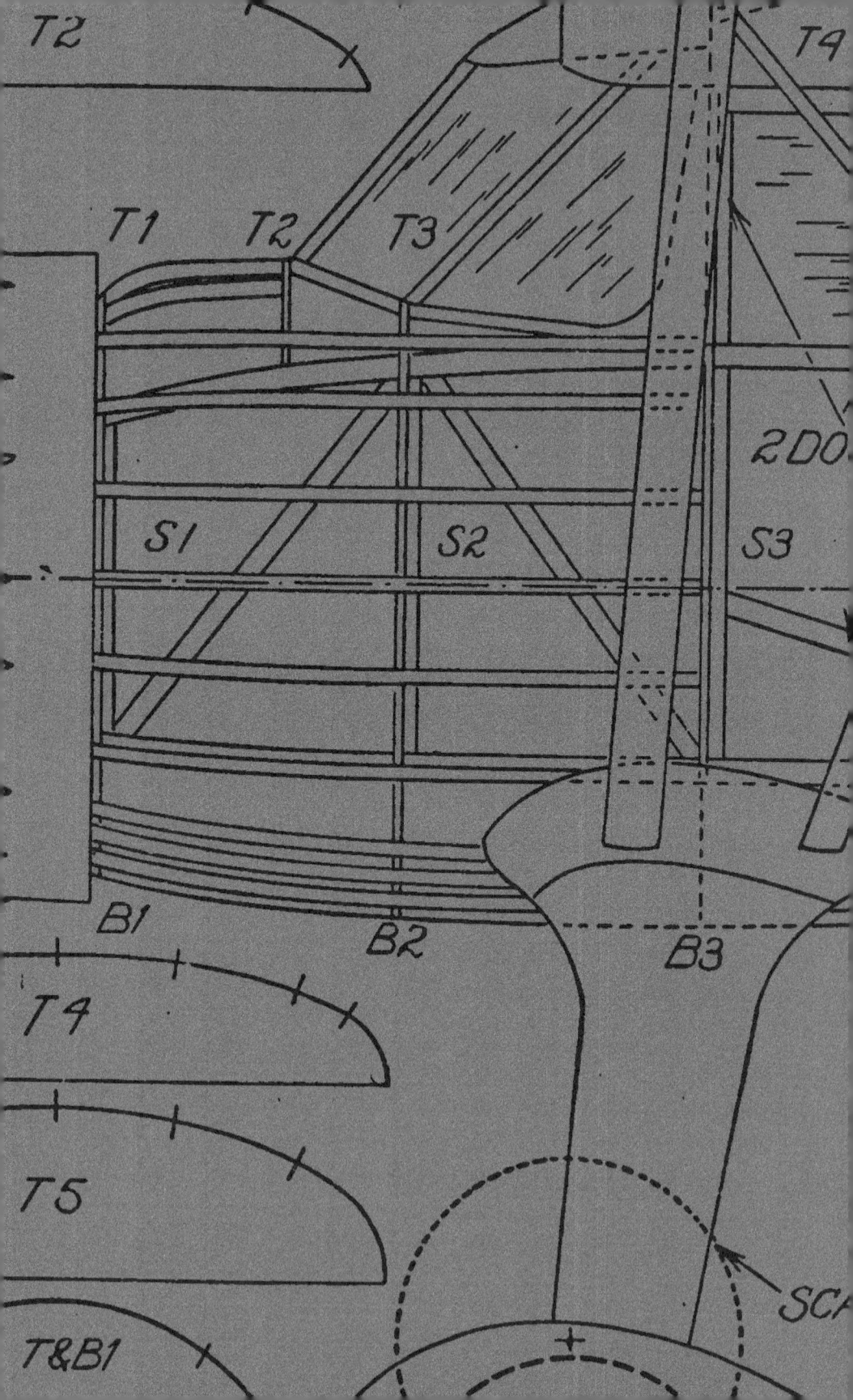

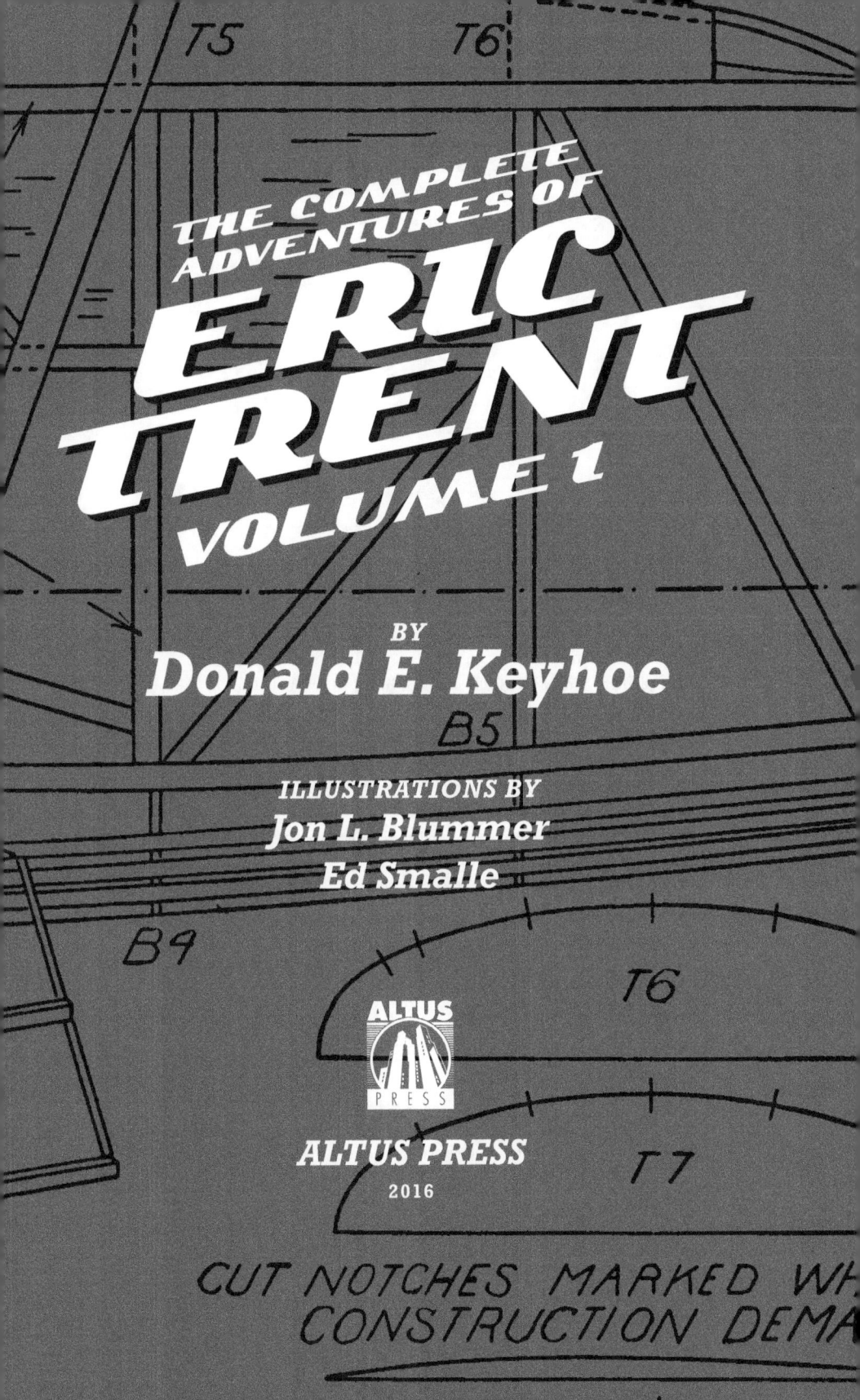

THE COMPLETE
ADVENTURES OF

ERIC TRENT

VOLUME 1

BY

Donald E. Keyhoe

ILLUSTRATIONS BY
Jon L. Blummer
Ed Smalle

ALTUS PRESS
2016

EDITED AND DESIGNED BY
Matthew Moring

PUBLISHING HISTORY

"Secret Flight Sixteen" originally appeared in the March 1940 issue of *Flying Aces* magazine (Vol. 34, No. 4).

"Death Flies Blind" originally appeared in the May 1940 issue of *Flying Aces* magazine (Vol. 35, No. 3).

"Junkers Juggernaut" originally appeared in the July 1940 issue of *Flying Aces* magazine (Vol. 35, No. 4).

"Swastika Scourge" originally appeared in the October 1940 issue of *Flying Aces* magazine (Vol. 36, No. 6).

"The Ace From Hell" originally appeared in the December 1940 issue of *Flying Aces* magazine (Vol. 37, No. 1).

"Television Tracers" originally appeared in the February 1941 issue of *Flying Aces* magazine (Vol. 37, No. 3).

THANKS TO

Louis Burklow, Everard P. Digges LaTouche, Ralph Laughlin and Chris Slembarski

Visit *altuspress.com* for more books like this.
Printed in the United States of America.

TABLE OF
Contents

I   SECRET FLIGHT SIXTEEN I

II   DEATH FLIES BLIND. 39

III   JUNKERS JUGGERNAUT 73

IV   SWASTIKA SCOURGE. 105

V   THE ACE FROM HELL. 137

VI   TELEVISION TRACERS 171

A LETTER FROM DONALD E. KEYHOE 204

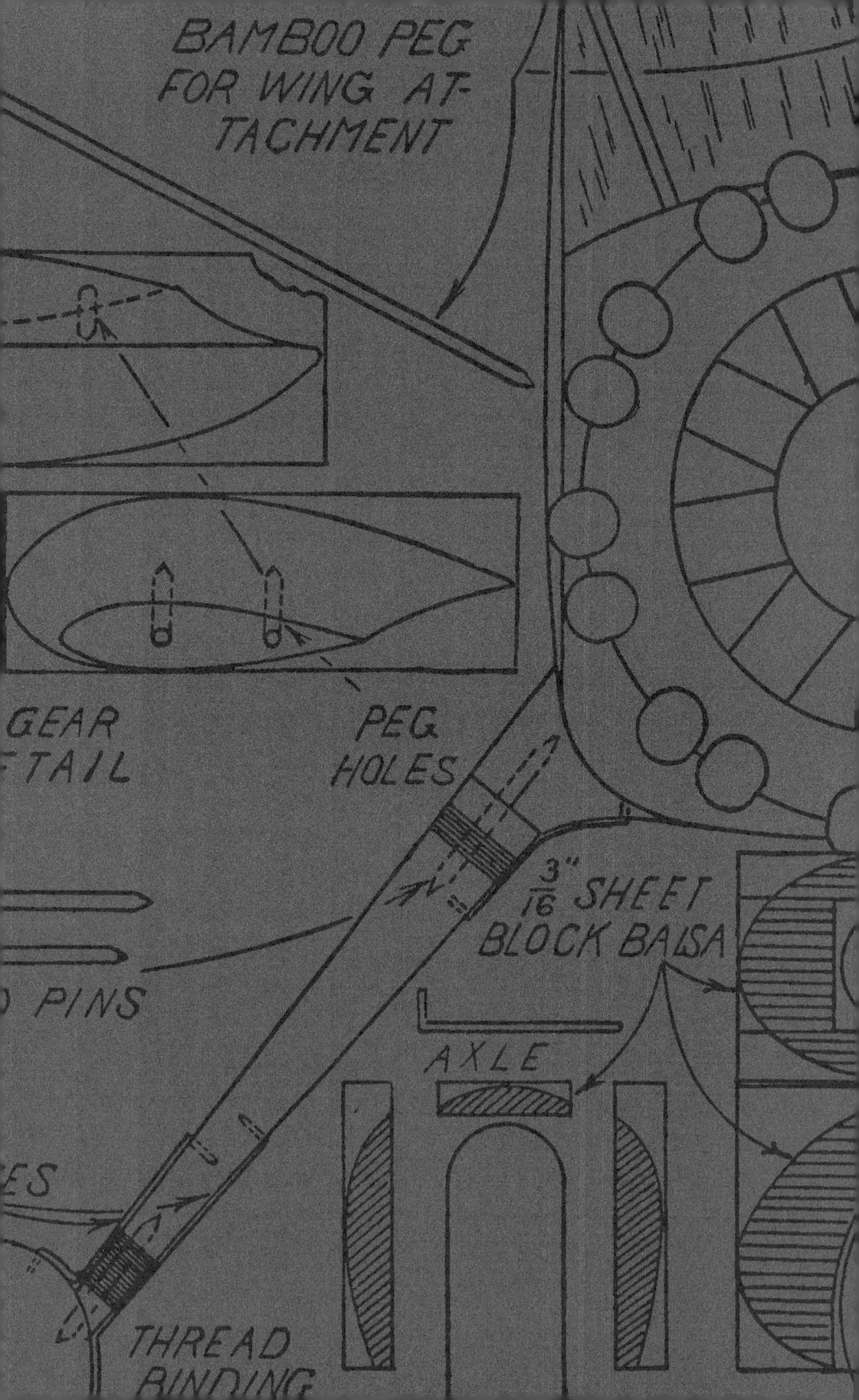

BAMBOO PEG
FOR WING AT-
TACHMENT

GEAR
TAIL

PEG
HOLES

PINS

$\frac{3}{16}"$ SHEET
BLOCK BALSA

AXLE

ES

THREAD
BINDING

Secret Flight Sixteen

CHAPTER I

Dutch Riddle

B *EYOND* the windows of the burgomaster's office, lights were starting to twinkle in the picturesque Netherlands city of Arnheim. The plump little Dutchman at the desk switched on a green-shaded lamp, then broke the seal of the confidential record which had just arrived by afternoon plane. On top he found a scrawled memorandum from the Amsterdam chief of police. It read:

Mynheer Voorst— Here, as requested, is our file on the American, Eric Trent. Take my advice and get him out of Arnheim before he turns your city upside down. Trent is a crazy adventurer, a modern D'Artagnan living by his wits—wits which unfortunately are entirely too sharp. He has been mixed up in a score of intrigues on the Continent, and it is a miracle the secret police haven't caught him. Don't try to trap him. He'll simply laugh at you. I know from experience.

Burgomaster Voorst looked out absently at the lights of a steamer beyond the pontoon bridge over the Rhine. After a moment he turned and pressed a button.

"Get the American, Trent," he told a uniformed police sergeant who answered. "And have some one bring the other man up to the anteroom."

The sergeant went out. Burgomaster Voorst bent over the confidential file, and with increasing amazement read:

February, 1937, Trent kidnapped two Gestapo agents who tried to arrest him near German border, later turned them loose in their underwear on Champs-Élysées, Paris, in broad daylight... April, reported in Singapore, with a small fortune in pearls, refused to pay duty, told British he found them in an oyster stew, collected five hundred pounds for false arrest.... Detained by Scotland Yard for masquerading as Guards officer, later privately released with apologies of Prime Minister, reasons unknown.... Reported executed in Manchukuo after scrape with Japanese.... Suspected in shooting of Greek blackmailer Nimopolis, no evidence... Secret rewards offered for his capture by

Nazis in Austria, Czechoslovakia, also by Spanish authorities, in last two years....January, 1939, broke the bank at Monte Carlo, purchased a flying boat with which he is said to have effected the mysterious Devil's Island escape of Jacques Gernay, later proved innocent of the murder for which he was sentenced....

BURGOMASTER VOORST raised befuddled eyes to the door as the sergeant reappeared with Trent. For a moment he stared, fascinated. He had expected to see a tense, wild-eyed Yankee, with recklessness written all over him. But this man might have been some polished European from the salons of Continental society. There was something reminiscent of the Riviera about him, a dashing, almost Latin darkness of hair and eyes, and white teeth under a close-clipped black mustache. With increasing bewilderment, the burgomaster noted that despite sixteen hours in a special detention-cell this incredible American was clean-shaven, his linen fresh, his clothes immaculately creased.

Trent returned the burgomaster's stare with a politely impudent grin.

"Come now, Burgomaster, you surely didn't expect me to be wearing horns?"

The burgomaster gulped.

"One moment, and I'll be at your service," said Trent. He reached inside his coat, handed some folded guilder-notes to the suddenly astonished sergeant. "Give this and my thanks to the detention-cell corporal for arranging the valet service and that excellent luncheon from the Cafe Grande."

The burgomaster's jaw dropped.

"Why wasn't this man searched?" he demanded furiously, in Dutch. "You know prisoners are not allowed money or special services."

"But I searched him myself!" moaned the sergeant. "I swear I emptied his pockets."

"May I cut in? I speak a little Dutch," Trent said pleasantly. "Don't blame him, Mynheer Burgomaster. It was a simple matter of palming a few bills—a little thing I once learned as a magician's assistant, before we came to a sudden parting."

"This is outrageous!" sputtered the little Dutchman. "I will charge you with theft."

"Of my own money?" Trent said amiably.

The burgomaster reddened. "Sergeant, place that blockheaded corporal under arrest."

"I'd hardly advise that," said Trent. "You see, he'd have to bring up the item of your wife's cousin at his trial, and she probably wouldn't like the publicity."

"*My wife's cousin?*" gasped the burgomaster. "What are you talking about?"

Trent smiled, carelessly took a gold-crested cigarette case from his pocket. While the sergeant goggled at the case, Trent extracted a monogrammed cigarette.

"Would you care for one, *Mynheer?* They're my own special brand—d'Artagnans."

"No!" roared the burgomaster. "Just what is this about my wife's cousin?"

Trent lighted his cigarette, withdrew a slip of folded paper from his packet of matches.

"I took the liberty of filling out one of those initialed inter-office blanks the sergeant conveniently had on his desk. Just a few words to the effect that I was your wife's cousin, temporarily in trouble, and that I was to be given special privileges. I showed it to the corporal later. A few remarks about my estimable cousin, the Burgomaster, and—" Trent swiftly touched the half-burned match to the scrap of paper, before the sergeant's frantic lunge brought him in range. The charred bits fell to the floor.

"Let them go," groaned the burgomaster. He glared up at Trent. "*Mynheer,* you and your companion were involved in a fight at the Rathskeller's on Zandort Street last night. There was something peculiar about that affair, and I intend to know what it was."

"Let me know what you discover," said Trent. "I've been wondering about it myself."

The burgomaster bristled. "I *demand* an answer! Why did you fly to Arnheim last night at such a late hour?"

"We were totally lost," said Trent. "We were heading for Paris—and when we landed, here we were in Arnheim."

The little Dutchman jumped to his feet. "For the last time, why did you go to that Rathskeller last night?"

Trent shrugged. "I suppose I'll have to tell you. You will keep it confidential?"

"If officially proper," snapped the burgomaster.

"Very well." Trent glanced toward the door, lowered his voice. "It was a strange thing; possibly you yourself have experienced it."

"Yes?" said the little Dutchman quickly.

"We were hungry," Trent said solemnly.

The burgomaster turned purple.

"Get that other man in here!" he shouted at the sergeant. "I will get the truth of this if it takes all night."

When he turned back, Trent was calmly reading the confidential report on himself that had come in from Amsterdam and which the burgomaster had failed to cover up when he came in.

"Interesting, but inaccurate," said Trent. "The *Gestapo* men were in Paris and tried to take me to the border. If you wish, I can fill in some gaps—"

The burgomaster snatched the record out of his hands.

"Mr. Trent!" he exploded. "You are insolent—you are mad—you are utterly impossible!"

"You can say that again," interrupted a funereal voice.

AT THIS, Burgomaster Voorst spun around. A mournful, gawky figure, a man about forty years old and dressed in rusty black, had ambled into the room ahead of the sergeant. His face was long and gloomy, and a protruding Adam's-apple worked up and down resignedly between the tips of his wing collar as he chewed on a wad of gum. The burgomaster looked at him twice, as though doubting his first glimpse.

"You are Mortimer Crabb?" he queried in passable English.

"That is my name," said the other man gloomily. His voice had a sepulchral sound, as though it came from the bottom of a well.

"I want certain information," the burgomaster announced. "Perhaps you will have more sense than your friend."

"He's no friend of mine," Crabb said dismally. "I was fool enough to let him talk me into this business—"

"What business?" demanded the burgomaster.

"I am an inventor," said Crabb. He looked bitterly at Eric Trent. "This young lunatic hypnotized me into buying a plane and flying over here with him to sell some of my ideas. We landed in Europe in August. Since then I have been arrested three times, shot at twice, and chased out of four countries."

Trent laughed. "Pay no attention to him, *Mynheer*. It's his dyspepsia that makes him so gloomy."

"What were you doing at that Rathskeller?" the burgomaster said grimly.

"This idiot got a mysterious phone call from some woman," Crabb replied in a mournful voice. "She wouldn't give her name, just told him to meet her in Arnheim, after midnight, at that place on Zandort Street. So we flew here. He said he liked the way her voice sounded, and it would be an adventure. What could I do? He hides my passport and my money, and I don't speak anything but English. I had to come. It was an adventure, all right. Four thugs tried to drag us into a back room, and I guess you know the rest."

"Yes, I have the report of damages," said the little Dutchman, dryly. "Four hundred guilders for the smashed window and the other breakage. To that I am adding three hundred guilders fine. Your romantic tendencies, Mr. Trent, will cost you and your companion three hundred and fifty guilders each."

Crabb groaned. Eric Trent smiled, squashed out his cigarette.

"Sorry to disillusion you, Burgomaster," he said politely, "but there is a provision in the existing America-Netherlands treaty that no American citizen shall be held more than twelve hours without giving him the right to appeal to the nearest American consular office. If so held, the American citizen can sue for damages to the amount of ten thousand guilders on the grounds—"

"Wait, I withdraw the assessment," said the burgomaster hastily. "You are both free," he went on, biting his lip in suppressed rage. "But I warn you, leave Arnheim at once. I will give you until seven to reach the airport. Your plane will be wheeled out and waiting."

"Tut! Tut!" said Trent. "Where is your famous Dutch hospitality?"

"We'll be there by seven," Mortimer Crabb said sourly. "You heard what he said."

"I'm afraid it's impossible," said Trent. "I've already planned a shower, a cocktail, and a good dinner at the Hotel les Bains. The burgomaster won't object—if we forget the little matter of the damage suit, will you, *Mynheer?*"

"Get them out of here!" the little Dutchman said wildly. "Give them their effects. Hurry up, before I go completely mad."

FIVE minutes later, Trent and Mortimer Crabb emerged from the old palace which now served as the Arnheim town-hall.

"It's a lucky thing you knew about that treaty," Crabb growled.

Trent laughed softly. "My dear Mort, don't tell me you fell for that story, too?"

"You mean there's no such thing in the treaty?" Crabb said, staring.

"Not a whisper. But that confidential file mentioned the time I nicked the British for five hundred pounds, and I had an idea our plump friend wasn't an expert on treaties."

"Some day your foot's going to slip," Crabb predicted gloomily.

Trent chuckled. "It's slipped more than once, Mort. "Didn't I ever tell you about the time in Venice when—"

Without warning, a large black sedan suddenly cut in from the street just as they started across an alley. Trent leaped back, snatching at Crabb's arm. But the inventor gave a jump to one side and was forced into the alley before he could turn back. The car's brakes went on hard, and one door was instantly flung open.

"Get in, you *Schweinhunde!*" a voice snarled, and a blocky face, marked with a saber cut, appeared above the muzzle of an automatic.

Crabb stumbled toward the car. Trent leaped around behind it, jerked open the opposite door. A blond girl frantically lifted a pistol.

"*Hoch*—raise your hands or I shoot!" she cried.

"Not so loud, you little fool," rasped the man with the scar. "Heintz, watch that devil while I get the other one in here."

The driver reached around and snatched at Trent's arm. Trent coolly climbed in, hands half lifted. The girl shrank back, but she kept the gun pointed at his middle. As Mortimer Crabb tumbled in on one of the kick-seats, the man with the scar savagely banged the door.

"Go ahead! Quick, before some one drives in here."

Gears clashed, and the sedan lurched forward. Trent looked at the scarred man.

"It's going to be a bit chilly out there in your underwear. No, not you, *Fraulein*," he added as the girl gasped, "I was referring to a little incident our friend Kleinert may remember."

"You'll pay for that smart trick, you *Teufel*," grated the man with the scar. "Elsa, watch the other man. I'll guard Trent, he's likely to trick you."

"Trick a beautiful young lady like our little Elsa?" said Trent. "You do me an injustice."

"*Stille!*" rasped Kleinert. He thrust his face close to Trent's. "Now, where is it?"

"If you're referring to your breath, even you shouldn't have any trouble locating it," returned Trent.

Kleinert's disfigured cheek twitched furiously. "You know what I mean! Where have you hidden it?"

"It's in the Douglas we flew here," said Trent. His eyes flicked for a split-second to Mortimer Crabb's gloom-ridden countenance.

"You lie!" snarled Kleinert. "A mechanic in my pay searched it thoroughly. You brought it into the city and left it somewhere."

Trent sighed. "Very well, it's in a lock-box at the railroad station. I have the key here in my—"

"Keep your hands up," snapped Kleinert. "I'll find it."

He reached out toward Trent's coat pocket, keeping the gun almost against the American's breast. Trent's gaze shifted sidewise. The driver had slowed as they neared a street. Trent's lifted right hand moved down with a sudden jerk, halted in mid-air as Kleinert's eyes swerved toward it.

"Get it up!" rasped the *Gestapo* man.

Trent obeyed—and simultaneously his unnoticed left hand threw the toggle-switch of the dome light. In a flash, the interior of the sedan was brightly illuminated.

CHAPTER II

The Stolen Box

KLEINERT started violently as the light went on. In the same moment a woman on the nearby sidewalk gave a scream at the sight of the German's gun against Trent's ribs.

"Turn that light off!" snarled Kleinert. "Heintz, get into that other alley! Faster, you fool!"

Trent threw the light off as ordered. In the swift darkness that followed, as the car plunged into the alley across the street, his lowered right hand went unseen. The door-handle gave under his surreptitious fingers, and the door flew wide open. Kleinert lunged half off his seat in expectation of Trent's attempt to dive from the car.

Trent threw himself sidewise, off the kick-seat, and Kleinert sprawled over the projecting edge. A shot roared from his gun, ricochetted from the opened door, as his trigger finger spasmodically contracted. Then before he could twist around for another shot, a swift boot from Trent's foot sent him headlong into the alley.

"Heintz—help me!" *Fraulein* Elsa cried desperately. Trent whirled in time to see Mortimer Crabb wrench the gun from the girl's hand. Heintz slammed on the brakes, spun around, clawing for his automatic. Mortimer Crabb's long arm lifted, came down like a piston. There was a thud, and the butt of the gun hit the driver's head. He slumped down in the seat, and the car angled toward the side of a building. Trent vaulted over, stopped the machine.

"Watch out, Mort—Elsa's giving you the slip!" he said suddenly. Crabb made a quick grab, but too late. The girl was out and running wildly into the darkness of the alley before he could reach the door.

"Too bad," said Trent. "I'd been looking forward to a glamorous evening once we got rid of Kleinert and Heintz." Then sitting calmly on the unconscious driver, he put the sedan in gear and sent it rolling ahead.

"Is that big ruffian clear out?" Crabb said uneasily.

Trent laughed. "If he isn't, he's giving a fine imitation. That was good teamwork, Mort."

"I didn't mean to hit him that hard," Crabb said, sepulchrally. He peered over at the hulking Nazi. "Oh, heavens, I'm afraid I've killed him."

"It would take a sledge-hammer to crack that skull," said Trent. "He's the bruiser I broke a chair on last night."

Trent quickly angled into the traffic at the next street, zigzagged two or three times to be sure they were not followed, then pulled into another alley and stopped. A search of the German's pockets revealed nothing of interest.

"Give me a hand with him, Mort," said Trent. "Then take those straps off the spare tires in the fender well."

In another minute Heintz was bound hand and foot. Trent looked around, rolled a trash-barrel behind the car, then took out a pencil and a scrap of paper. A few moments later Heintz was doubled up and wedged halfway into the barrel, with a note pinned on his chest.

"What's that for?" said Crabb, suspiciously eyeing the Dutch words.

"Just a little note for the police to deliver him personally to Burgomaster Voorst—with my compliments."

"The burgomaster won't like it," Crabb said gloomily. "Let's get out of this town while we're still able."

"And leave a lovely little mystery like this behind us?" said Trent. "No, Mort we can't let Fate down."

"You're not taking this car?" demanded Crabb.

"Certainly. Why walk when we can ride? Kleinert wouldn't risk using a stolen car."

"I'll bet ten dollars we're back in jail before midnight," Crabb said pessimistically.

"Taken," Trent said. He started the car.

"Why didn't you tell me there was something else to this business?" the inventor said dourly. "What was Kleinert after?"

"I haven't the least idea. That lock-box story was just to get him to search me, so I could reach the light switch. But in case you've forgotten, it's only about seven miles to the German border, and there's bound to be a lot of shenanigans in any border town with a war going on."

"Or any town where you are," said Crabb tartly.

WHEN they reached the Hotel les Bains, Trent drove around on the side street and parked.

"Leave Elsa's gun in here," he told Crabb. "It might be a trifle embarrassing if we were picked up on a concealed weapons charge."

"You don't think the police found out about our stopping here under fake names?" Crabb said morosely.

"No, or Voorst would have mentioned it." Trent led the way into the bar, ordered a dry Martini. "Better break that long abstinence, Mort, and have a cocktail. Life will take on a new glow. Who knows, you might even unloosen those facial muscles and find a smile lurking in there, unsuspected all these years."

"You know I don't drink," said Crabb sadly. "Besides, remember my weak stomach. With all I've gone through since I met you, my ulcers have probably come back."

Trent finished his cocktail, glanced at a short, bearded man who had just ordered a vermouth. As they went out the man gulped down his drink and followed.

"We seem to be popular tonight," Trent said in a careless aside to Crabb. "I've an odd feeling I've seen that chap before—but without that foliage on his chin."

"He looks like a Bolshevik to me," muttered Crabb. "You can stay here, if you want to, and get killed sticking your nose into other people's business. I'm going home, even if I have to cable that fathead stepbrother of mine for money and a passport."

Trent laughed. When they stepped off the elevator at the fourth floor, he handed their room key to Crabb.

"Go ahead. I'll be there in a minute."

"Now what?" Crabb said suspiciously.

"Just an idea about our bearded friend. I'll be back."

The inventor ambled down the hall, with a walk like a tired camel plodding across the sands. Trent drew back into a side corridor and waited. In a few moments the bearded man emerged from the service stairs, furtively went toward the room Crabb had entered. Trent tiptoed after him, caught up just as the bearded man stooped to peep through the keyhole.

Breathing hard, the stranger reached toward his hip, and his lifted coat-tail revealed a pistol. Trent's fingers closed on it a fraction of a second before the other man's. The bearded man spun around with an oath.

"I hope you don't mind," said Trent, genially. "I left my artillery downstairs."

"You—you traitor!" said the other man hoarsely. "You won't get away with this, Trent!"

Mortimer Crabb suddenly opened the door, and his long face dropped as he saw the tableau on the doorstep.

"Here we go again," he groaned. "What is it this time?"

"Just an old friend, come to pay a visit," said Trent. He reached out, and the stranger's beard came away in his hand, disclosing an angry, bulldog face. "An atrocious bit of sagebrush, my dear Colonel. Next time try the little costumers on Brevoort Street. Not that I blame you for trying to conceal that visage. It must be a daily shock to look at it in the mirror."

"Silence, you insolent scoundrel!" said the other man furiously. He wheeled to Mortimer Crabb. "Where is it? What have you done with it?"

"Don't look at me," Crabb said gloomily. "I'm just an innocent bystander. I don't even know what you're talking about."

Trent pushed the colonel into the room, closed the door.

"Just for the record, Mort, this unbearded gentleman happens to be Colonel Leffingwell Potter, our Army G-2 attache at Paris. We once had a trifling difficulty, and I regret to say the colonel lacks a sense of humor."

"Well, you can count me out, whatever's up," said Crabb. "I just phoned the desk. That clerk who speaks English said he'd call the airport and have the ship out and ready to go. I'm going to get a pilot and cross over to—"

So that's it!" broke in Colonel Potter, harshly. "You traitors are going to sell it over in Germany! Trent, you'll pay for this! G-2 will hound you to the ends of the earth! I'll see to it!"

Trent shook his head admiringly.

"I'll bet you were the toughest cadet at West Point, Colonel. Now suppose you calm down and explain—"

"Ah!" said Potter, with a sharply indrawn breath. He sprang across the room, pounced on a leather-covered box with a lock and handle. With a frenzied leap, he whirled into the bathroom with the box in his hand. The door banged shut.

"Come back here with that!" Mortimer Crabb said with sudden indignation. He hammered against the locked door. Trent stepped to the window, saw Colonel Potter climbing from the bathroom onto the fire-escape landing.

"Come on, Mort!" he said quickly, and turned to the hall door.

"But he's got my lightning position-calculator," protested the inventor.

"We'll get it back—I think he's mistaken it for something else," said Trent. "We'll catch him down below."

CRABB followed sourly, and they went out to the service stairs. Trent went down two at a time, almost knocked over a startled chef as he plunged into the kitchen on the first floor. With Crabb at his heels, and the Dutch cook howling profane comments on the two Americans, he ran out onto the delivery platform at the rear. Colonel Potter had just reached the ground, with the box tucked under one arm. As he glimpsed Trent he sped, puffing, for the side street.

Trent was gaining on him when a hatless figure stepped abruptly from back of a tree and swung viciously at the colonel. Potter went down, and his assailant snatched up the box, whirled toward the curb. Headlights flashed on, and Trent recognized Kleinert. The *Gestapo* man was bruised, his coat torn. Before Trent could reach the curb, the Nazi agent sprang into the car and it swept past. He saw that it was the black sedan, and he recognized Elsa bent over the wheel.

"There goes my calculator!" mourned Mortimer Crabb.

"Follow me!" said Trent. He dashed to the delivery platform, jumped into the front seat of a light truck parked there. The motor roared to life.

"Stop—thieves!" bawled the Dutch chef, as Trent sent the truck charging out into the street.

"Now you've done it," Crabb said unhappily. "He's got our descriptions, and we'll probably get ten years for stealing this thing."

"Hang on," said Trent. He sent the truck around a corner on two wheels, grazed a tram-car. The sedan was racing through the evening traffic, scattering frightened pedestrians. Trent bore down on the horn, shoved the throttle to the floor. A policeman fiercely blew his whistle. Trent dodged around him, missed a bus by less than a foot. The sedan turned again, away from the downtown section, began to outdistance them. Trent was looking feverishly for another, faster machine to commandeer, when the spies' car swung into the airport road. He followed, and three minutes later braked the truck to turn in through the airport entrance.

Above the rumble of idling motors he heard a shot, then the emergency siren blared furiously. A Dutch airport attendant was struggling to his feet, holding his side. And beyond him a Douglas DC-3 was pivoting away from the line.

"Eric, they've stolen our ship!" moaned Crabb.

Trent looked swiftly to one side, as a Dutch Air Service mechanic ran toward a ship. It was a Koolhoven escort fighter, an F.K. 52 two-seater biplane, and lined up next to it was another escort fighter and three Koolhoven F.K. 58's, single-seater monoplanes, used on border patrol.

The 840 horse-power Bristol Mercury engine of the first escort fighter thundered as its mechanic pulled the prop through. More mechanics were tumbling from an emergency barracks near the airport office, and Trent saw a pilot coming on the run, fastening his helmet.

"Quick, get into that rear pit!" he told Mortimer Crabb.

"Steal a ship?" ejaculated Crabb. "You must be insane!"

Trent grinned. "Maybe. See you later, Mort!"

He raced to the side of the two-seater, jerked the chocks and was into the front pit before the open-mouthed mechanic could stop him. The Dutchman sprang back to block the wheels. Mortimer Crabb suddenly appeared, snaked out a long arm and jerked the mechanic back onto the seat of his pants. The next second Crabb was tumbling into the rear cockpit.

"Good boy, Mort!" Trent was chuckling as he opened the throttle. An automatic rifle flamed, off to the right, and Plexiglas flew from the bulge of the enclosure above Mortimer Crabb's head.

"I knew it!" groaned the inventor. "I'll be killed."

Trent kicked the ship around, and the rifle burst swerved away. A hangar loomed up, directly in their path.

"Look out, you idiot!" bawled Crabb. "We'll hit it!"

Trent backsticked at the last second, and the Koolhoven shot up at a dizzy angle, wheels barely missing the roof. He nosed down swiftly to keep from stalling, dived under the wires of the airport radio antennae. Directly below, pilots and mechanics were falling all over each other getting out of the way. Trent laughed, zoomed after the fleeing DC-3. Moonlight shining through breaks in the clouds caught the dural wings of the Douglas as it banked toward the German border.

TRENT flung a quick look at the Koolhoven's upper wing. There were two fixed machine-guns in the leading edge, outside the prop arc. He pulled the remote-control charging lever, set the hydraulic gear, and rapped out a warming-up burst. Crabb pounded frantically against Trent's shoulder.

"Stop, you crazy loon! That's my ship—and besides, the girl's in there."

"Relax, Mort," Trent tossed back, "I'm not going to shoot the ship down."

He triggered a blast close to the DC-3's right wing. The big ship twisted hurriedly to the left. He shifted the Koolhoven's nose, sprayed a burst near the other wing, then started to edge in closer. But a stream of tracers from below sent him into a swift chandelle. An F.K. 58 was lancing up on their tail with all the fury its 1080-h.p. Hisso radial would give it. Trent made a lightning estimate, suddenly renversed. The Dutch fighter streaked after them, its four guns blazing. Trent hurtled across in front of the DC-3, twisted into a vertical bank. The single seater's tracers smoked across the path of the Douglas, and the big ship whipped back toward the airport to escape being hit. Trent grinned, flipped a salute toward the Dutch pilot.

"Thanks, *Mynheer*. Now another like that—"

Br-r-r-r-t-t-t-t! Above the roar of the Bristol Mercury, a faint, ominous pounding became audible. The next second a gray German Messerschmitt fighter plunged out of the night. At terrific speed, it charged in at the F.K. 58. Like shadows abruptly come to life, two more gray Messerschmitts whirled into sight. One went after the Dutch single-seater, and the other raced in at the F.K. 52.

A furious blast flamed out at the escort fighter—and on into empty space. Wings screaming, the Koolhoven stood on its tail as Trent savagely jerked the stick. The ship flashed over the top and down in a headlong dive. A gray blur showed beneath, as the first Messerschmitt came rocketing back for another strafe of the Dutch pilot.

"Say your prayers, Fritz!" Trent shouted. His fingers closed on the stick-trigger, and the wing-guns thrashed into action. Two fiery streaks shot in front of the Messerschmitt's nose, raked the Nazi fighter from prop to tail. A puff of flame swirled back from the Messerschmitt's cowl, was fanned instantly into a roaring inferno. The Nazi ship rolled over, went down like a meteor, smoke pluming far behind it.

The Dutch pilot stared across the flame-lit sky at Trent, pointed helplessly to his motor as his ship nosed down. The two Messerschmitt pilots plunged in fiercely at the escort fighter, ignoring the crippled singe-seater. A jagged hole appeared in the madapolam fabric of Trent's right upper wing. He jerked the throttle, and the faster Nazi ship overshot.

A sudden clattering roar came from the Koolhoven's rear cockpit. Trent cast a surprised look back. One eye closed, Mortimer Crabb stood hunched behind the spouting tourelle-gun. His lips were moving furiously, and his gloomy face was a picture of wrathful determination.

Trent gave a laugh of pure delight. "Mort, you old war-horse— I knew you had it in you!"

"You tend to your end—I'll handle mine!" roared Crabb.

The two Messerschmitts whirled around behind the slower ship, came in at converging angles. Trent feinted a hasty dive, yanked the stick back and banked tightly. The fighter on the right skidded sharply to avoid collision. Crabb's long hands swung the rear-pit gun, and the tracers swept over the Messerschmitt's tilted left wing. A zigzag crack ran through the wing as Crabb's bullets gouged it, then the outer section broke off. The Messerschmitt went into a crazy spin, and the remaining Nazi fighter fled before Trent's guns could range it.

Crabb let go the gun, stared incredulously over the side.

"What have I done?" he groaned.

"Unless my eyes deceive me, you've shot the pants off of one of the swastika boys," said Trent. "Don't let it worry you. He'll probably bail out."

"This is terrible," mourned Crabb. "I never shot at anybody before in my life."

"A neat job, for a beginner," said Trent. "Keep your eyes open. You may have to pick off a few more before we're through."

"You mean you're going on, after all *this?*" Crabb said in a hollow voice.

"Why not?" said Trent. "It's a beautiful night—and anyway, we're already across the border."

CHAPTER III

Mystery Chateau

THE TWO-SEATER droned eastward, while Trent searched the vague shadows. The DC-3 had turned toward the border after first being driven back, and he had managed to note its general course during the brief fight. After a few moments he caught the gleam of moonlight on dural wings and banked to follow. Mortimer Crabb was fumbling around in the rear seat.

"What's the trouble, Mort?" said Trent. "Drop your chewing gum in the excitement?"

"I was looking for a parachute," Crabb said gloomily. "I don't suppose there's any chance of persuading you to land me in Holland before you commit suicide?"

"We'd better let things cool off at Arnheim," said Trent. "Surely you aren't giving up a hundred thousand dollar ship without a battle? To say nothing of the calculator."

"The ship's insured," Crabb said morosely. "One week with you and I had the policy changed to cover everything but an act of God. And my life's worth more than that calculator."

"Somebody doesn't seem to think so," observed Trent. "Hello, our friends appear to be landing!"

He closed the throttle, held the Koolhoven just above stalling speed as he nosed down. Two or three miles eastward a light showed momentarily on the ground, flashed out a signal. Trent quickly switched off the motor. A moment later a searchlight flickered up, probed around the sky. He ruddered away, and the beam slanted across the border, picked up two or three Dutch fighters circling near Arnheim.

The DC-3's landing lights went on, and as the ship banked Trent saw a chateau half-hidden in trees, and a cleared area stretching nearby. Then the DC-3 leveled off, and the lights went out. A second later the searchlight went dark.

"Don't tell me you're fool enough to land down there," Crabb said unhappily.

"Just a little reconnoitering," replied Trent, "We can take off if things get too warm."

"We'll probably crack up, landing," Crabb said in a pessimistic voice.

"Why, Mort, you wound me to the heart," chuckled Trent. "This is child's play. You should have been with me one night in Ethiopia. It was raining so hard I had to use a periscope, and I landed smack against the wall of a native chief's harem. He thought I was trying to kidnap his favorite wife, and I had quite a time."

"It'll be a brick wall this time, and we'll be standing in front of it, blindfolded," the inventor predicted dismally.

"They go in for the axe in Germany," laughed Trent. "Well, brace yourself. Here we go!"

"Take it easy, Eric," pleaded Crabb. "You know my weak stomach. That fight back there almost finished me."

Trent slid the enclosure open, leaned out, brought the two-seater down at bare flying speed. He skimmed over a dark spot where a tree dimly loomed, set the ship down in a pancake stall. It rolled less than a hundred feet.

"Dumb luck," mumbled Crabb.

"The point is, we're here," said Trent, "While we're waiting to make sure nobody heard us, we might check up a point or two. How many people have seen that lightning calculator of yours since we flew the Atlantic?"

"Nobody but that squint-eyed Frenchman you tried to sell it to," growled the inventor. "I'd have stored it with the other things in Paris—if we hadn't left so suddenly after that row with the gendarmes."

"Count out Squint-Eye," said Trent. "His interest didn't go higher than five hundred francs."

"Wait," broke in Crabb suddenly, "There *was* a fellow who acted peculiar when the customs man at Amsterdam made me open up the case. I thought he was just some nosey foreigner."

"Ah!" said Trent. "And that night I got the phone call—which I'm pretty sure was from dear little Elsa. Light begins to dawn. Your nosey chap was a Nazi spy. He tipped off Kleinert. Kleinert had Elsa phone me, knowing my romantic soul would bring me trekking along to see what was up. He arranged that trap at the Rathskeller. Object—to get that box. But why? I'm not belittling your brain-child, but the Nazis would hardly go to such lengths for an avigation gadget. And there's Colonel Potter, too. Mort, it's obvious there's a case of mistaken identity somewhere."

"So what?" said Crabb in a gloomy voice.

"So we do a little quiet checking up—around that chateau over there." And Trent climbed out, after setting switch and throttle for a hasty start. The inventor followed, groaning.

"If my stomach felt less wobbly, I'd start this ship and head back for Holland. I'd probably break my neck trying to land, but that's better than getting my head chopped off."

"I still have Colonel Potter's pistol, in case we find the going rough," said Trent. "Keep close behind me."

THEY made their way carefully along the edge of the woods, listening now and then for outposts. They were within two hundred yards of the chateau—in front of which the DC-3 and the third Messerschmitt fighter were visible in the wan moonlight—when they heard an approaching car. Trent pushed Crabb back of a tree as two slits of light appeared. The slits were from headlights almost covered with black tape. A sentry with a rifle hurried to intercept the car. Trent and Crabb drew farther behind the trees as the machine stopped.

"*Halt. Wer da?*" barked the sentry.

"I am *Leutnant-Oberst* Brahnner," said a cold voice. "Examine these credentials—quickly!"

The sentry focussed a faint bluish light on the German's papers. "*Gestapo!*" he muttered, and jerked to rigid attention.

"*Herr* Kleinert has landed?" said Brahnner.

"*Ja, Herr Oberst.* In the big plane. But two of the fighters were shot down by Dutch."

"Unfortunate," said the *Gestapo* officer. "Now listen closely. You will return to the chateau without mentioning our arrival. As soon as you can get Major Wiessen's attention quietly, or find him alone, tell him a Lieutenant-Colonel Brahnner, of Army *Gestapo* Section, is here and to come at once. Be sure *Herr* Kleinert does not overhear or see you, even if it takes you some little time."

"*Ja, Herr Oberst.*" The sentry clicked his heels, spun around. Trent peered around a tree, saw another man in the front seat beside the *Gestapo* officer.

"Why not arrest Kleinert at once?" said Brahnner's companion. "It's clear that he's trying to steal the money given him for this mission, since I myself secured the stolen American bomb-sight."

"All except the part your *verdammt* Spaniard held out on you," Brahnner said in a curt voice. "But we will go into that later and pay him the agreed amount, if necessary, to obtain the missing piece. The question of the moment is what Kleinert is up to. His code, evidently sent just after he crossed the border, said he had the bomb-sight and had paid the full amount. He must have something he intends to pass off as the stolen device—unless the Spaniard tricked you."

"Impossible!" said the other man. "I myself made the contact in Amsterdam. The bomb-sight was intact, then. This Pedro Rodrigo agreed to let me fly him to the chateau for final settlement. He must have hidden the missing part somewhere in Amsterdam during the few minutes when we were separated. I opened the case before we took off, but the sight is complicated, and I did not notice any difference then."

"Well, *Herr* Lemler, we shall soon know. You left your bomb-sight and the Spaniard in this man Wiessen's care. I checked Wiessen's record and he seems to be all right. Now we will see what Kleinert has to match against your evidence. Whichever of you is… er… mistaken, the *Gestapo* will handle accordingly."

There was a heavy silence. Trent warily stepped back, put his lips to Crabb's ear.

"Fate's dealt us a royal flush. Come on!"

Crabb clutched wild at his arm, but Trent was already tiptoeing toward the rear of the car. Brahnner sat at the wheel, fingers drumming restlessly on the spokes. Trent stole closer, his gun covered with his hand to prevent any gleam in the moonlight. Brahnner jerked around suddenly. In a twinkling, Trent had the pistol against the *Gestapo* man's head.

"Not a sound, *Herr Oberst,* if you please. And as for you, *Herr* Lemler, my companion has you covered on the other side."

"Who are you?" snarled Brahnner.

"The identity's unimportant," said Trent. "Climb out, both of you—and I'll take that gun, if you don't mind."

BRAHNNER cursed under his breath, lifted the hand he had tried to thrust inside his uniform tunic. Lemler, a smaller, stockier man, was dressed in civilian clothes. He had raised his hands, but as he saw that Crabb was unarmed he ducked suddenly to one side. Trent stuck out his foot, and Lemler sprawled headlong. With an oath, the young Nazi sprang up—and ran squarely into one of Crabb's piston-like fists. There was a thud as he hit the side of the car, and he slumped to the ground with a moan.

"Excellent, Mort," Trent said softly. "Truss him up with his belt, and gag him before he gets his wind back "

"You *Teufel*, you'll die for this!" fumed Brahnner.

"What an unpleasant future you depict," said Trent. "Now let me look in the crystal. I see a beautiful bump on the top of that square head of yours—if you aren't out of that uniform in ten seconds!"

Hastily, the *Gestapo* officer started to disrobe. Trent cast a swift look toward the chateau, loosened his tie and shirt while covering the German. By the time Brahnner was out of his tunic and uniform slacks, Trent was also nearly undressed, and Mortimer Crabb had finished with Lemler.

"Cover our long-flanneled Adonis here," said Trent, "while I make a quick change. His outfit isn't exactly a smart fit for me, but I can't be particular."

"Eric, you're stark, raving crazy!" groaned Crabb. "Kleinert will know you—you won't have a chance."

"There's no time to give you the details," said Trent, "but it seems that our friend Kleinert isn't exactly in good repute. We'll play along and see where we land."

"*We?*" said Crabb in a horrified voice. "But I don't know a word of German."

"I'll take care of that. Take our guest's shirt and belt and tie, and see if you can make him snug alongside his little pal."

In another minute Brahnner was securely bound and gagged. Trent finished buttoning the *Oberst's* tunic, swung the cape over his shoulders, and put on Brahnner's cap. He and Crabb carried the two Germans back under the trees, placed them well apart.

Trent was tightening Brahnner's gag when he heard a door open, and light briefly shone from the side of the chateau.

"Get into the car!" he whispered to Crabb. "I'll tell them your name's Muller. No matter what anybody says to you, don't answer. Just repeat what I say when I look at you and say '*Nein*,' or '*Ja*.'"

"Oh, Lord!" Crabb said despairingly. "A time like this—and you start giving lessons in German."

Trent snatched up his coat, transferred its contents to one of his tunic pockets, tossed the coat into the shadows. He was pacing impatiently up and down beside the car when the sentry approached with a bulky Nazi in field-gray uniform.

"That's all, sentry," Trent said sharply in German, to keep the man from getting too close. "I'll speak with Major Wiessen alone."

The sentry about-faced, strode back to the chateau. The major halted nervously, staring at Trent through the faint moonlight.

"My credentials," snapped Trent. He brought out Brahnner's *Gestapo* identifications, switched on the shielded headlights. As Wiessen stepped close to the slit of light nearest him, Trent saw that the major's pudgy face was a trifle pale. He followed up the man's evident fear of the secret police.

"Major Wiessen, there is a traitor here!" he said sternly.

Wiessen started, almost dropped the credentials. "B-but I don't understand, *Herr Oberst*."

"I refer to *Herr* Kleinert," said Trent, and Wiessen let out a sigh of relief. "There is a matter of two American bomb-sights, instead of one. What do you know about this?"

"Only what has just occurred, *Herr Oberst*," Wiessen said shakily. "I thought it was odd—the agent named Lender landed here—"

"I know all that," Trent said crisply. "He thought he had tricked the Spaniard—but it seems the reverse. You have the man and the bomb-sight?"

"Yes. But Kleinert insists the other sight is false, that he has the right one. He was very much upset when he heard about the second one. He was for shooting the Spaniard who claims he stole the other bomb-sight—"

"We'll see about that," cut in Trent. He jerked his head toward Mortimer Crabb. "This is *Herr* Muller, one of the *Gestapo's* undercover men. Muller, I think we are safe in assuming Major Wiessen is innocent, ja?"

"Ja," said Crabb, in a rusty voice.

"Thank you, *Herr* Muller," Wiessen said hastily. He wiped his forehead. "I swear, *Herr* Oberst, I knew nothing—"

"We will go inside," interrupted Trent. "Get two armed men— but not that sentry I sent after you. He acted suspicious, and I intend to check up on him later."

"If you will wait at the side entrance, I shall be there in a few seconds," said Wiessen. He hurried around to the front of the chateau. Mortimer Crabb gave a hollow groan.

"Eric, for the love of Heaven, let's run for it while we've still got our heads."

"And miss the look on Kleinert's face when he sees us?" said Trent. "I'd never forgive myself. Just remember *'nein'* and *'ja'*—and keep this gun of Brahnner's handy."

Major Wiessen quickly reappeared, followed by two husky Nazis. At Trent's gesture, Wiessen cautiously opened the side door.

CHAPTER IV

Secret Flight Sixteen

J UST beyond the portal, a lighted central room could be seen. Kleinert's voice came savagely from somewhere in the room.

"Never mind what *Fraulein* Elsa says. Keep her locked in that room, and bring that lying Spaniard in here."

Trent pushed by the two Nazi soldiers, motioned for them to follow. As he reached the entrance to the room, he saw Kleinert and a small group of Germans, some in uniform, some in civilian clothes. The spy was glaring at a lieutenant.

"And don't forget, I'm the senior *Gestapo* agent here."

The young *Leutnant* mumbled something, then got to his feet quickly as he saw Trent's uniformed figure and the men behind him. The rest of the group jumped up, and Kleinert looked around hastily. A look of utter amazement came into his eyes as he saw Trent and Crabb. For a moment he stood paralyzed, the blood receding from his bruised face.

A faint, mocking gleam came into Trent's eyes, then he coolly lifted his pistol.

"*Herr* Kleinert, in the name of the German *Reichsfuehrer,* I arrest you for high treason!"

The two Nazi soldiers sprang forward and seized the astounded agent. Kleinert lunged away from them frantically and faced Wiessen.

"Have you gone crazy?" he screamed. "Wiessen, I tell you these men have tricked you! Let me go, you fools!"

"Keep him quiet," Trent said calmly. "If he starts yelling again, give him a touch of the bayonet."

"Wiessen, listen to me!" Kleinert cried wildly. "I—I" He broke off with a howl as one of the soldiers gave him a smart jab between the shoulder-blades. Trent looked around at the staring Germans.

"I am sorry, gentlemen, but it will be necessary for you to remain here while I conduct a brief investigation. Major Wiessen, have the Spaniard brought in here."

"Yes, *Herr Oberst.*" Wiessen gestured to one of the men, and in a few seconds the Nazi returned with the prisoner. Rodrigo was a slight, sallow-faced man, with a crafty face just now a trifle sullen. He glared at Kleinert, then as he saw the Nazis holding the *Gestapo* agent he looked relieved.

"I brought the bomb-sight he claims is the right one, *Herr Oberst,*" said the German who had gone for Rodrigo. He opened a leather-covered case similar to the one containing Crabb's position calculator. Trent hid his real feelings behind a satisfied look as he saw the inscription, "*Mark V, Model XII, U.S. Army Air Corps Bomb Sight.*"

"Have no fear, my colonel," Rodrigo said in broken German. "It is the famous American bomb sight—twice as accurate as any other in the world. I regret it is not all here. To protect myself, I removed the curved linkage-bar on which the speed-altitude equation ratio is determined. Without that mathematical equation the sight is useless."

"Where is it? And what is the price?" Trent said coldly.

"It is safe in Amsterdam," Rodrigo said with a smirk. "When I am safe there, also, I will deliver it to anyone you designate—when I have been paid the agreed sum of five hundred thousand marks."

"Search *Herr* Kleinert," Trent ordered Wiessen. "He was given the money to negotiate this deal."

"I find only a few hundred guilders," reported Wiessen, after searching the fuming secret agent. "He told me, *Herr Oberst,* that he had paid the entire amount for this other bomb-sight."

Trent looked at Mortimer Crabb. The inventor was tightly gripping Brahnner's automatic and swallowing convulsively.

"Muller and I have other ideas on that, *ja?*" said Trent.

"*Ja,*" Crabb said in a hollow tone. Trent saw two or three of the Nazis look curiously at the gloomy-faced inventor.

"*Herr* Muller was once an official executioner," he said, with a chuckle. "He has used the axe on so many necks his Adam's-apple bobs up and down like a condemned man's whenever an execution is in the offing."

Wiessen glanced at Kleinert, shivered. Trent beckoned to the major.

"Question *Fraulein* Elsa privately. Ask her about the five hundred thousand marks."

As Wiessen disappeared, Trent turned to one of the Nazi lieutenants. "Have the motors of the American plane started. *Herr* Muller and I will be flown to Berlin with the prisoner."

The *Leutnant* hurried out. Trent glanced at Kleinert's sweating face. "You see, *mein Freund,* it is unwise to try to trick one's superiors."

Kleinert's mouth opened, but a prick from a bayonet kept him in agonized silence. Trent closed the bomb-sight case, was securing the cover of Crabb's lightning calculator when Wiessen returned.

"She says Kleinert went to see one of our resident-agents named Schule at 93 Ten Eyck Street, in Arnheim," the major reported. "She thinks he must have left the money there on some pretext, probably intending to return and claim it secretly. I am convinced she is innocent."

"Nevertheless, hold her until I send you word from Berlin," said Trent. "We are taking Kleinert—"

THE FRONT door of the chateau opened suddenly, and a Nazi *Unter-offizier* burst in through the entry-hall.

"Your pardon, Major!" he said breathlessly to Wiessen. "But one of the men just found a Dutch plane, a Koolhoven two-seater, down near the end of the clearing!"

Trent broke in before Wiessen could answer. "Probably the pilots were forced down. Start a search—they'll be making for the border."

"But, *Herr Oberst*, the soldier says the plane was undamaged," exclaimed the *Unter-offizier*. He wheeled before Trent could stop him, and a sentry hurried in from the hall. Trent swore under his breath.

It was the man who had talked with Brahnner.

"*Ja*, the plane was not—" the sentry broke off, jerked his rifle up with a startled exclamation. "Major Wiessen, this is not the man who sent me to get you!"

"I told you they'd tricked you!" Kleinert burst out fiercely. "Seize them, you idiots! They're spies!"

A look of horrified understanding dawned on Wiessen's face.

"Arrest them!" he flung at the *Unter-offizier* and the sentry. "*Herr* Kleinert, I was not to blame—I had no way of knowing—"

"I'll attend to you later!" rasped Kleinert. There was a new, frightened look in his eyes, and Trent knew he had guessed at least part of the truth about the real Brahnner's visit. "Take all but these four of the guard detail and start searching across the field for those Dutch pilots. This lying swine was right on one point—they're undoubtedly trying to reach the border."

Wiessen barked an order, and all but the four enlisted men dashed out. The major turned back at the door, uncertainly.

"There is something I don't understand. If the real *Gestapo* men were intercepted by these two, then they must be—"

"I'll do the thinking here!" snarled Kleinert. "You've botched everything. I was trying to trick Rodrigo—Lemler and I were working together, with Schule. Now I'll have to take Rodrigo and recover that missing part. If you've caused me to fail, your head will be the penalty."

"Play your hunch, Wiessen!" Trent now said swiftly. "You'll find the—"

Kleinert whirled, struck him furiously.

"Do as you're told!" he shouted at Wiessen. The major hastily went out. Kleinert spun around, struck Trent another savage blow, as two men held him helpless.

"You damned coward!" grated Mortimer Crabb.

"Never mind, Mort," Trent interrupted. Blood was trickling from his lips, but his smile mocked Kleinert. "There's a lot of rat in him; it has to come out some way."

"You'll stop smiling before I'm through with you!" raged Kleinert. He snatched the pistol one Nazi had taken from Trent, then looked tensely at the clock as the engines of the DC-3 rumbled into life.

"Get *Fraulein* Elsa," he flung at one of the two Nazis who had guarded him. "And you—tie that Spaniard's hands behind him. Quick, before I even the score for that bayonet work!"

The two men sprang to obey. Kleinert swung the pistol toward Mortimer Crabb. The inventor glared back with a gloomy defiance.

"All right, get it over with, you butcher."

"Quick and easy, *hein?*" snarled Kleinert. "You will see."

He put his gun under his coat, un-snapped the bayonet from the sentry's rifle, and stepped toward Trent. Crabb closed his eyes, and the *Unter-offizier* shivered. But *Fraulein* Elsa's appearance at the doorway halted Kleinert's half-raised hand.

The girl had cringed back before Kleinert's murderous glare.

"Take her out and put her in the big ship," the spy said thickly. "If she tries to scream, choke her. Stand guard over her until I get there."

There was dread in Elsa's eyes, but she offered no resistance as she was led out. Kleinert jerked his head at the man guarding the Spaniard.

"Take him to the side entrance. I'll be there in a second."

HE HURRIEDLY opened a large drawer in a flat-topped desk, laid the bayonet down while he stuffed two or three papers into his pocket. The two remaining Nazis exchanged uneasy glances, but their guns did not swerve away from the prisoners.

"The complete double-cross, eh, Kleinert?" said Trent. "Too bad it's wasted. Unfortunately, Pedro *doesn't* have the linkage bar."

Kleinert wheeled furiously. "No smart trick will save you now, *Herr* Trent!"

"I'm aware of that," Trent said coolly. "But I'll have the last laugh, even when you finish me off. Pedro sold that linkage bar to the Soviet—plus the full plans for the rest of the bomb-sight. He tried to collect twice by selling the other part to Germany. So your little scheme to get paid double will blow right up in your face."

"I had no such scheme," retorted Kleinert, with a darting look at the two Nazis. "As for Rodrigo, you're bluffing."

"Am I?" said Trent. "Ask him why he met Sergius Kivosilov in the Hotel Metropole, Rotterdam, three nights ago."

"Get that Spaniard back in here!" Kleinert rasped at the *Unter-offizier*. He drew the gun he had holstered, flipped it toward Trent. "Get over here. If you're lying, you won't live two seconds."

Trent stepped beside the desk. For a fraction of a second his eyes rested on the bayonet lying there. Kleinert saw the look.

"Raise your hands!" he snarled.

Trent's hands started up, then with incredible swiftness he caught the edge of the desk and hurled himself down behind it. A shot blazed through the collar of his cape. The next second the desk went crashing onto its side, hurling Kleinert off his feet. The bayonet clattered to the floor. Trent snatched it up by the tip of the blade.

As he whirled, Crabb's guard frantically leveled his rifle. There was a swish, a flash of steel, and the German's right arm thudded against the wall, with the bayonet through his sleeve. Mortimer Crabb dived after the fallen rifle. Kleinert jumped around one corner of the desk, but before he could fire the front door of the chateau was flung violently open Brahnner and Lemler, still half-clad, burst into the hall, with Major Wiessen and a Nazi pilot at their heels.

"Stop that man Kleinert!" cried Brahnner. "He is a member of Secret Flight Sixteen!"

A panic-stricken look flashed into Kleinert's face. Two shots roared from his gun, and both Brahnner and Lemler toppled to the floor. Kleinert then jumped up, snatched the bomb-sight case, and ran madly for the side entrance. Trent had jerked Mortimer Crabb down back of the desk as the front door flew open. As Wiessen dashed back outside with the pilot behind him, Trent sprang to his feet.

Just as he and Crabb emerged from the front doorway there was a crash of pistol shots at the side of the chateau. Trent ran for the DC-3, Crabb close behind. They were within fifty feet of some boxes which had been lined up to serve as a gangway when a Nazi with a light machine gun appeared near the tail of the ship.

Trent leaped in just as the man took aim. He flung himself at the German, feet first, like a runner sliding for a base. Raising one foot, he slammed his heel against the man's knee-cap. With a scream, the gunner went over backward. Trent snatched up the machine gun, dashed for the ship.

Fraulein Elsa suddenly appeared in the cabin doorway, struggling with the Nazi assigned to guard her. As the German saw Trent and the gun, he released the girl, jumped frenziedly to the ground, and fled.

Trent leaped up to the cabin, thrust the gun to Crabb as the inventor scrambled in, with his position-calculator jammed under one arm. Elsa made a desperate attempt to get past Trent, but he hastily closed the door.

"Sorry, *Fraulein*—there's no time for that. Mort, knock out a window and blast a few shots to keep them away till we're off."

He raced to the cockpit, threw himself down at the controls. The motors revved up thunderously, and the DC-3 began to roll. Tracers sparkled out from one side, ricochetted like fantastic fireworks as they hit the side of the ship. Trent rammed the throttles full on.

A car was speeding along the side of the clearing, with guns blazing at it from back at the chateau. He saw the machine whirl up beside the Koolhoven and stop. Somewhere near the chateau, a searchlight went on, and he saw mechanics starting the lone Messerschmitt as the beam angled past it toward the Koolhoven.

Trent retracted the landing-gear, banked steeply toward the Dutch border. The searchlight flashed across his wings. He looked back into the cabin, saw Elsa huddled at a window, staring toward the Nazi base. Mortimer Crabb's angular figure was hunched over the machine gun, with the barrel projecting through a broken window. The searchlight shifted abruptly. Trent switched on the radio, hurriedly tried several wave-lengths. A harsh German voice grated into his earphones.

"Leutnant Schneider—not the American ship! Force down the two-seater!"

Somewhere back in the vague moonlight, tracers flamed across the sky.

"Goodbye, Mr. Kleinert," said Trent. A minute passed, and he could see the lights of Arnheim begin to take shape. But suddenly Crabb gave a shout of alarm.

"Eric! Look out—there's a ship on our tail!"

TRACERS smoked and blazed past the left wing as Trent swerved. He shoved the controls forward, dived the big Douglas across the border. The tracers came again, angling in from the right. He heard Crabb's machine-gun chatter fiercely. Jerking off the headphones, he leveled out at five hundred feet, then ran back into the cabin.

"Take the controls, Mort! Keep S-ing her, but head for Arnheim!"

"It's no use," moaned Crabb. "He's got us—he dodges before I can nail him."

"Never mind, take the controls," cried Trent. He seized the machine gun. A burst from the Koolhoven's guns tore through the top of the cabin as Crabb loped forward to the cockpit. Trent hastily drew the girl to one side.

"Roll under the lounge, *Fraulein*. We can't risk that pretty head of yours."

The Douglas went into a shaky turn, and the Koolhoven shot by. Trent crashed the gun-barrel through two more windows. As the two-seater darted in again, he sent a lightning burst through a starboard window, then leaped across to the other side with the rifle. The Koolhoven came whirling in on the left, with a swift change of direction. Trent crouched, without firing, as the first burst flamed toward the tail. Coolly, he aimed the weapon between the spurting wing-guns of the two-seater. Shattering glass and bits of dural were flying from the rear of the cabin as he pressed the trigger.

As his burst hit, the Koolhoven's nose pitched down, and its guns abruptly went dark. With its prop shot off, the two-seater went into a hasty turn. Trent dropped his gun and ran forward. Kleinert was now floundering the Koolhoven in a vain attempt to stretch his glide back to the border. Trent laughed as he saw the spy desperately turn to cross the Rhine.

"I'll give you ten to one, Mort, he doesn't make it. Oh, oh—there he goes!"

The two-seater fell off from a sudden stall, struck the river with a splash. Lights from steamers and from a pier angled across the water and focussed on the wreck.

"Take this wheel before we do the same thing," said Crabb hoarsely. "If we keep her wide open, maybe we can get to Belgium before they catch us."

"There's a little unfinished business," said Trent. "Let's see—we can't risk the airport. Go back and tell little Elsa to get in a seat and fasten her belt. She's under the lounge."

Crabb groaned, climbed down—Trent throttled the motors, lowered the landing-gear, and put the Douglas into a fast forward slip. The plane howled across the center of Arnheim, leveled out near the steeple of the Groot Kerk of St. Eusibius, and settled, flaps down, into a long municipal garden beyond the church. With a crashing of trellises, the DC-3 charged to the end of the garden, where Trent braked it to a stop with one prop almost nicking a small fountain. The American cut off the motors and hurried aft, discarding the German cap.

"Mort, you stay with the ship. When the police come, tell them you've a message for Burgomaster Voorst. But don't tell him a thing—except that I'll be there inside of an hour."

"You lunatic—we're in deep enough now," Crabb said unhappily. "If we make a clean breast—"

"Don't tell him a thing!" Trent picked up the calculator-case, turned to the girl. "Come, *Fraulein*, we'll have to hurry."

The girl stared, then, followed him to the door. He jumped to the ground, caught her as she swung down. He grasped her arm, and they ran across the disheveled garden to the nearest street. When they stopped, in semi-gloom in the middle of a block, startled Arnheimers were already scurrying toward the stranded DC-3. The girl looked up into Trent's face.

"What are you going to do with me?" she whispered.

Trent sighed. "Much as I hate it, *Fraulein*, I'm afraid I must say goodbye to you. I'd looked forward to a pleasant evening with you in a cozy cocktail bar or somewhere out in the moonlight—"

"You mean you're letting me escape?" she said, incredulously. "You won't turn me over to the Dutch police?"

Trent laughed. "Frankly, I don't approve of their jails. And besides, this isn't my war—now that Germany's lost the American bomb-sight. But if I were you, I'd go into some other more innocent business. Bullets might mar your really pretty face."

"You—you're very kind," she said huskily. "I won't forget you."

Trent bent over, whispered in her ear: "*Auf Wiedersehen*, little Elsa... perhaps some day we'll meet again."

Then he turned and walked swiftly away toward the shrouding gloom of the old Groot Kerk.

THE CLOCK on the wall of the burgomaster's office showed five minutes to eleven. Mortimer Crabb sat gloomily silent before the burgomaster's desk, as he had sat for almost an hour. Back of him stood Voorst's office sergeant, and pacing savagely back and forth nearby was Colonel Leffingwell Potter of G-2. Burgomaster Voorst wiped his plump, perspiring face for the hundredth time, glowered at Crabb.

"*Mynheer,* I give you one last chance. It is obvious that your friend—" Voorst stopped abruptly to answer the phone. After a moment he hung up, muttering a Dutch oath under his breath.

"Send out an alarm for a missing ambulance," he told the sergeant. "The men in that wrecked plane were brought ashore nearly drowned, and some one called an ambulance. But nothing's been seen of it since it drove away from the river. Now, *Mynheer* Crabb, you'd better tell what you know. It's obvious Trent has deserted you."

"Always mistrust the obvious, my dear Burgomaster," said an amiable voice. Voorst leaped to his feet in blank amazement. There in the anteroom doorway stood Eric Trent, a neat Van Dyke beard on his chin, his dark eyes twinkling behind gold-rimmed glasses. He wore a Dutch military overcoat, and a general's gilt-braided cap.

"Oh, Lord!" groaned Mortimer Crabb.

"You contemptible traitor!" shouted Colonel Potter. "What have you—"

"Keep still!" howled Voorst. "Sergeant, add impersonation of a Dutch officer to the other charges."

"This reception really overwhelms me," said Trent. "But don't forget the dangers of false arrest, *Mynheer* Burgomaster."

"We've got you this time," snapped Voorst. "You're charged with espionage, assault, theft of a truck, violating five traffic rules, refusing to halt at police order, theft of a military plane, and murderous assault of the unidentified man you left with that insolent note."

"Quite a list," said Trent. "But you'd better add breaking and entering of the costumer's shop on Breevoort Street. I didn't have time to phone the proprietor."

Voorst plumped back into his chair, speechless. Trent laughed.

"Naturally I've a good explanation. It goes back to Colonel Potter and his stolen bomb-sight. Never mind glaring, Colonel.

Anyway, a chap named Pedro Rodrigo is your man. He made a deal with a Nazi, but another agent mistook one of Crabb's inventions for the bomb-sight.

You people evidently found the Germans were shadowing us, and came to the same conclusion. You stole Crabb's avigation plotting device, and a spy named Kleinert who's an agent for an insidious independent spy group called Secret Flight Sixteen, snatched it thinking it was the bomb-sight. We chased him to the airport, borrowed a plane to try to recover our stolen ship, and after a trifling misadventure across the border recovered the Douglas and returned. We had to shoot down that Koolhoven in self-defense. The chap in the trash-barrel was Heintz, one of the spies. A little third-degree will probably loosen his tongue."

Potter sneered. "You're slipping, Trent. A child could think up a better lie."

"Take them both below," ordered the burgomaster. "We'll finish this investigation when they're safely behind bars."

Mortimer Crabb looked gloomily at Trent as the group entered the elevator. Trent grinned. "Don't worry, Mort. I expected this.

"When they emerged near the detention cells, a homely little corporal looked eagerly at Trent. "Now, *Mynheer?*" he exclaimed.

"Now," said Trent, and the corporal sprang to rear-courtyard door.

"What the devil?" spluttered Voorst and Potter in unison, both of whom had decided to put Trent safely in a cell.

"Just a little surprise," Trent said nonchalantly.

THE CORPORAL flung open the door and an ambulance was revealed. At Trent's nod, the driver and an interne swung the doors open. Strapped to the stretchers inside were the shaken-up Kleinert and Rodrigo, eyes glaring, their lips taped shut.

"Colonel Potter, there's a box that may interest you," said Trent. The Army man seized a dripping leather case and lifted the cover.

"The bomb-sight!" he cried. Then his jaw dropped. "But the ratio-bar—it's gone."

"Rodrigo told me where he hid it, after a bit of persuasion," Trent said pleasantly. "If you let him off lightly, he'll also tell you."

"Thank the Lord!" said Potter. "Trent, I misjudged you terribly. If there's anything—"

"You might tell the Burgomaster I've done him a service," chuckled Trent. "It looks bad to have German agents with a stolen American bomb-sight operating on Dutch soil, while the police persecute patriotic Americans who try to recover it."

Voorst managed a ghastly smile. "A—a slight misunderstanding, *Mynheer* Trent. Forget the charges."

"Thanks," said Trent. "Sorry about your gardens. I'll be glad to pay for the damage after we haul the ship out. But you might get that costumer out of bed for me—I've a German tunic under here, and it might become embarrassing. Also, you can explain about these various borrowed items."

"Of course," Voorst said hastily. He looked down at the prisoners. "There was another spy—a girl, was there not?"

"Yes, brown-haired, black eyes, a bit on the scrawny side," said Trent. "Had a mole on her nose."

He grinned down at Kleinert, gave him a mock salute. "Come on, Mort. Good-night, gentlemen—it's been a pleasant evening."

With the astonished ambulance men staring after him, he removed the Van Dyke beard and glasses, sauntered out to the street. As Crabb caught up with him, Trent took out a wallet, handed him a huge roll of bills. The inventor's jaw dropped.

"I dropped in at *Herr* Schule's," said Trent. "Brahnner's *Gestapo* card did the trick. He thought I was carrying on for Kleinert."

"You stole that spy-money?" Crabb said hoarsely.

"I simply sold your calculator for you," said Trent. "And it's probably an excellent device—for peacetime commercial flying. Anyhow, was it my fault if Schule took it for the bomb-sight in the dark? By now he's half-way to the border with it. By the way, you owe me ten dollars—for we're not in jail."

Mortimer Crabb looked at the roll of bills, and something almost like a smile came into his mournful face. Then he gazed up at the clock in the Groot Kerk steeple and shook his head pessimistically.

"We've still three minutes to land in jail. I might collect even yet."

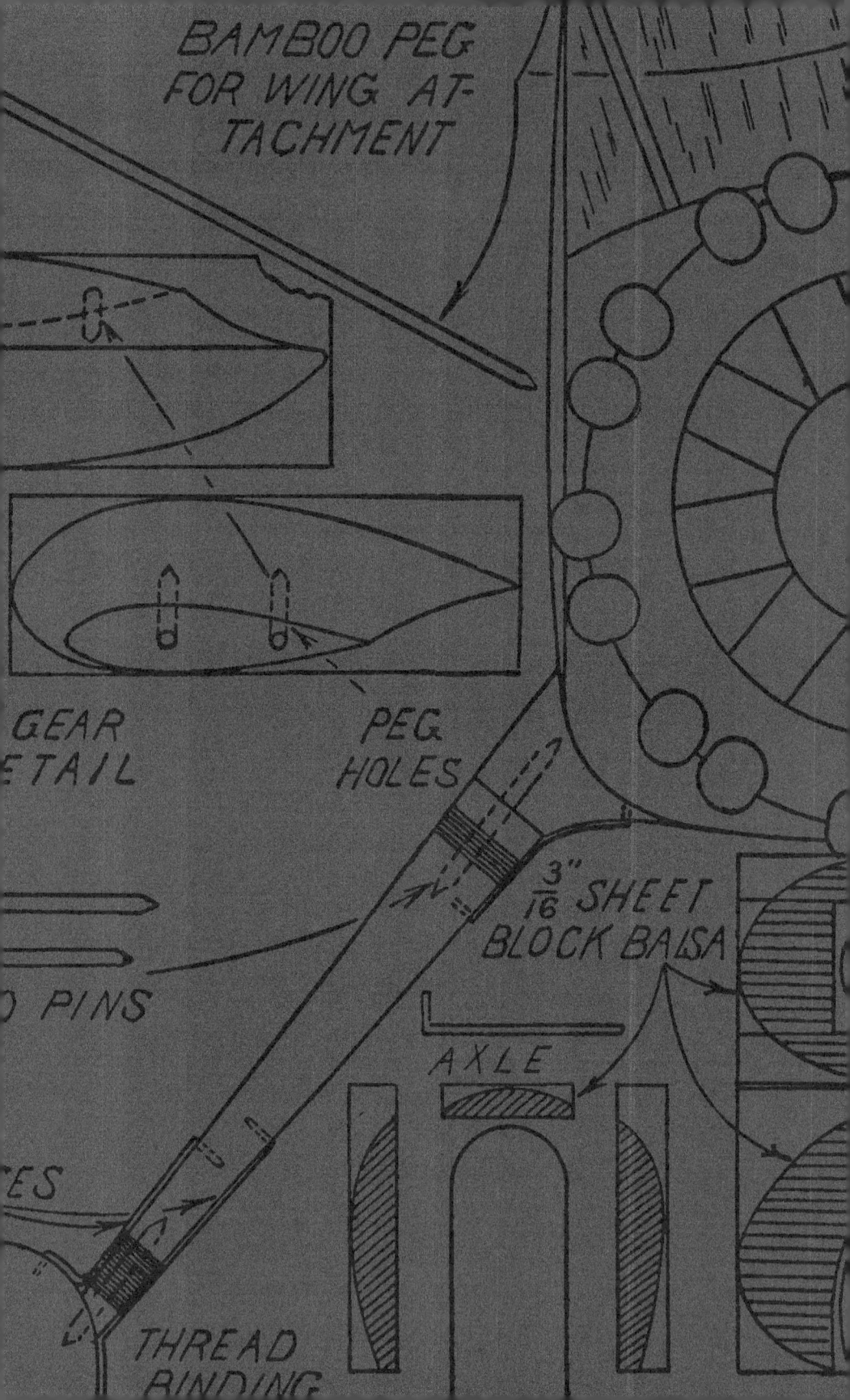

BAMBOO PEG
FOR WING AT-
TACHMENT

GEAR
ETAIL

PEG
HOLES

PINS

$\frac{3}{16}$" SHEET
BLOCK BALSA

AXLE

ES

THREAD
BINDING

Death Flies Blind

CHAPTER I

Voice From the Fog

THICK, sluggish, yellowish-gray fog closed in around the Deuxieme Bureau car, hiding all but a dim stretch of the road to Le Bourget Field. Eric Trent skidded around a slower-moving machine that suddenly loomed through the mists. He swung the wheel expertly, missed a pole by less than a foot. Flicking an ash from his cigarette, he bore down on the accelerator again. Two minutes later, recognizing a familiar crossroads, he pulled to one side and stopped.

"Now what?" said a dismal voice. Trent looked back and grinned at the mournful face of his partner, Mortimer Crabb. In his rusty black suit, Crabb looked like an undertaker who had seen better days. Between the tips of a wing collar, a large Adam's-apple worked up and down dispiritedly as he chewed on a wad of gum. He was perched on a long, shapeless bundle which now and then gave a convulsive jerk.

"Mort," said Trent, "much as I shall miss your cheerful countenance, you'd better submerge again. We're almost to the sentry-post."

The bundle twitched violently. Mortimer Crabb lifted the rug which formed the cover, and a glaring face appeared, red from the vain effort of trying to loosen a gag.

"He seems a trifle upset," observed Trent. "Maybe he doesn't like you to sit on his head."

"We'll never get out of *this* jam," Crabb said gloomily. "That crazy business in Montmartre was bad enough. But kidnapping a French cop—"

The captive made a furious gurgling sound.

"Now look what you've done," said Trent. "Don't ever call a *Surete* officer a cop. You've offended the poor chap."

"Glub—waw—oogle," the Frenchman said wildly.

"An interesting point, but not conclusive," Trent answered him. "After all, that's only *one* man's opinion."

The Frenchman gave him a murderous look, chewed savagely on the gag.

"Mort, this poor fellow is famished," Trent exclaimed. "I'd no idea the French Army was on such short rations."

"Oh, Lord," groaned Crabb, "I think I'll give myself up. If anybody had told me six months ago I'd leave my factory and go chasing all over Europe with a lunatic, getting into one mess after another—"

"—And doing the German spy-system out of five hundred thousand marks," put in Trent, amiably.

"You're the one who made them think that position-calculator was the U.S. Air Corps bomb-sight," Crabb said in a hollow voice. "You can have the money—if you'll give me back my passport, and enough change to get home on. I'll even toss in the DC-3 and the inventions I brought over."

Trent shook his head reproachfully. "Here I work my fingers to the bone, slave to make you happy—and now you want to toss me aside, like an old shoe."

Crabb moaned, slid down beside the bound Frenchman, and drew the rug over his gawky figure. Trent took out a gold cigarette

case, lighted one of his private brand of D'Artagnans and drove on, humming *Faithful Forever* in a pleasant baritone.

Change that to *Scatterbrain* and I'll make it a duet," came Crabb's dismal accents, muffled by the rug.

To appease the drab one, Trent changed his tune. Crabb, though did not join in as promised.

TRENT chuckled. And he was still laughing softly to himself when he slowed the car at the airport entrance. Even in a tight spot, Eric Trent never lost that gift for laughter, nor his *sang froid*. There was something reminiscent of the Riviera about him, a dashing, Latin darkness of hair and eyes. The lips under his closely-clipped mustache had an audacity verging at times on pure impudence.

But Trent knew when to veil that audacious look, and his manner was crisp and official when the sentry approached ghost-like through the fog.

"Vite—hurry up!" barked the American. "I am Captain Deschalle of the *Surete*, on important business." He held out the credentials taken from the captive, and the sentry saluted. Trent drove past, halted the car in the shrouding mists, then swiftly checked his wrist-watch with the clock on the dash.

"All right, Mort. Two minutes—on the dot."

Crabb's gloomy face emerged from under the rug. "All I hope is they don't put us in the same cell at the Bastille."

"When you shoot, aim at the ground," said Trent. He grinned at an afterthought.

"Don't get your feet in the way.... *Au voir, Capitaine*—being arrested by you has been a real pleasure."

"Wuggle—moo—gluff!" said Captain Deschalle hoarsely.

"And the same to you," Trent said politely. "Remember me to the Prefect." He strode into the fog, and in a few moments a Douglas DC-3 with American registration became visible. The ship apparently had not been moved since their landing, the day before. But, as he had expected, there was an armed *poilu* guarding it. He started toward the man, saw a moment too late that a *sous-officier* was leaning against one of the wheels. The sergeant straightened abruptly, and the *poilu* jerked up his rifle for a hasty challenge.

"Captain Deschalle, *Surete*," said Trent. He let both men see his borrowed identifications. "I just received a flash from Paris that the Americans who came in this plane were last seen heading for Le Bourget. Be on your guard—they may even have reached here under cover of the fog."

"*Que le diable*," muttered the *poilu*. "No sane men would fly into this fog, even to escape arrest."

"We are not talking of sane men," said the sergeant. "This Eric Trent is a mad Yankee. My lieutenant just told me he is the one who turned loose two *Gestapo* agents in their underwear—in broad daylight, and on the Champs Elysees, mind you—for trying to kidnap him and take him to Germany. It seems he meddled with some of their plans in Poland and elsewhere. They would like to cut off his head."

"I have heard him called a little peculiar," admitted Trent.

"Peculiar is not the word," insisted the *sous-officier*. "Who but a madman would go into a Montmartre dive filled with the toughest thugs in Paris, take over the piano in the middle of an Apache dance and start to play the *Hitler Youth Marching Song*?"

"*Oui*, it does seem eccentric," said Trent. He glanced at his wrist-watch. "The report from Paris gave no details. How did this Trent escape from the place?"

"It seems he has a companion—an inventor named Crabb," began the sergeant. "And—"

"I have seen him," nodded Trent. "A very sad-looking man."

"I venture he will be even sadder, *mon Capitaine*, when you of the *Surete* are through with him. It appears that when Trent started the riot, the man Crabb was hidden by the light switch, or Trent would certainly have been knifed. When the police arrived and put on the lights, the Americans were gone, an Apache had been stabbed, and the male dancer was behind the bar, unconscious."

"There was something about a code letter," suggested Trent.

"It was found on the rear stairs by which the Yankees escaped. My lieutenant told me it was in a Soviet code and that Trent was evidently expecting to meet a Russian spy in that den."

"Ah, then he is a Communist pig," said the *poilu*.

"*Non*, that is the strange part. The *Ogpu* has a price on his head, dead or alive."

"If I were the Prefect, I would question the dancer and the Apache who was stabbed," offered Trent. "They might turn out to be a German and a Russian spy working together to—"

THE BARK of a pistol cut him short. Both Frenchmen spun around, staring into the fog. There was another shot, then Deschalle's voice came in a frantic shout.

"*Garde a vous!* Help! The Americans, Trent and Crabb—"

The cry was abruptly stifled. Trent seized the sergeant's arm.

"Search over that way! you go with him!. I'll guard the plane."

The two men darted into the mists. Trent peered under the left wing, and in a few seconds Mortimer Crabb appeared by a circuitous path, somewhat out of breath. With Crabb as a stepladder, Trent managed to open the cabin door and scramble inside. He reached down, hauled his mournful partner aboard and ran to the pilot's compartment. Just as the right-hand motor stuttered into life, the *sous-officier* came dashing back to the ship. Trent released the parking-brake, gunned the protesting motor and kicked the DC-3 around, away from the hangars.

A shot blazed from the sergeant's automatic, and a hole appeared in the left window of the cockpit. Trent switched on the other engine, looked out and saw *Capitaine* Deschalle hopping on one foot, his half-loosened bonds jerking at his ankles. The *poilu* came suddenly from the other side, lifted his rifle. Trent shoved the rudder, and the *poilu* threw himself flat as the DC-3 roared at him.

Trent opened the throttles as much as the cold engines would take, sent the ship rolling out into the fog. For the next minute he taxied wildly back and forth, warming the motors. The administration building loomed from the murk. He pivoted hastily, missed a row of parked cars by less than two yards.

Panicky Frenchmen ran for shelter, and Trent edged the throttles up to take-off settings. The hangars swept mistily by on his left, then the ground slipped away and the ship thundered up into the gray world of fog. He retracted the landing gear, climbed until the altimeter showed two thousand feet. Mortimer Crabb gloomily opened the cockpit door, took the other seat.

"Excellent work, Mort," Trent said gaily. "What's the matter with your thumb—get it caught in the door?"

"That Frenchman bit it when I pushed the gag back into his mouth," Crabb said unhappily. He watched Trent set the gyro-pilot. "Well, what place do we get chased out of next?"

"We're visiting merry old England," said Trent, "providing we can find it. I had a slight misunderstanding with the British last summer. But that spy-lead we picked up at Montmartre ought to even matters. If you'd dragged that dancer outside instead of leaving him *hors de combat,* we'd have had all the details."

"I suppose I should have let him break that bottle on my skull," Crabb said sourly. "I was crazy to go along in the first place. Playing that song to see if he was a disguised Nazi—"

"The way he jumped up, there wasn't any doubt," said Trent. "Too bad the French didn't see through that code letter I left. I tried to plant a hint with a non-com back at the airport, but maybe we'll have better luck with the British. It's pretty obvious that the

Nazi Air Force is ready to let loose with something in the next twenty-four hours. Suppose you turn on 'Charlie McCarthy' and see if he can help us spot Croydon."

"I'll thank you not to make fun of my talking-beacon," Crabb said with dignity. "Anyway, how are you going to identify a British station even if we catch one?"

"We're on the course to Croydon," Trent explained, "and if you get a signal on this same bearing, then that's the new emergency station just beyond the village."

Crabb bent forward, tinkered with an odd-looking dial. He pressed a button, and a green light glowed at the top of a cylindrical box. There was a faint hissing from a concealed amplifier, then the box said, *Off, off, off,* in a deep, sepulchral voice startlingly similar to Mortimer Crabb's. He pressed another button marked "Test," then turned the dial, and the box said gloomily, *Right— Left—Right.*

"You'll have to teach Charlie to speak Italian, if we're going to sell him to Mussolini," said Trent. "Try up in the short-wave. Maybe that Croydon station has shifted."

Crabb complied, but without success.

"Leave it on that bearing," said Trent. "Maybe we'll pick it up later, if they're on reduced volume."

FOR FORTY minutes the DC-3 droned through the fog, and still the talking-beacon gave an "off" signal on the Croydon bearing whenever Crabb tried it.

"We ought to be near the English coast," Trent observed. "Test it again."

Crabb switched on the device. Hardly had the tubes warmed up when an angry voice erupted from the speaker-unit:

"Du Lieber Gott! Get in position—it is only eight miles yet!"

Mortimer Crabb's jaw sagged, Trent looked at him with arched eyebrows, then chuckled.

"Mort, you old joker, I didn't know you had it in you. Who fixed up the German speech-tape?"

"The thing's gone crazy!" Crabb said hoarsely. "I never fixed—"

"*Achtung—attention!*" rasped the talking-beacon. "*Come in on course 320, altitude 300 meters, speed 290 kilometers. Give constantly your signal and watch for the beam. Acknowledge.*"

"*Sehr gut,*" muttered the talking-beacon, after a pause. Trent looked at Crabb's bulging eyes, whistled softly.

"Our Charlie seems to have picked up some quaint friends. Keep him set at maximum volume while I drop down to 300 meters."

"I can't understand it," Crabb said dazedly. "It can't say anything but what's on those speech-tapes—unless that relay coil is overloading from— Hey, where are you going?"

"I've a sudden curiosity to find out who's prowling in this fog," said Trent.

"You idiot!" groaned Crabb. "We're liable to smack right into another plane."

"*Drei! On course, speed and altitude,*" blared "Charlie McCarthy."

"*When should I—Gott im Himmel!*"

Simultaneously with the exclamation, a blinding red light stabbed out of the fog almost squarely ahead of the DC-3. Trent rolled the big ship into a vertical bank—and the hurtling shape of a Heinkel He.111 bomber whirled by his tilted wings, into the weird red glow.

"*Drei! An Amerikaner plane!*" screamed the talking-beacon.

The blinding red light had shifted, sweeping to one side as Trent banked. Suddenly it whipped back, and with a two-tongued blast of tracers a torrent of machine-gun bullets raked across the DC-3's right wing.

Trent rammed the throttles full on as he slammed the ship into a tight climbing turn. The mysterious light probed through the fog, caught the light wingtip, and another burst of machine-gun fire hammered at the Douglas.

CHAPTER II

Blind Battle

"**GET BACK** in the cabin and break out the Bren gun," Trent ordered. "Aim at that light." Thereupon, Crabb jerked open the cabin door, disappeared. Trent swiftly reversed the DC-3's turn, and for a moment the strange red light swerved away. Back of it he caught a vague blur, but the fog made it impossible to tell what it was. A grayish bulk suddenly crossed the red beam, and Trent saw the pointed, transparent nose of the Heinkel bomber. The Nazi bow-gunner sent a fiery blast smoking at the nose of the Douglas. Trent zoomed the DC-3 over the Nazi bomber, chandelling before the gunner in the turret could swing his air cannon.

A clatter sounded back in the cabin as Crabb cut loose with the Bren gun. The Heinkel lurched crazily, and Trent saw one of the pilots tumble out of sight, just as the red beam flashed back across the ship. Before Crabb could fire again, the weird light stabbed straight into the side of the DC-3's cabin, and his next burst went angling off into space. Trent, likewise half blinded, rolled the Douglas away from the beam. For a second he thought they would crash headlong into the Heinkel, then the Nazi bomber zoomed frantically and the DC-3 roared beneath with only a few feet to spare.

As the Heinkel zoomed, the mysterious red light again probed up through the fog, whipping back toward the Douglas in an obvious attempt to guide the Heinkel. Trent shielded his eyes with one hand, banked to give Crabb a better aim.

"Get that light, Mort!" he shouted.

"I can't see anything—they've got me blinded!" came a lugubrious howl from the inventor. Nevertheless, the Bren gun hammered again, and tracers lanced out through the fog, pallid in the red glow. The light shifted suddenly, and in the same instant Trent saw the Heinkel charging back into the fight. Guns were blazing from all three turrets of the Nazi bomber, and as the red beam whirled again toward the Douglas two streaks of tracers shot from behind the dazzling light.

Trent cast a swift look through the cockpit window, hauled the controls back. Crabb's tracers lifted up, crossed the bow of the Heinkel, and smoke puffed out from the nearer engine nacelle. The red light whipped madly toward Trent's cockpit, and he had a split-second of total blindness from that eerie crimson glow. Then the light went out. In the ensuing darkness he saw a tongue of flame, quickly spreading, where his hasty zoom had sent the Bren gun's bullets into the Heinkel's engine.

The Nazi ship nosed down steeply, plunged through the fog with a plume of flame and smoke trailing behind. Trent shoved the controls ahead and followed with half-throttled motors. There was now no sign of the mysterious red light.

Mortimer Crabb stumbled into the cockpit, hauled himself into the copilot's seat. His gloomy face had a dazed, unbelieving look.

"That bomber—what hit it?" he said hoarsely.

"A little gift from Messrs. Crabb and Trent. I angled up so your shots would get it. And I think we hit the light, too—or at least something back of it."

The howl of the DC-3's wings almost drowned the last words. Trent flicked a glance at the altimeter, pulled out of the dive. The burning Heinkel vanished in the fog, and three seconds later a terrific explosion shook the sky.

The Douglas shuddered, slid off on one wing. Trent caught it, looked down through a clear space which had been literally blasted through the fog. A rugged cliff was visible and beyond it the edge of a large town, almost hidden by the dusk and mist Directly beneath the DC-3, a gigantic wave was rushing in to fill a crater at the foot of the cliff, where the Heinkel's bombs had exploded as the ship struck. Fragments of the bomber were falling back onto the beach and into the sea.

As the mists slowly began to close the hole in the fog, a search-light blazed up from the far end of the cliff. Trent nosed down hurriedly, scanning the piers and buildings momentarily revealed.

"It's Folkestone," he told Crabb. "There's a new field near the old Shorncliffe camp. We'll try to land there."

"That red light—what do you make of it?" mumbled the inventor as Trent lowered the landing-gear.

"Couldn't tell much—it evidently pierced the fog for the chaps behind it. Must have been mounted on—"

T-t-t-t-t-t! The DC-3 quivered as a burst of machine-gun fire pelted the left wingtip. Trent ruddered hastily, and the next blast from the ground guns went wide. He heard Mortimer Crabb groan, saw a Spitfire come zooming up through the murk just as a Bristol Blenheim swung in from the right, its nose-guns flaming at long-range. Trent whistled.

"Mort, I'm afraid we're getting too popular!"

He whipped the Douglas into a vertical bank, eased off the rudder and let the ship scream down in a fast forward slip. The Spitfire lanced after them, blanking off the Blenheim gunner's fire. The Leas promenade swept past beneath, and the Douglas grazed the steeple of an old church atop the west cliff. Trent pulled out of the slip, jerked the throttles, as the murky outlines of a flying-field showed ahead.

TWO MORE searchlights had now blazed up, frost-white, and along the front of the hangars Trent glimpsed row after row of bombers and fighters, at least two hundred ships. He made a shallow turn, missed the top of a hill beyond the field, and let the Douglas settle to the mist-covered ground.

"Left—left—left," the talking-beacon suddenly spoke up in a gloomy tone.

"Thanks, Charlie, but you're a bit late," said Trent. "Mort, your little pet certainly has an odd sense of humor. A left turn now would put us smack into that third shed."

"Stop this plane and let me out of here," Crabb said dismally. "I'm going to make a clean breast of everything before these Englishmen stand us up in front of a wall."

Trent laughed. "Always the optimist. Better let me handle this. I've an idea—"

"You and your ideas!" groaned Crabb. He reached up, cut off the master switch, and yanked the parking-brake back as the DC-3 slowed. "Go ahead and cook up your crazy idea—I'm getting out!"

"*Right—right—right,*" said the talking-beacon dolefully.

"You, too, Charlie?" Trent said in mock reproach. He went back into the cabin. "Before you depart, Mort, perhaps we'd better get together on our stories—and, by the way, the British are sticklers for passports."

"You won't bluff me this time," Crabb retorted sourly. He opened the cabin door, swung down, and let himself drop. Trent sighed, lighted one of his D'Artagnan cigarettes, and followed his sad-faced partner. He dropped into a misty darkness relieved only by the futile probings of the searchlights which sought to locate the Douglas. Crabb stalked off toward the nearest light.

"That's up on Castle Hill," said Trent amiably. "There are some fine old ruins up there, if you like that sort of thing. Personally, I never cared for falling into old moats on dark nights."

"I could stand anything after that flying lunatic asylum," said Crabb, in a hollow voice.

The roar of a car speeding in second gear cut short Trent's answer. A few moments later, lights showed dimly through the mists.

"Here comes the reception committee," he observed. "They seem to be in a bit of a hurry."

The car loomed through the fog, jolted to a stop near the tail of the Douglas, Mortimer Crabb started toward it, but the lights instantly went out.

"Drive up closer, *Dumkopf!*" came a harsh whisper from the rear seat. "Quick, before *der Englander* pigs get here!"

Eric Trent's fingers closed on Crabb's arm, and he silently drew the inventor back into the fog.

"Good Lord, you've landed us in Germany," Crabb said in a hoarse undertone.

"No, it seems our British friends have termites," whispered Trent. "Stay back here out of sight."

He tiptoed closer to the car. By now, it was alongside the Douglas, and a shadowy figure was climbing from the hood to the door of the ship. Two others were scrambling up onto the hood.

"*Ach,* the door is unfastened!" said the first man in an alarmed tone. "They must have escaped."

"I hear some one talking up forward," muttered one of the others. "Get in there—and remember, no noise! Use the butt of your gun!"

Trent had stepped on his cigarette the moment he heard the first German words. He waited until two of the men had crawled into the cabin, then he stole toward the front of the car. There was a sudden exclamation from one of the two spies who had gone inside the Douglas.

"*Mein Gott!* There is no one here—it is a robot pilot that talks!"

"They must be hidden aft!" snarled the man left standing on the car hood. "Richter's message said he was attacked. A robot pilot does not fire a machine gun. Back with you fast—quick!"

Trent was so near now that he caught the faint gleam of a pistol in the speaker's hand. He reached out, seized the man's ankle and gave a vigorous jerk.

"*Himmelherrgott!*" howled the spy. He came down with a resounding thud, and his gun clattered from the hood to the ground. "Hans! Max! We've been trapped!"

Trent scooped up the fallen pistol, jumped back. The Nazi had plunged headlong to the ground on the other side of the car. And now with an oath, he sprang up and dashed into the mists. The two spies in the ship ran to the door just as a searchlight beam mistily swung across the Douglas. A gun blazed, and a bullet ricochetted from the hood of the car back of which Trent had crouched. Trent triggered a quick shot at the man's leg, and the spy stumbled, fell to the ground.

"Eric!" Mortimer Crabb yelled hoarsely. "I've got one of the—OW!"

TRENT whirled as Crabb's words turned into a howl of pain. The inventor was struggling with the Nazi who had escaped, and both men fell, rolled over, as Trent ran to the spot. The spy had jerked out a knife, but when he saw Trent he leaped to his feet and fled. Trent aimed a shot after him, but the headlights of a car suddenly appeared almost directly beyond, and he held his fire.

The Nazi lunged to one side, away from the blurred lights, and vanished. There was a grinding of gears, back near the Douglas, and the spies' car raced away. When Trent reached the ship, there was no trace of the Nazi he had shot. With a squeal of brakes, a khaki-colored R.A.F. machine drew up. A lanky major sprang out, followed by three armed Tommies.

"You're a trifle late, Major," said Trent, pleasantly. "The official greeters have left—they seemed to be in a hurry."

The major stared at the American, covering him meanwhile with an automatic. He had a hard jaw and the look of a man seasoned by service under a blazing sun.

"I'll take that pistol of yours," he said grimly. He jerked his head at a beefy corporal. "Get that other man and search him."

The corporal stuck a gun against Crabb's ribs. "Lift yer paws up, Fritzy, and be quick about it."

"My name is Mortimer Crabb, and I am not armed," said the inventor gloomily.

"Be careful, Corporal," the major said tersely. "They may be desperate enough to try some trick. They know what happens to belligerents wearing civilian clothes."

"I'll tyke no chances," said the corporal. " 'E's a killer, if I ever see one."

Trent chuckled. The major eyed him coldly, reached out and warily began to search his pockets, keeping the automatic poised.

"I could save you a lot of time," said Trent. "For instance, our passports are up here—" he negligently thrust his fingers inside his coat.

"Put your hands up," said the major, sharply. Trent shrugged, obeyed. As he raised his right hand, a lighted cigarette appeared in his fingers, as though plucked from the air. The major jumped. Trent smiled, took a puff at the cigarette and exhaled.

"D'Artagnans—my private brand," he told the startled Englishman. "Would you care for one?"

The major stared, and the Tommies looked open-mouthed at the gold case which materialized suddenly in Trent's left hand.

"Lord help us!" groaned Mortimer Crabb. "We get arrested as spies—and you start playing magician again."

"Now you've spoiled the illusion," said Trent. "I wish, Mort, you'd be more considerate."

"Smart tricks won't help you," the major said curtly. "If you'd been in uniform, that bombing would be a simple act of war, but—"

"Bombing?" said Trent. "And where is the bomber?"

The major wheeled, then a blank look came into his face as he took a closer look at the mist-shrouded DC-3. He was turning back to Trent when another R.A.F. car roared through the fog and skidded to a halt nearby. A big man in flying gear jumped from the running-board, followed by two mechanics in flying suits.

"So you've got them, Major Hawes?" said the big pilot. He shoved up his goggles, looked savagely at Trent and Crabb from under bushy black eyebrows. "Spies, eh? Did you get the whole crew?"

"I don't know. But there's something peculiar about it, Smeade. This ship isn't a bomber—it's an American Douglas, an airliner."

"There was another plane—a German bomber!" Mortimer Crabb blurted out. "This is a privately-owned American ship. We were just trying to find a place to land—"

"Listen! What's that?" said Major Hawes, as a guttural voice sounded from inside the Douglas, speaking in German.

"—*drei, eine, acknowledged,*" said the talking-beacon. "*Confirm advance zero-hour to seven. Das ist alle.*"

Major Hawes sprang past Smeade, who was staring in amazement at the Douglas.

"Come out of there—and come running!" he grated.

"Now that," said Trent, "will be something to see."

"Keep quiet," snapped Hawes. He glared back at the cabin doorway. "I'll give you ten seconds to come out—then I'll start shooting."

"It's only a talking radio beacon," Crabb said dismally. "Something's gone wrong with it, and it's been picking up German messages in the ultra high-frequency band."

HAWES stepped on the fender of his car, peered cautiously into the ship, then climbed inside. In a few moments he reappeared.

"Captain Smeade, take a mechanic and taxi this plane back to the line. Then have that device in the cockpit brought into my office, along with a six-volt battery. It's apparently some new type of radio these spies were using."

"Then you're convinced they're spies?" said Smeade, with an ugly look at Trent and Crabb.

"There's a machine-gun in the cabin," Major Hawes told him significantly. "I'll get to the bottom of this affair. Corporal, have your men bring the prisoners to my office. You can use Captain Smeade's car."

Ten minutes later, Trent and Crabb were marched into Hawes' office at the rear of a portable barracks. Heavy black cloth covered the windows. The major turned from the phone as the prisoners were brought in, and Trent saw a gleam in his eye.

"All right, Corporal, you and your men can wait out in the hall. I've got a pistol here if they should try anything."

"Beggin' the Major's pardon, hi'd keep a close eye on this un," said the corporal, with a dark look at Trent. " 'E might pull a gun right out o' nowheres, like 'e did that cigarette."

"Hardly likely," said Hawes. "And here comes Captain Smeade, if I need any help."

The big captain came hastily in from the hallway, carrying the talking beacon. Behind him was a stolid-faced mechanic with a battery.

"I brought one of the lab men to test this apparatus," said Smeade, putting down the talking beacon and looking quickly at Trent and Crabb. "Did you get anything from these two, Major?"

"Not *from* them, but *about* them," said Hawes. "Have you ever heard the name 'Eric Trent?'"

Smeade's bushy brows drew together. "Not the American who caused all that trouble on the German-Holland border two months ago?"

"Yes, this is the man," nodded Hawes. "And I just learned he has an amazing record. Up till now he's been able to wriggle out of every scrape. But this time—"

"Before you go on with this interesting dissection," said Trent, "I'd like to make a call."

"Put down that telephone!" roared Hawes. "Of all the cheek!"

"I'm only trying to save you from sudden retirement from the military service," Trent said genially. "I'd suggest you call Number 10 Downing Street and ask the Prime Minister why an apology was made to a certain Eric Trent a year ago—and why Colonel Hilary Beems resigned shortly after."

"You can't bluff me, Trent!" shouted Hawes. "You and this sour-faced friend of yours are working for the *Gestapo!*"

CHAPTER III

Secret of Shop Three

"*THAT'S FINE,*" said Trent. "I wish you'd tell the *Gestapo*, too—they've been a little annoying lately."

"Try to talk yourself out of *this*," snapped Hawes. He picked up a scribbled memorandum, began reading: "*Digest of a radio warning just received from our Intelligence in Paris: Be on lookout for Eric Trent and Mortimer Crabb, Americans, escaped from Le Bourget Field—*"

"—After a fight in Montmartre. Yes, something to do with leaving a Soviet code message, knocking an Apache dancer unconscious, and kidnapping a *Surete* officer," Trent finished amiably.

"Then you admit it!" gasped the major.

Trent grinned. "Frankly, I thought it a neat bit of work. You might tell your Intelligence johnnies in Paris that the dancer is a Soviet spy. The chap who was stabbed is a Nazi, by the way. Clumsy chap—fell on his own knife when I tripped him. If it's of any interest, that code message hinted at some skulduggery by the Nazi Air Force—within the next twenty-four hours."

"Major, we'd better turn these men over to Intelligence," Smeade said harshly. "This fellow Trent sounds like a dangerous man—if he isn't completely insane."

"You don't know the half of it, mister," said Mortimer Crabb sadly. "If I'd only listened to that half-brother of mine and stayed in Vermont...."

"Sergeant, is that thing hooked up yet?" Hawes cut in, as the mechanic looked stolidly from Trent to Crabb.

"Yes, sir," the man grunted. "But it ain't workin'."

"Something's been disconnected, or the 'on' light would, show," said Crabb. "I can prove it's nothing but a—"

"Keep away from that," ordered Hawes. "Smeade, I think I've figured out this whole thing. These men were after that secret projector. That bombing was a trick to distract attention so they could land in the Douglas and raid the laboratory shed in this fog. They didn't know, of course, that the projector was being tested in the Blenheim."

Trent's eyes rested for a second on Hawes' automatic. "This 'projector' wouldn't by any chance be a red fog-piercing light?"

Hawes started, and Captain Smeade's eyes bore into Trent.

"So you *did* know! That's what you *were* after!" Hawes said fiercely.

"You're crazy!" erupted Mortimer Crabb. "Somebody else must have got your idea already. We ran into that red fog-light—and somebody was guiding the German bomber with it."

Hawes stiffened. For a second he stared at Crabb, then his eyes flicked up at Captain Smeade, and there was a sudden, horrified look on his face. Smeade's face was deathly white.

"You!" whispered Hawes. "Insisting on that test today—"

His hand snatched up the pistol. Smeade leaped back, clawing inside his flying-suit. But Trent hurtled against him and knocked him to the floor.

A shot crashed, and Trent whirled. The mechanic held a smoking gun, and Hawes was tottering back, fumbling at his breast.

"Smeade—you devil—" Hawes whispered. Then his knees buckled and he sprawled across the desk. There was a shout from out in the hall, the sound of running feet. The mechanic hurled the gun across the room just as the door burst open, followed it with a wild leap at Trent.

"Grab him!" Smeade shouted hoarsely as he scrambled up from the floor. "He's killed the Major!"

The guard-corporal and two enraged Tommies slammed Trent back against the wall, and Smeade hastily drew his gun, covered Mortimer Crabb. A lieutenant and three or four Headquarters men came dashing in from the hall. The lieutenant, a redheaded youngster with R.A.F. wings, looked down in horror at Hawes' body.

"This damned spy shot him!" Smeade rasped, with a furious lunge at Trent.

"Lieutenant, check the prints on that—" Trent's swift warning was cut off as Smeade struck him viciously across the mouth. Two Tommies had seized Mortimer Crabb, and his frantic attempts at an explanation were lost in the hub-bub.

"Get them out to my car!" snarled Smeade. "When the men hear the C.O. has been murdered by these Nazis, they might take things into their own hands. Not that I'd blame them—but a firing squad will take care of them fast enough."

A HASTY glance passed between him and the spy-mechanic, and as Trent and Crabb were hustled out of the building, the mechanic went back into the office. Trent knew he had gone to recover his service pistol, but the American's attempts to be heard were futile. A thickset lance-corporal was waiting near Smeade's car, and he hurriedly started the motor at a signal from the big pilot.

"Where are you taking them?" said the red-headed lieutenant sharply. Smeade hesitated for a fraction of a second.

"To Folkestone jail, for tonight," he answered. "I'll have them taken to London in the morning."

"Then I'll go with you," said the lieutenant. "I'm Intelligence Officer for this outfit, and these spies should be questioned as quickly as possible."

"All right, get in," snapped Smeade. Trent saw the grim look on his face, then the door to Headquarters closed off the light, and the car rolled away into the fog. Trent felt the hard snout of a gun in his side, knew that Smeade would fire at the least pretext. The young lieutenant sat on the other side of him. Crabb was huddled in the front seat beside the driver, and the spy-mechanic was wedged between him and the door, turned half around so that his gun could be pointed back into the rear as well as against Crabb's side.

"Duncan, perhaps you'd better go back and phone Corps what's happened," Smeade said suddenly to the lieutenant. "You can follow in a Headquarters car."

"I told the O.D. to take care of that," said the red-headed pilot. "I'd like to get all the facts on this thing—it all happened so quickly—poor old Hawes—"

"I know," Smeade said, with a gruff pretense of sympathy. "If I did it my way, I'd finish these two swine here and now. But we can't—"

"What are we stopping here for?" exclaimed Duncan, as the car slowed beside a dark structure. "Why, this is Number Three Shed—the special lab."

Trent waited for Smeade's gun to shift, but the pseudo-captain never moved. The spy-mechanic spun quickly and in the same instant Trent caught the glint of the driver's pistol as he covered Crabb.

"Sergeant, have you lost your mind?" Duncan said dazedly.

"Get out, and keep still, *Englander!*" rasped the mechanic.

"Captain Smeade, for heaven's sake, shoot!" cried Duncan. "This mechanic is a spy!"

"Shut that fool's mouth!" Smeade said in a harsh undertone. The spy-mechanic lunged over from the front seat and brought his gun down at Duncan's head. Trent instinctively jerked the young Englishman to one side, but the barrel of the gun struck Duncan a glancing blow and he reeled against the side of the car. Smeade's pistol was hard against Trent's ribs.

"Hans," barked Smeade to the driver, pointing to Crabb, "take that walking tombstone inside. Then come back and help Schmidt drag out this dumbhead of a *Leutnant.*" He prodded Trent with the gun, forced him cut of the car and to the door of the shed. He knocked swiftly, and the door was guardedly opened.

"Richter! What's happened?" exclaimed the man inside.

"Not so loud," muttered the spy who had called himself Smeade. "Open up—we've three prisoners."

Trent and Crabb were hurried into the shed and through another doorway into a space fitted up as a combination chemical laboratory and electrical workshop. Coils of wire hung on pegs, and reflectors, lenses, and vacuum tubes of various types and sizes were scattered on workbenches. Part of an odd-looking searchlight was assembled on a table in the center of the room, with wires trailing to a power socket.

Trent also noticed a bank of red tubes at the center of the reflector. Nearby was a cabinet filled with vials of chemicals, and adjacent to it was a table on which was a litter of test-tubes and bunsen burners. The floor was covered with odds and ends of it wire, solder, tape, and other débris.

A MAN in dungarees lay groaning on a cot in one corner, and Trent saw a bloody bandage on his right leg. The spy who had admitted Richter and the others, a sullen-faced man in private's uniform, looked vindictively at Trent. There was a bruise on his face, and Trent recognized the man he had tumbled from the hood of the spy-car.

"So you got the *Amerikaners,*" the spy said savagely.

"*Ja,* but we've no time to waste on them, Wolfe," Richter said in a tense voice. "Help carry Max out to the car."

"What are you going to do with me?" moaned the man with the injured leg.

"Hans will take you to Margate. The agent on King Street will hide you."

"What about me?" said Wolfe. His heavy, brutal face had an alarmed look.

"You're going with Schmidt and me in the Blenheim. I'll explain in a minute. Take Max out and help Schmidt bring in the other prisoner. Hans, you go ahead with Max. If the sentry tries to stop you, yell at him that it's Captain Smeade with the prisoners and keep going."

The wounded man was taken out, groaning. Richter grimly covered Trent and Crabb.

"Well, Eric, I guess this is the end," Crabb said gloomily.

"You might try to buy the gentleman off," said Trent. "You'll pardon me, *Herr Richter*, if I call you a gentleman? It's merely a figure of speech."

Richter glared at him over the gun. "What's this about—this buying me off?"

"My esteemed partner has 500,000 marks cozily tucked away in an Amsterdam bank," Trent answered. "Profit from the sale of one of his inventions to—ah—one of the belligerents."

Richter's face turned a mottled purple. "You thieving *Schwein!* I heard all about that trick. An Amsterdam bank, *hein?* Well, the Reich will soon have that money back."

Trent's dark eyes had an amused look. "Really, *mein Herr*, you do my partner an injustice. He is not simple enough to make it an ordinary matter of presenting a passbook. He must appear in person and be precisely identified even down to a mole on—shall we say—his empennage."

"The *Gestapo* can arrange many things," Richter said harshly. "A week or two at Deschau prison-camp, you know. Then *Herr* Crabb will be only too glad to cooperate."

The conversation had been in German. Mortimer Crabb looked helplessly at Trent. "What are you up to, Eric?"

Before Trent could answer, Wolfe and Schmidt, the spy who had shot Hawes, came in with Lieutenant Duncan stumbling between them. Blood was trickling down Duncan's face. He looked around glassily as the men halted him, saw the sneering grin on Richter's face.

"Smeade—you traitor!" he said hoarsely.

"Tie him and throw him on that cot," Richter directed. "We may take him with us. He's the Intelligence officer for this post, and he's had access to important information."

"We'd better not waste time on him," Schmidt said nervously. "I didn't tell you, but Hawes isn't dead—he was still breathing when I went back."

"You imbecile!" rasped Richter. "Why didn't you finish him off?"

"There were three men in there—I had to lie about the gun, tell them you wanted to keep it for evidence."

"He's not likely to recover his senses soon enough to bother us," muttered Richter. "But we must lose no time. Tie up Duncan, then break open the locked compartment in the safe. I want the blueprints and the formula for the gas in those vacuum tubes, in case our engineers can't analyze it."

Duncan was too weak to struggle, and the spies quickly bound him to the cot. His agonized gaze shifted to Trent's face, as he realized that the two men were actually prisoners and not spies.

"Try to stop them," he moaned. "They're stealing the fog-piercing light—England will be at the mercy of their bombers."

"Sorry, old man," said Trent. "We're a bit handicapped at the moment."

"What of these two?" Schmidt demanded brusquely.

"The *Gestapo* has been after Trent for two years," said Richter. "But he's a dangerous man—he was once a magician's assistant. If we've time to tie him up securely in the ship, we'll take him. The other man goes with us—we'll get a special reward for bringing him in. He stole 500,000 marks from the Reich."

WOLFE had hurried into the adjoining room, and Trent heard the sound of a chisel biting into steel. Schmidt looked hastily at the laboratory clock.

"The Blenheim's engines should be started soon. By now, the Heinkels must be half-way here."

"I've timed everything," Richter said in a taut voice. "We don't want to take off too soon or those accursed Englishmen may get suspicious. I have allowed twelve minutes from the take-off to the moment when the Heinkels will be ranged behind us, ready to drop their bombs. Even if somebody investigates when they hear the Blenheim, they won't have time to do anything. The bombs will be falling before they could more than warm up a few fighters, and in this fog they'd be helpless, anyway. We'll blot out the entire two hundred planes and the *Englanders* along with them, just by way of a start in the new Nazi air drive."

"You're sure that Heinkel making the first test today didn't have time to radio back what happened?" Schmidt said dubiously.

"No, they crashed too quickly." Richter scowled at Trent. "If it hadn't been for this Yankee *Teufel* blundering in on us, that test would have been perfect. I had to flash word that it had succeeded, and they haven't had time back at Dusseldorf to realize the Heinkel is missing. But have no fear. When the others return to Germany after blowing this place off the map, the *Generalstab* will not worry about one ship. They will probably think it was lost in the Channel."

Trent's gaze strayed idly past Richter's head while the spy was talking. On the opposite wall was a sheet of reflector metal, with a section cut out at one corner. Trent could see a clear image of the wall behind him. A few feet to the right of where he stood was a shelf with several vacuum tubes lying on it. He let his glance shift to the work-bench before him, which stood to the left of the chemical cabinet. There was a pair of shears close to the edge. He made an apparently furtive movement toward it.

"Get back! *Handen hoch!*" snarled Richter.

Trent backed away, hastily raised his hands. In the reflector he could see that his left hand was now only a few inches from the shelf with the vacuum tubes. Richter glowered from him to the shears.

"I've heard about your knife-throwing, *Herr* Trent. Try another trick like that and it will be your last."

Trent let a disappointed look come into his eyes. A moment later Schmidt came in from the other room, handed Richter some folded papers. As Richter slid them inside his flying-suit, he jerked his head toward Wolfe.

"Clip some wire and bind *Herr* Crabb's hands behind him before we take him out. Schmidt, go prime the Blenheim's motors and unlock the controls. Set the fog-light in the tail to fan out at its widest angle so the Heinkel pilots will have no trouble. We will be there in a minute."

Schmidt hurried out. Wolfe took down a roll of wire, started to cut off a section. Richter backed around so that he could cover both Americans and also see Duncan. The Englishman was straining desperately at his bonds. Trent's eyes caught Mortimer Crabb's for a split second. His lifted hand was within an inch of the nearest vacuum tube when from out on the field an alarm siren suddenly shrieked.

CHAPTER IV

Red Death

R **ICHTER** whirled with a look of consternation. *"Himmel!* They must have caught Hans and Max—or else Hawes has recovered his senses!"

Wolfe made a wild leap for the door.

"Come back here!" snarled Richter. He snatched the roll of wire, jammed his gun against Crabb's back. "I'll take him out to the ship—finish off Duncan, and bring the other man!"

Wolfe jerked out his gun as Richter rushed Crabb from the room. Covering Trent, he hastily stepped backward toward Duncan. His eyes flicked sidewise toward the struggling Englishman and he lifted the gun for a murderous blow. Trent's nimble fingers instantly closed on the vacuum tube.

"Get your hands up!" he snapped.

Wolfe's head jerked around just as Trent hurled the tube. There was a sharp report as the tube struck squarely in the German's face. Wolfe staggered back with a scream, clawing at his eyes.

"Gott! You have blinded me!" he shrieked.

There was no pity on Trent's face. He picked up the shears, sprang across to the cot, hurriedly severed the wires that held Duncan.

"Warn Headquarters!" he said swiftly. He snatched up Wolfe's gun, raced out into the murk. An engine sputtered just as he emerged, and in a few seconds he heard a second one start. Guided by the sound, he ran at top speed through the fog. The siren was still shrieking, but he could dimly hear excited voices as men ran by him in the darkness.

The blurred shape of a Bristol Blenheim bomber became visible directly ahead, its engine exhausts flickering in the gloom. Just as he reached the steps to the cabin doorway, the engines revved up, and the door whipped against him. He forced it back, plunged into the darkened bomber.

"Schmidt—where are you?" he shouted in German. Above the roar of the motors he heard a faint answer, then a flashlight suddenly stabbed at his face. He had a fleeting glimpse of Mortimer Crabb lying prone on the catwalk between the side-gunner positions, with Schmidt back of him, his face a pasty yellow above the light.

A look of dismay shot into Schmidt's eyes when he saw Trent. He jumped back, fired as the motors went full on for the take-off. The bullet drilled the side of the ship. Trent's pistol jetted flame and Schmidt toppled over, a dark hole between his eyes. Mortimer Crabb was struggling to free his hands from the wire twisted about them. Trent knelt after a swift glance forward. The thunder of the motors had evidently drowned the shots. He laid down his gun, quickly freed Crabb's hands.

"I thought you'd be dead by now," the inventor said with a gloomy grin. "You've got more lives than a cat."

"Never mind that," said Trent. "We've got to move fast. Take Schmidt's pistol and come—"

He broke off as a tiny blue light flickered on a panel a few feet away. By the rays of the flashlight he saw a helmet with a telephone headset hanging near the empty gunner's-seat. He swiftly put it on, threw the toggle switch.

"This is Schmidt. *Was ist?*" he said harshly into the telephone mouthpiece.

"Did you set the tail fog-light for a full-angle flare?" came Richter's taut voice from up forward in the cockpit.

"*Ja,*" Trent answered.

"Did Wolfe get aboard?"

"He is here, yes," Trent said. "But he is hurt—one of the *Englander* sentries shot at him."

Richter swore. "Then get up here yourself—I will need help."

"I'll be there as soon as I tie the *Amerikaner* securely," Trent told him. He jerked off the helmet, peered out through the gunner's turret. They were now in the air and there was a faint glow beneath, where a searchlight vainly strove to pierce the fog. It faded as Richter climbed.

"What crazy business are you up to now?" Crabb said dismally.

"Bring that coil of wire," said Trent. "We're going to pay *Herr* Richter a surprise visit—I hope."

He switched off the flashlight, felt his way forward between gun turrets, tanks, and bomb-bays. At the end of the narrow catwalk was a dim glow from the instrument board in the bomber's cockpit. Abruptly, a crimson light appeared, and he could see Richter silhouetted in the pilot's seat. The spy's left hand was on a knob connected with the powerful fog-piercing light in the nose of the ship. He set it to point downward, reached for the radio microphone.

"*Drei* calling Heinkel Group Two. *Drei* calling Heinkel Group Two...."

There was a brief pause as he switched to receiving and plugged in his helmet earphones. Then he cut in the generator again.

"*Jawohl*, hold speed, course and altitude as ordered. I am at 400 meters, course 90. I will circle three kilometers out, until I see you fly under me. When you see the light, reduce speed to drop behind until I am ahead and below."

RICHTER pronged the microphone, reached up and turned a switch. Above his head a mirror instantly glowed with red light.

Trent could see that it was connected with a periscope turned aft to show the area illuminated by the fog-light in the tail. He came a step closer.

"Too bad, *mein Herr,* all this effort is wasted," he said pleasantly.

Richter whirled, and a stark look came into his eyes.

"I wouldn't try for that gun," said Trent, "unless you want to explore Valhalla with your friend Schmidt."

The spy sagged at the controls, as though beaten, then with a furious kick at the rudder he hurled the bomber into a skid. Trent saw the motion, but not quite in time. The violent lurch threw him to the catwalk on top of Mortimer Crabb, and the pistol slipped from his numbed right hand.

Triumphantly, Richter snatched for his own gun. Trent's left hand flashed behind him to the wire Crabb had dropped. The coil went whizzing through the air. Before Richter could draw his gun, the coil whirled down over his head, pinning his arms to his sides. With a furious oath, he jerked one arm loose, but Trent was already on his feet. He gripped the spy's free arm, whirled him out of the seat. Richter landed on his back, lay glaring up in helpless rage.

"Keep him covered Mort," Trent said coolly. "If you have to shoot him, make it a leg. We'll need him for evidence."

He reached down and pulled off Richter's helmet, quickly climbed into the pilot's seat. As he put on the helmet and plugged in the headset, he saw a penciled diagram clipped at one side of the instrument board. It showed the Blenheim at the head of a long, narrow Vee which consisted of twelve ships. A profile sketch at one side showed the twelve bombers in two levels, with the point-ship of the Vee 60 meters lower than the second and third bombers, and the same alternation throughout the formation. Two fluctuating lines from the point-ship ran back through the Vee, and Trent surmised that the Heinkel leader was using a low-wattage transmitter with two short-range directional beams for his pilots to guide on in the fog.

The last detail of the Nazi scheme was now clear. Richter had planned to guide the Heinkels the last three kilometers to the

Folkestone base, spotting the massed British planes and squadron buildings with the fog-piercing lights. Helpless to see the Nazi raiders roaring above them in the mists, the British would have been massacred, their grounded armada totally destroyed.

Trent's eyes flitted to the clock. The Blenheim was approximately ten miles out from Folkestone, if his estimate was correct. Almost the three kilometers Richter had stipulated. He picked up the hand-mike.

"*Drei* calling Heinkel Group Two. *Drei* calling Heinkel Group Two."

The answer came the instant he switched to receiving: "*Group Two. Go ahead, Number Three!*"

"What is your estimated position?"

"*Five kilometers from Folkestone, on bearing 270. Altitude, upper half of formation, 300 meters. We are still spread out. Cannot close in until we see the light for fear of collision.*"

"I am starting to circle," Trent said quickly. "Watch for the light."

As he pronged the mike, he looked back at Mortimer Crabb and Richter. The inventor was sitting mournfully on the German's stomach, the muzzle of the gun rammed into Richter's mouth. The spy's face was distorted with fear and rage.

"I'm warning you, mister," Crabb said in a sad voice, "if you make another jump like that your brains are going to be in a mess."

"Watch out for your thumb, Mort," grinned Trent. "Remember that Frenchman."

"Never mind me," retorted Crabb. "What the devil are *you* doing? Who's that you were talking to?"

"A dozen Heinkel bombers are headed for that field," said Trent. "They're expecting this ship to guide them in."

"Then cut off that light, you idiot!" howled Crabb. "Get away from here. They won't find the place in this fog."

"They'd go ahead and drop their eggs blind," said Trent. "They might hit Folkestone, too, and kill hundreds of—"

"Drei! I see the red light!" the excited voice of the Heinkel leader rasped into Trent's phones. *"Tilt it down, or you will blind us."*

TRENT grasped the knob which controlled the fog-light in the tail. But instead of tilting it down, he flicked it upward. As he leveled out, heading back toward Folkestone, he seized the mike.

"Group Two! Close in—keep *under* the light. I will point it down to spot the targets when the Vee is aligned."

Back of him, Richter gave a strangled yell. Trent kept the mike in one hand, watching the periscope mirror overhead. A tingling went up his spine as the turreted nose of a black Heinkel He.111 emerged from the fog, and dimly back of it, two more, to right and left. The Heinkel edged in under the up-stilted fog light, so close that he could see the bomber-gunner in the bow. Midway of the black hull, the top turret was pointed forward, with an air-cannon ready for action. The leader's ship was directly on their tail.

Trent cast a hasty glance at the clock, lifted the microphone to his lips. "I am nosing down. Keep at my altitude. We will make the lowest possible approach directly over Folkestone."

The tense voice of the Heinkel leader grated into his ears as he released the transmitter button: *"Drei! There are three planes not yet in line—wait until they—"*

Trent jumped. Out of the mists on the right, a black shape suddenly angled down steeply. Blinded by the upward beam, one of the three Heinkel pilots was heading straight for the Blenheim's right wing!

Trent hurled the Blenheim into a dive. There was a muffled shout from behind him as the sudden maneuver threw Mortimer Crabb headlong under the co-pilot's seat. Richter leaped across the inventor's sprawled figure, snatched the dangling microphone which Trent had dropped.

"Group Two!" he screamed. A crazed, fanatical light blazed into his eyes. "Shoot down the Blenheim! It's a trap—"

Trent snapped off the transmitter switch a split second before Mortimer Crabb's frantic lunge carried Richter to the cockpit floor. There was a sudden bright flash in the periscope mirror, and a gaping hole appeared in the top of the Blenheim's cockpit. By the red glow of the rear fog-light, Trent saw the leading Heinkel plunge in, the mid-turret air-cannon twitch down for another shot. He booted the rudder, snatched at the control-knob which operated the rear light.

Through the weird red tunnel made by the light in the Blenheim's nose, the mast of a freighter suddenly showed, dead ahead, then the piers of Folkestone leaped swiftly out of the fog. Trent whirled the bomber into a lightning turn. In the periscope mirror he could see the leading Heinkel charging blindly in, machine-guns blasting from its nose-turret. For another second he waited.

Then like a wall of doom the East Cliff sprang out of the fog!

Trent hauled the controls back, and the Blenheim shrieked up in a furious zoom. For an instant he thought they were lost—then the ship cleared the top of the cliff. A terrific blast of flame shot up through the mists, then a second, and two more in swift succession as the first bomb-laden Heinkels crashed head-on into the cliff.

Trent leveled out, banked away from the city, switching off the fan of red light at the tail. The crimson beam in the nose slanted down through the fog, picked out the fragmentary details of a dreadful scene. Now utterly blinded, the remaining Heinkels were twisting wildly back toward the sea, as leaping flames shot through the murk where the first four ships bad crashed.

As Trent watched, two Nazi bombers whirled out of the mists and into headlong collision. The blast as their bombs went off shook the Blenheim's wings. A third Heinkel, revealed in that frightful explosion, banked wildly away—and spun down into the sea.

Somewhere off in the gloom there was another flash of flame, then suddenly the remaining Heinkels were gone, fleeing desperately into the night. Trent turned the control-knob of the bow light, swept it over the blazing wreckage below the cliff, then slowly banked the ship back toward the British air base.

When he looked around into the cabin Mortimer Crabb was dismally regarding a set of bruised and bleeding knuckles. Richter lay on the catwalk, his left eye closed, two upper teeth missing. He showed no desire to get up.

BEHIND the black curtains of the C.O.'s office, lights were brightly burning. Lieutenant Duncan, smiling despite his bandaged head, put down the telephone and looked across the room at Eric Trent and Mortimer Crabb.

"They caught Max and Hans near Margate. So that winds it up. But if it hadn't been for you two—"

"Thank 'Charlie McCarthy' here," Trent said, motioning to the talking-beacon. "If 'Charlie' hadn't talked out of turn, we'd all probably be scattered around the countryside."

"I just found out how that happened," grunted Crabb, straightening up from an inspection of the circuit. "There was a short from an ultra high frequency coil to the speech-tape amplifier, and that simply turned it into an extremely high frequency radio receiver. Those Germans were using a frequency they thought nobody else could receive."

"Yes, we found a radio-sending set hidden in Shed Three," nodded Duncan. "Richter was a resident spy, and he must have been planted in England years back, according to a hasty Intelligence check-up. He was the test-pilot for experimental apparatus here, and it was easy for him to get those other spies brought in on fake orders. But there's the phone ringing—I'll join you outside in a moment."

Trent and Crabb went into the ante room. Two grim-faced Tommies had Richter by the arms. His battered eye was purple now, and the missing teeth gave him a vacuous expression, plus a decided lisp.

"You devilth!" he said thickly. "The *Gethtapo* will even our thcore!"

Trent chuckled. "Mort, you've knocked *Herr* Richter clear back to his cradle days. You really ought to pull your punches a bit."

Richter gave him a baleful glare from his one good eye. A moment later Duncan came into the anteroom.

"Just heard from Corps. Major Hawes is going to pull through. And the General says to do everything in our power for you chaps until he can come down in person."

"Well, come to think of it, there's a trifling matter of a kidnapped *Surete* officer and a little misunderstanding in Paris," said Trent. "Perhaps a kind word—"

"Consider it done," said Duncan. "I'll have Intelligence tell the French you were working with us, special duty, and all that we'll fix it. Matter of fact, I'll wager you could both have majors' commissions for the duration, after what you did."

"Thanks a lot, old man," said Trent. "But if there's one thing I heartily detest, it's the sound of a bugle early in the morning. Now Mort, here, would make an excellent Brass Hat. I can just see the subalterns quaking in their boots."

Crabb looked at Duncan, shook his head sadly.

"Much as I would like to be free from this young lunatic, I could not accept military service, except to defend my own country. Essentially, I am a man of peace."

"Man of peath!" moaned Richter. "Take me out of here before I looth my mind. Man of peath—*Gott im Himmel!*"

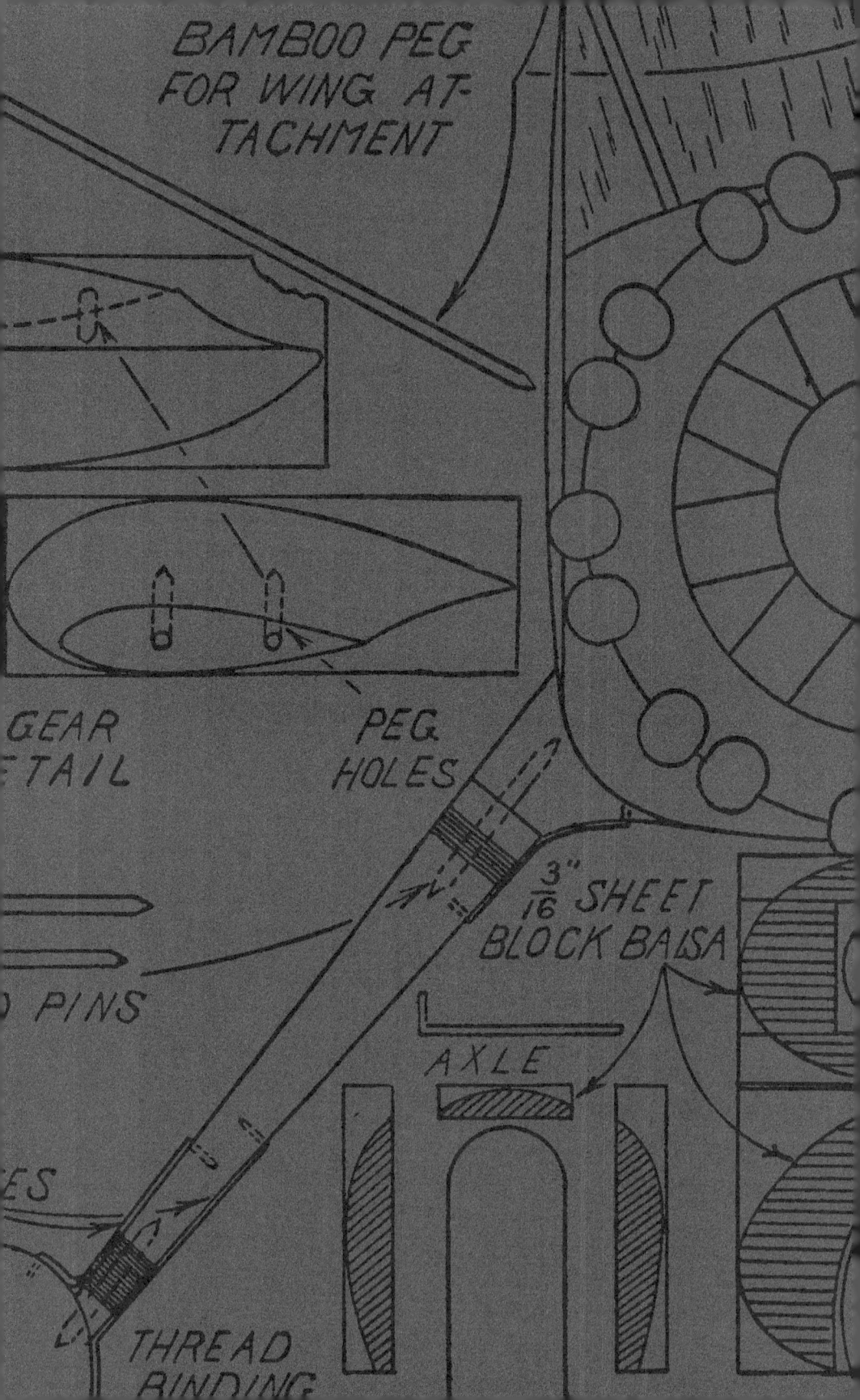

BAMBOO PEG
FOR WING AT-
TACHMENT

GEAR
TAIL

PEG.
HOLES

PINS

$\frac{3}{16}$" SHEET
BLOCK BALSA

AXLE

ES

THREAD
BINDING

Junkers Juggernaut

CHAPTER I

The Man With the Cane

IT WAS the third time in as many minutes that Eric Trent had seen that Royal Air Force lieutenant limp past the entry to the reading-room alcove. Trent watched him idly in the cracked mirror above the magazine rack, meantime continuing his pastime of palming a coin and plucking it out of the air.

The lieutenant now paused and peered into the canteen reading-room, a curious, almost frightened expression on his face. Then he glanced hurriedly at his wrist-watch and limped on toward the main room of the barn-like structure which the British Expeditionary Force had erected in the edge of the Foret des Fiemes near the fighting lines.

Trent's dark eyes took on a sudden gleam. He looked across the scarred reading-table at the long and mournful countenance of Mortimer Crabb, the Vermont inventor who for eight hectic months had been his unwilling partner in European intrigue. Craft was gloomily playing solitaire.

"Mort," he said in an undertone, "I've a feeling Fate is about to relieve our boredom. Yes, things are about to happen; for my jaded olfactory nerves detect some kind of an Ethiopian in some kind of kindling."

"Oh, Lord," groaned Crabb. "I knew this couldn't last. What now?"

"Our presence here seems to disturb a certain red-faced individual. You don't happen to have a stout, meaty-looking R.A.F. lieutenant among your bosom friends? A chap who limps, uses a cane?"

"How could I know anybody here?" Crabb said dismally. "We just got in at noon, and they've parked us here ever since. Where is this guy, anyway, and how's he bothering you?"

"He's been patrolling, the doorway as though he'd like to come in, but he's nervous as Sally Rand with a broken fan."

"I'll bet a plugged nickel we're under arrest again," spoke up Crabb in a doleful voice. "I told you it was a trick to turn us over to the French for that fracas in Paris, having us come over here to show my magnetic gun to some Limey general."

"British Intelligence would hardly have gone to the trouble of supplying us with these war correspondent uniforms," said Trent, unperturbed. He watched the mirror again, absently juggling three coins while he waited.

Even in repose, there was plenty of nerve about Eric Trent, partly from the almost Latin darkness of his hair and eyes and close-clipped mustache. But mostly it was veiled eagerness back of his smooth manner, and the look of audacity which clung to him, hinting at an impudent humor that would be no respecter of persons or rank.

But now, as the frightened-looking pilot failed to return, some of the eager look faded into brief puzzlement. "Odd," he said, half to himself. Then he tossed a grin at Crabb. "Maybe it was your lugubrious countenance which scared him, Mort. You look as sad as a poorhouse Christmas."

"It's my dyspepsia," the inventor said, frowning. "What I've been through with you has ruined my stomach. I'll *never* be the same again."

"But think of the fun you've had," chuckled Trent. He glanced back at the mirror, shrugged. "Fate seems to have fired a dud. So how about a little penny ante while we wait for our aloof hosts to invite us to mess?"

"And have you pulling cards out of your sleeve?" retorted Crabb. "No, thanks, I've seen enough of those card-shark tricks of yours."

Trent laughed. "Mort, you cut me to the heart. Any trifling skill I have with the cards is only a hangover from those days when I used to be a sort of aide-de-camp to that magician 'The Great Mysto.' I wouldn't dream of putting such monkeyshines to unethical use."

"Ha!" said Crabb, with a sepulchral sound that was intended for mirth. "Just the same, I'll play by myself."

Trent grinned. "In that case, I'll take a turn out in the canteen and see if I can locate the limping lieutenant. He still interests me a great deal."

"I hope you get thrown in the guard-house, if they've got a guardhouse," Crabb said in a rusty voice. "Then maybe I can get my passport back and head for home."

TRENT stood up, a tall, striking figure in the gray noncombatant's uniform which British officials in London had provided for use at the Front. He was almost to the doorway, when an R.A.F. corporal appeared, carrying a small tool-kit. The man's slate-blue eyes met Trent's for a second. Then he went on past, halted before a gum-vending machine in the corner, and tagged it with a placard sticker reading, "Out of Order."

A quick glance into the main part of the canteen showed Trent that the lieutenant had gone. He strolled back after a few moments, saw the corporal working at the rear of the slot-machine, the unlocked mechanism concealed by his body. The man seemed to be working with unwonted nervous haste.

A screw-driver clattered to the floor. Mortimer Crabb, until then absorbed in his solitaire, glanced up at the mechanic, then ambled over to the corner.

"Been wanting some gum. Had a notion to work on the thing myself, but I thought—"

He stopped and Trent came a step closer. The corporal had jerked around, face suddenly white.

"It's not working," he said hoarsely. "Go see the canteen clerk. Maybe he has—"

"What's that thing you've got there?" said Crabb. The corporal jumped back, thrusting something behind him. His right hand flicked under his uniform coat, and a gun gleamed in the light.

Trent's hand flashed to the man's wrist, twisted it hard. The corporal gave a howl of pain, and the pistol dropped from his grasp. It struck the floor, went off thunderously. But then the mechanic ducked past Mortimer Crabb as Trent snatched up the gun.

Trent had a glimpse of a small, compact mechanism that looked like a miniature radio, which the man held in one hand, with a wire trailing as he ran.

It was the mess-hour, and the canteen was almost deserted. But two uniformed attendants came dashing from behind the counter as Trent and Crabb pursued the fleeing mechanic. The corporal made for the side entrance, raced out into the camouflaged road which led to the hidden gun emplacements in the woods.

The sudden transition from the lighted room to the dusk of the forest made it harder to see, but Trent saw the corporal's shadowy figure dart behind a nearby Staff car. Crabb started for the man at the same moment. The crippled lieutenant now abruptly stepped from the gloom, stuck his cane between Crabb's legs. The inventor fell, and the R.A.F. pilot lifted his cane intending a vicious blow at Crabb's head.

AT THAT instant, Trent's fisted hand started down with paralyzing force at the side of the man's neck. The pilot's knees buckled, and he slid on his face. The two canteen men now burst out of the doorway, shouting for help. Trent shot a swift glance around, but the corporal had vanished. Dim blue flashlights stabbed through the shadows, and three or four armed Tommies descended upon the scene.

" 'Ere now, what's all this abaht?" demanded a cockney sergeant.

"That civilian—the tall one—he tried to shoot a mechanic," blurted out one of the canteen workers. "And he knocked down Lieutenant Brummley—the amusement detail officer."

"It's quite difficult to shoot at a man without a gun, sergeant," said Trent amiably.

" 'E's right," grunted the sergeant, after a brief search. "No gun on 'im."

"But I saw it—and he didn't drop it inside," insisted the canteen clerk. "Ask the lieutenant—he's coming around now."

Trent gave a sidewise warning look at Crabb, who had got to his feet and was being held by two Tommies. Brummley groaned, fumbled for his cane, then let one of the men help him up. As his eyes fell on Trent, his befuddled manner underwent a quick change.

"Hold him, Sergeant! Arrest both of them! They're Nazi spies!"

"It won't work, my dear fellow," said Trent. "Sergeant, this fine officer and his corporal are a couple of crooks. Look here—he's got my wallet in his pocket."

Before anyone could stop him, he thrust his hand inside Brummley's tunic. The lieutenant jerked back—and there in Trent's hand was his leather wallet, apparently snatched from the pilot's inner pocket. As Brummley gaped at it, Trent opened the card section, displayed the credentials which British Intelligence had furnished him.

"It's a trick!" Brummley howled. "I tell you they're *spies!*"

"What's all this about spies?" broke in a stentorian voice. A bow-legged colonel with an enormous nose strode across the camouflaged road from the entrance to a headquarters dugout—part of the Maginot Line rear section. Behind him came two junior Staff officers and an orderly. As the colonel saw Trent he stopped, jaw sagging.

"So—it's *you* again!" he roared.

"Well, this is indeed a pleasure," Trent said, happily. "Mort, let me present my old friend Colonel Roscoe Wittington-Leeds, V.C., D.S.C.—not to mention Knight of the Bath."

"Then you know this man, Colonel?" Brummley said hastily. Trent saw that his frightened look had come back into his eyes.

"Know him?" Whittington-Leeds bellowed. "The infernal blighter almost caused me to be court-martialed. Tricked me into arresting him—cost His Majesty's Government a cool two thousand pounds and an apology from Downing Street. What's he done now?"

"Apparently it's all a misunderstanding," Brummley said in a hurried voice. "They had a little argument with a mechanic—I saw the chase—thought they were spies. And now the tall man accuses me of lifting his wallet—just now pretended he found it on me—"

"Another of his smart tricks!" the colonel roared. "Used to be a magician, or some such rot. Pulled a mouse out of Admiral Sleasy's beard down in Singapore one night. What are you doing here, Trent—and in that uniform? You're no correspondent!"

"The King sent us over to check up on the war," said Trent. "Confidentially, he doesn't like the way it's being run."

"Why, you impudent Yankee!" sputtered Whittington-Leeds. "Of all the cheeky blighters I've met! Why—"

"Don't pay any attention to him," Mortimer Crabb interrupted dismally. "We were sent over here to demonstrate a new aerial gun, an invention of mine, to some general by the name of Ironside."

"To General Ironside?" The colonel's manner underwent a change. "Oh, so you're the two men that my aide said—" He paused. "Well, the General's still busy down below—important conference with Allied staffs. Maybe in an hour—"

"I'll be running along, Colonel," Brummley broke in. "And, by the way, I'll arrange that Saturday night show as you suggested."

"One moment," said Trent, smoothly. "There's a little matter of a gum-machine—"

"See here, Trent, I've no time for nonsense!" roared Whittington-Leeds.

"And you might ask Lieutenant Brummley why he carries a gun in a shoulder-harness," Trent went on unruffled. "Or is that standard equipment for an amusement-detail officer?"

BRUMMLEY'S meaty face twisted into a mirthless smile. "You're a great joker, Mr. Trent. I should put *you* in one of my shows—considering that it's been my job to keep the men *well* entertained ever since the flight-surgeons scratched my name from the combat list."

He turned toward a motorcycle side-car across the shadowy road. "If one of you men will run me out to the field—"

"Colonel!" a wild voice broke in from behind. A Staff major, hair disheveled, came dashing out from the dugout entrance. "The tracing of the new map—it's been stolen!"

"Impossible!" bawled the colonel. "No one but the devil himself could—" he broke off, spun around with an oath. "Trent! What do you know about this?"

"I'd suggest beating the bushes for a stocky R.A.F. corporal, light hair, close-set eyes," Trent said calmly. "And you might ask—"

"If this is some more of your infernal magic you'll regret it!" thundered Whittington-Leeds.

"Colonel, a corporal like that did run up the road, to the left," cut in one of the canteen workers.

The colonel whirled. "Major Slade, take that first car and three men. Get to the field and don't let anyone take off!"

The Staff machine roared away, the orderly at the wheel. Whittington-Leeds turned to his two aides. "Get down below—one of you phone the field, and the other warn the road-posts and patrols."

The two officers scurried to the dugout entrance. Brummley was about to step into the sidecar, and the sergeant was climbing into the saddle, when the colonel peremptorily stopped him.

"What about that corporal, Brummley? And what made you think these two men were spies?"

In the dim bluish light from the cockney sergeant's flashlight, Brummley's face was a ghastly color. Trent saw his hand clench tighter on his cane.

"I saw Trent pass something—I couldn't tell what it was—to the corporal," Brummley jerked out. "I'd know the man again—I'll dash on out to the field—"

"Hold on there!" bellowed the colonel. "Why are you in such a—" his mouth suddenly popped open. "Why, dammit, you were down there only twenty minutes ago! Grab him, Sergeant!"

Brummley jumped back, frantically reached inside his tunic. Eric Trent's right hand made a flashing motion upward and the missing pistol now magically appeared in his fingers.

"Surely, old chap," he said genially, "you didn't expect to get away with it?"

Brummley shakily lifted his hands still holding the cane. The sergeant gaped at Trent's gun.

"Always look under a man's hat, Sergeant," Trent advised him. "Handy place for a gun—though a bit hard on the skull."

Whittington-Leeds recovered his breath with a roar.

"Search that officer, Sergeant! Amusement detail, eh? I'll amuse you with a firing-squad, before I'm through with you!"

The cockney had Brummley's pockets almost emptied, with no sign of the stolen tracing. Then abruptly a faint, whining sound, like an approaching shell, sounded from off in the night. Almost simultaneously, two searchlights blazed up from positions in the forest.

CHAPTER II

Mystery Crater

B **RUMMLEY** went rigid, terror distorting his face as the whine grew into a piercing attack. With a violent lunge, he threw the sergeant aside.

"You fools!" he screamed. "It's coming here—we'll all be killed!"

The non-com scrambled to his feet, dashed for the dugout entrance. Before anyone could follow, something black flashed down through the slanting beam of a searchlight, disappeared. A terrific explosion instantly followed, with a blinding flash that lit up sky and ground. Trent was knocked flat by the concussion.

As he got up, still a trifle dazed, he saw Mortimer Crabb paw a blob of mud from his face and sit up groggily. Whittington-Leeds was on his feet, but swaying drunkenly, a cut along his forehead where some hurtling fragment had struck him.

The clamor of excited voices back at the dugout entry was abruptly drowned by the roar of a motorcycle engine. Trent snatched up the gun, which had been knocked from his grasp. But Whittington-Leeds staggered in front of him, and the cycle raced away with Brummley in the saddle before he could fire.

"Come on, Mort!" Trent said swiftly. He seized Crabb's arm, propelled him toward the remaining Staff car. He heard the colonel shout something in a hoarse voice as he started the motor, and a bullet crashed through the windshield as the machine charged after the fleeing pilot.

"Stop, you idiot!" groaned Crabb. "He thinks we're in on it and trying to get away."

"This is no time to explain," said Trent. "He'll probably dope it out later—when he gets his brains untangled."

"What if he doesn't?" Crabb said gloomily. "We'll get shot as spies."

"I haven't got you shot yet, have I?" Trent bantered.

"There's always a first time for everything," Crabb retorted unhappily. "Why do we have to stick our noses into— Hey, look out!"

Trent whirled the wheel, and the machine careened wildly away from a tangle of shattered trees which the dim headlights had barely revealed in time. The road had been completely obliterated by an enormous crater which stretched into the woods on both sides. Smoke and dust were still hanging over it, like a pall. Trent gazed back at it a second, then threw the car in gear again and sent it bumping along between jagged stumps and trees devoid of leaves.

"What kind of a shell could that have been?" Crabb said, amazed. "That was big enough for a mine crater."

"It wasn't a shell," said Trent. "I saw something go through a searchlight beam, but though I couldn't tell what it was, it surely wasn't a shell."

"When they start tossing stuff like that, I'm getting out of here," Crabb said dismally. "No wonder that pilot was scared. If he knew—"

"Listen, there's a ship starting up!" Trent cried. He tramped on the throttle, and the car shot crazily between the trees, heading back toward the other section of the road.

As they came out of the woods, faint lights appeared a few hundred yards ahead. Three Hawker Hotspur two-seater fighters had been rolled out from their underground hangar in the side of a hill, and mechanics were starting the engines. Brummley's motorcycle sped straight for the nearest ship, and Trent saw him jump out, point back toward the road. All but one of the mechanics ran to the hangar opening, came back with rifles.

"He's told them we're spies!" moaned Crabb. "Turn around before it's too late."

"We can't let him get away now," Trent flung back. "If Whittington-Leeds' gray matter doesn't unscramble itself, we've got to have Brummley to clear this thing up. Anyway, I don't like Brummley's face."

"You don't like his face—so we get killed! And to think I joined up with you of my own free will."

"Duck!" said Trent. Two rifles blazed, and a bullet ripped through the top of the car. He swerved, skidded to a stop between two of the Hotspurs, just as Brummley and another man climbed into the third ship. In the headlights, Trent recognized Brummley's companion as the mysterious corporal, then Brummley slammed the cockpit enclosure shut and the two-seater spun around into the wind.

Trent sprang out of the car, took a hurried look toward the hillside base. Several pilots were coming on the run, but they were too far away.

"They'll never stop those birds, Mort," he exclaimed. "It's up to us."

"Not me!" howled Crabb "I've had enough—"

A rifle bullet ricochetted from the hood of the car, and another sent shattered glass showering onto Crabb's knees. He dived out of the car like a jackrabbit, tumbled into the rear pit of the Hotspur. The 1500-h.p. Rolls-Royce Merlin engine was already revving up under Trent's expert fingers. A bullet creased the top of the dome-like rotating power-turret which covered Crabb's cockpit just as Trent let off the brake and sent the ship trundling ahead.

LIEUTENANT BRUMMLEY had already taken off, was climbing steeply. Trent flicked his safety-belt shut, shoved the throttle full on. The Hotspur gave a furious leap, hurled itself down the field. A searchlight lifted up sharply, and Trent saw the other ship cut back in a tight bank, four jets of flame stabbing from hastily-warmed guns. He snapped on the key-switch for the Hotspur's four forward guns, cast a swift look at the air-speed meter. The hand swept past 95, and the fighter tugged fiercely to lift.

The other ship pitched down, guns blazing. Above the roar of the motor, Trent heard Crabb's frantic yell: "Look out, you lunatic! He'll get us cold!"

Trent let the ship lift a few feet, so the tail would not hit the ground, then slammed the stick back and corkscrewed up in a terrific zoom.

"Get ready, Meat-Face!" he shouted. "Here we come!"

Brummley's tracers fanged down like red-hot wires—and suddenly whipped aside as Trent booted the rudder. With a lightning half-roll, Trent was outside the spy's furious burst and his own guns were flaming across the corporal's power turret. The tremendous speed threw the two ships half a mile apart in a few seconds. Trent renversed, saw Brummley twist back, climbing fast.

"Pick off that corporal, Mort!" he flung over his shoulder, as he retracted the landing-gear. "I'm going to force old Meat-Face down, if I can."

"Wait till I figure out this blasted turret thing!" ejaculated Crabb. "It's got me shut in like a turtle."

Trent tossed a look back, grinned at Crabb's perspiring face. The inventor was desperately pawing at knobs and toggle-switches, but the turret refused to rotate.

Brummley unleashed another fusillade, at long range. Trent back-sticked, cut inside the spy's answering chandelle and hurled a blast at the rear turret. His tracers grazed the edge of the helmet-like enclosure, and the corporal's fire went wild as the man threw himself aside. Brummley made a hasty turn, less than three hundred feet from the ground. An instant later, Crabb's turret gun clattered into action, tracers streaking earthward and curving around in a crazy arc. Trent looked down as he banked to follow the other ship.

"Great work, Mort. You just shot the top off our borrowed car—not to mention chasing the Limeys back into their cave."

"Don't blame me," Crabb said morosely. "How was I to know" you were going to bank just when I got this blamed thing figured out?"

"Well, don't worry about it," replied Trent. "You didn't hit anybody. And what's one car-top when the Allies are spending fifty million dollars a day?"

CRABB leaned forward under the dome, peered out into the beam-slashed night sky. Brummley had abandoned the fight, was speeding for the German lines. "Well, that's that," the inventor said gloomily. "Let's land and get it over."

"And let old Meat-Face laugh up his sleeve? It would haunt me the rest of my days. A chap like that ought to be taught a lesson—a sort of permanent one, if you follow me."

"Now I know you're crazy," moaned Crabb. "We just got out of Germany two months ago by a miracle—"

"—Plus a little Trent luck. It's never failed me yet."

Crabb gave a hollow groan. "I'd have been better off if I'd stayed in that car. At least, they might have only wounded me."

Trent eased the stick back for a brief climb, keeping his eyes on the other Hotspur, where the Allied searchlights intermittently spotted it.

"Listen, Eric," pleaded Crabb, "let's be reasonable. With all the trouble the Nazis are having up in Norway, now that the Allies have finally got tough, they're not going to be in any mood for visitors. You wouldn't—you couldn't be thinking of landing over there in Germany, could you?"

Trent looked back, laughed. "Relax, Mort. I'm only trying to corral *Herr* Meat-Face and force him back into Whittington-Leeds' welcoming arms. We're gaining on him; he's evidently slacked off on his throttle. And we're not over the West Wall yet, so there's a good chance of bringing home the bacon."

"Looks to me like he's nosing down already," Crabb said pessimistically. "If he—hey, cut in your main tank. You're running on the reserve, and it's two-thirds empty."

"I know it," replied Trent. "They must have started on the reserve and forgotten to—oh, oh! This may be a bit embarrassing. See if you can turn that valve-rod where it comes through your pit."

"What's wrong?" demanded Crabb alarmed.

"One of our friend's bullets has jammed the valve-rod up here."

"It's stuck here, too," Crabb said gloomily, after pounding on the valve. "Hurry up and turn back—maybe we can still make it."

"Yes, but there's still plenty of time," said Trent. "We can make one try, anyhow, at old Meat-Face."

"Twenty minutes' gas, and you want to start a fight right over No-Man's-Land," Crabb said hopelessly. "I give up."

Trent grinned. "Anything can happen in that time, Mort. A thousand babies will be born in the next twenty minutes. People will be divorced and married again."

"And we'll be dead. If I could find a spare stick back here I'd use it on your head and fly this ship back myself."

"Get ready," said Trent. "Here we go."

THE SPY ship was almost invisible in the deepening twilight, but Trent could distinguish it slowly descending toward some point beyond the Siegfried Line. He took a swift look at the small sector map clipped on the instrument board. The Nazis seemed to be gliding down toward the town of Schallsburg, which he knew had been evacuated at the outbreak of war. Apparently there was a field somewhere near, though none showed on the map.

He shoved the stick forward to out-dive the other Hotspur, intending a surprise attack. If he could silence the rear-pit gun, there would be an even chance of driving the spy-pilot back into France. As his altimeter showed three thousand feet and he was about to cut loose his guns, a battery of searchlights came to life, probed steeply up at the ship.

Trent kicked out of the first two beams, thumbed a burst at the spy plane. The other ship banked hastily. But before Trent could fire again, a stream of tracers blazed past his left wingtip. He slammed up into a lightning zoom, twisting as he climbed. A Henschel Hs.123 single-seater came streaking down a light-beam, guns flaming swiftly, and from right and left, higher up, flashes of red marked where two more fighters were diving in to join the attack.

"Hold him off, Mort!" he shouted, after one quick burst as the Henschel overshot. "I'm going to try a trick!"

He rammed the nose down, plunged after the other Hotspur, hoping to confuse the single-seater pilots. The spy kicked off into a steep slip, flashing his landing-lights. Trent hurriedly snapped on his own lights, flicked the toggle back and forth, following the spy-ship in a screeching forward slip. The deserted city of Schallsburg loomed from the shadows, directly ahead.

But to Trent's surprise, the other ship ruddered into line for a hasty landing in one of the dim streets below. He made a split-second decision. If he tried to pull up and escape now, the three fighters would be on them like vultures. He closed the throttle, started to come out of the slip, following the other Hotspur.

With a vicious pounding, a hail of lead from the first Henschel's guns cut through their right wing. Crabb's turret gun beat out a fierce answer, but the fighter twisted in for another burst. Trent booted the rudder just in time, and the smoking blast missed the two cockpits, slanted across the engine. The Rolls-Royce broke its smooth roar, and smoke began to pour back from the riddled cowl.

Trent had already snapped the switch to lower the landing-gear. The jammed fuel valve made it impossible to cut off the flow of gas, but he switched off the engine, threw the enclosure open and leaned out, straining his eyes to see through the smoke.

"Be ready to snap open your belt, Mort," he tossed over his shoulder. "It's going to be nip and tuck!"

The other Hotspur had landed in a street which was parallel on the left. Trent ruddered away from a building that suddenly appeared in their path. The smoke eddied aside, and the landing-lights revealed the street below. But instead of being deserted, it was filled with scores of gray-clad Nazis piling out of several lorries.

As the ship swayed down upon them between the buildings, the Nazis broke and ran. Trent zoomed over three lorries, felt the wheels crunch to the pavement. The ship bounced, rolled for another block, and scraped the right wingtip against the side of a huge trailer coach parked near a square building. Trent kicked left rudder and the Hotspur came to a jolting stop against the curb.

IN A TWINKLING, Trent had the lights off, his belt open, and was shoving the latch on the rear-pit turret. As Crabb jumped, Trent snatched out a packet of matches.

"Get clear, Mort! I'm going to set her off!"

The leaking gasoline caught with a loud puff. Trent ducked under the wing, raced into the shelter of an alley at the rear of the squarish structure. He thought for a moment no one had seen their escape from the Hotspur. But a hoarse voice suddenly rasped from the shadows: "Fritz, seize the second man! I have this one!"

A tall man attired in a flowing black cape and silk hat leaped out at Trent and a steely hand gripped his arm. Trent flung himself down on one knee, jerked at the cape. The other man did a somersault, hit the ground with a spine-jolting thud.

Mortimer Crabb meanwhile was exchanging blows with a husky German in a garb like a bell-hop's. As Trent sprang up to help him, one of Crabb's ham-like fists landed on the Nazi's jaw and sent him headlong against the side of the trailer-coach. The man groaned, made one last futile swing at Crabb. The inventor uncocked a long arm, hammered the Nazi clear off his feet.

"Come on!" said Trent, as the German slumped to the bricks. "If we move fast enough, we may be able to grab old Meat-Face's ship. He landed in the next street to our right."

But they had gone hardly ten yards when a door opened at the alley side of the square structure, and a rectangle of light cut through the shadows which were already lessened by the glare of the burning ship around the corner.

"Back behind the coach!" whispered Trent. He dragged the black-caped figure out of sight, and Crabb hauled the other German behind the trailer. Half a dozen uniformed Nazis ran out into the alley and toward the burning plane.

"There comes a car down the alley," groaned Crabb. "Now we're finished."

"Quick—into the coach!" ordered Trent. "We'll drag these two inside and change clothes with them."

"What good will that do?" said Crabb dismally. "I can't speak German."

"We'll work that out later." Trent slung the tall Nazi into the trailer, scooped up his silk hat which had rolled to one side. Crabb lifted the other German inside.

They had barely closed the door when the approaching car halted, unable to pass the coach in the narrow alley.

CHAPTER III
"On With the Show!"

A FAMILIAR voice reached their ears. *"Was ist?"* came the query, and the spy who had called himself Brummley jumped out of the auto, followed by a squatty Nazi in major general's uniform.

"One of Goering's soldier-show circus-trailers," growled the general. He stopped an excited *Unteroffizier* who came running back into the alley. "What happened? Were the Allied airmen captured?"

"Nein, Excellenz," said the non-com, with a hasty salute. "It seems they must have been caught in the plane when it burst into flames."

"Zum Teufel!" muttered the spy pilot.

"Why this sudden sympathy for the Allies, *Herr* Sturmme?" demanded the general.

"Not sympathy—I'd be glad to see those two burn," the spy said grimly. "But it happens they were not Allied pilots. They were those two *Amerikaners* who have caused us so much trouble—Eric Trent and that imbecile Crabb."

Trent grinned, in the darkness of the coach.

"How did they get mixed up in this?" grated the general.

"The British ordnance men at London sent them over to see Ironside about some kind of magnetic gun." Sturmme hurriedly explained what he had heard Trent tell Whittington-Leeds. "And they came—of all days—when we had everything timed. Not only that, but the colonel's aides had them wait in the alcove where Bischoff had hidden the guide-unit. I had planned to retrieve it when everyone was at mess and re-plant it directly beside the dug-out entrance. Ironside and the Allied Supreme Command would have been finished—"

"I heard of the plan," cut in the general. "And the explosion was reported by our sound-rangers. I thought all had gone according to schedule."

"It would have, but for the *verdammt* Americans," said Sturmme bitterly. "I had Bischoff try to sneak the guide-unit from the gum-vending machine where he hid it two days ago. But Trent and Crabb must have seen it. They chased out of the canteen after him, and he had to put the device the first place he could think of so as not to be caught with it. He put it in a Staff car, then escaped. Trent caused me to be trapped, and but for a miracle I would have been killed. That long-nosed colonel sent some men in the Staff car...."

Inside the trailer, the man in the black cape moaned faintly. Trent knelt swiftly, took out his handkerchief. In a few seconds he had the man gagged. He then removed his cape, stripped off the full-dress suit the German wore.

"Here's my belt, Mort," he whispered to Crabb. "Fasten his hands behind him. Then get into that monkey-jacket the other man's wearing. Never mind changing trousers— yours will come close enough to matching."

"We'll never make it," Crabb mumbled. "They'll be looking for us—"

"They think we're dead," Trent said in an undertone. "And that's what I was hoping for when I set the ship on fire."

He could hear Sturmme and the general talking as he and Crabb completed the hurried change of clothes and tied up the other German. But the words from outside were now indistinct. The Yank now brushed dust from the black cape and silk hat, put them on, and stepped close to the window. The glare from the burning Hotspur had diminished, but he could see Sturmme and the general coming back toward the car, followed by two Nazi officers. Sturmme was no longer limping, but he still carried his cane.

"The performers who came in this trailer-car must have witnessed it," said one officer. "They had just driven up. They're probably in the theater—I can go ask them."

Sturmme paused, shook his head. "Not if you're sure the plane caught fire the instant it crashed," he said.

"Hardly two seconds elapsed," said the Nazi. "They could not possibly have escaped."

"Then I'll go on to von Freyhausen's headquarters," Sturmme told the rotund general. "I've important information for him—to be specific, the exact positions of every Allied force behind the Maginot Line. There's real action coming, General Brucke—and when the new torpedo proves itself on the next test, we'll have the *verdammt* Allies on the run!"

"I'll be glad to see action," growled Brucke. "The men in this sector are getting soft—playing at war—and Goering's fool idea of keeping them amused with vaudeville and dancers, bah!"

"Well, the entertainment idea served me well across the lines," said Sturmme. "After I faked that air-battle and gashed my leg, it was easy to get assigned as amusement-detail officer with the privilege of going anywhere. But the Allies haven't risked using theaters in any evacuated front-line cities."

"What danger is there here?" snorted Brucke. "We've used it—and the entire Staff has lived in Tendelyn Hotel—for months. Time enough to hole up when action finally starts."

"I wouldn't wait too long," warned Sturmme. He hesitated, looked back toward the flames from the burning ship, then climbed into the waiting car and backed it away.

"Well, *mein Herren*," said the general, "we may as well go in and see this magician pull his white rabbits out of the hat. Cheap vaudeville bores me—but I understand there are some pretty dancers to follow the magic act. If they prove interesting, we might have them over for a champagne supper afterward."

"*Gut!* A fine idea, *Excellenz!*" chorused the Nazis. The group moved around to the street toward the front of the theater. Trent grasped Crabb's arm.

"Now's our chance at that Hotspur. If we meet anybody, don't run. I'll try to handle it."

"But what are these bell-hop duds for, anyhow?" Crabb muttered, as he climbed out of the trailer.

"You're evidently supposed to be a magician's assistant—my old role, Mort. Only the costume I used to have wasn't quite so gaudy. It seems we ran into one of Goering's entertainment-corps outfits. If we had more time I'd go in there myself and show them a few real tricks."

"Good heavens!" said Crabb, horrified.

Trent chuckled. "I thought you'd appreciate that idea. But this time I guess discretion is in order."

THEY STARTED along the empty alley toward the street where Sturmme had landed. The glow of the burning ship had almost died out.

"We'd better move fast," said Trent. "If they happened to discover there aren't any bodies in that—"

Without any warning, the stage door opened, flooding light across their path. Two Nazis in dungarees, apparently acting as stage-hands, came out, followed by a Nazi with a military police arm-band and a pistol at his belt. Crabb took a hasty step backward, but Trent nudged him to stand still.

"Act natural," he told Crabb. "I've the gun under my cape—but maybe I can bluff it out."

"There they are," exclaimed one of the stagehands. "What are you waiting for?" came the call. "The general and his officers will be taking their seats in a minute."

Trent breathed again. The light was on his face enough for them to have gone into action if they had recognized an impostor. Evidently, the real magician was some obscure entertainer; at least these men did not know him.

"We were going to the front of the theater," he said easily, in German. "I often make my entrance through the audience, with one or two tricks before I reach the stage."

"There's no time now for that," insisted the other stagehand. "And it throws out the schedule your assistant gave us this mor—" he stopped, peering at Crabb. "Why, this is not the same assistant who got your props ready this afternoon."

"Well, that stupid fool got drunk tonight on *schnapps*," Trent said in a disgusted tone. "This is his understudy."

His hand tightened on the gun under his cape. He was ready to whip it out and cover the three men if his insistence on an "audience entrance" failed. Then two more armed Nazis with armbands came out into the alley. There was now only one thing to do.

"Since time is short," said Trent, "we will dispense with the trick entrance. Lead the way."

Mortimer Crabb's mournful face took on a look of utter despair, as Trent motioned him to follow the Germans into the theater. The backstage lights were on, with the curtain down. Trent's quick glance showed him that the usual magician's equipment had been put in place—two trick cabinets, a magic table beside a rack, and a side table with a variety of colored handkerchiefs, cards, a prop pistol, smoke-grenades, bottles, and other accessories. A loud buzz of voices came from out in the theater. An electrician and three more stage-hands stood in the wings.

TRENT took a relieved breath when he saw the magic cabinets. He looked at the middle of the stage, spotted the outlines of the usual trapdoor, then turned to the Nazi who seemed to be the senior stage-hand, a stolid, bald-headed man of about forty-five.

"Hold the curtain for a minute or two. I want this understudy to be sure he can work the cabinet trick."

"It's an ordinary trap with counter-weights," began the German, but Trent beckoned to Crabb, led him over to the trap.

"Get on it—you'll land in the basement," he whispered, lips hardly moving. "Wait till I come down."

Crabb, a ludicrous figure in the tight-buttoned jacket and round bellhop hat, ambled onto the trap, his Adam's apple working up and down convulsively. The trap promptly descended, and after Crabb stepped off, below, the counterweights brought it up again flush with the stage.

Trent snapped his fingers, made believe he was irate. "I should have told him to re-set the counterweights, so he can come back up for the reappearing act later on!"

"I will tell him, *mein Herr*," said the bald-headed stage-hand, starting for the steps to the basement.

"Never mind, I'll go down and make sure he gets it right," Trent said quickly. "Go tell someone to inform the general the performance will begin in a few moments."

The Nazi went into the wings. Trent stepped on the trap, was rapidly lowered to the basement section behind the empty orchestra pit. It was dimly lighted, the floor littered with old scenery and other debris.

"How do we get out of here?" Crabb said hoarsely, as Trent stepped off and the trap rose back into position.

"There's probably a door to the alley. If we can find it before they get suspicious!" Trent jumped over a tangle of stage-settings, hurriedly glanced behind a row of boxes piled at the rear. "Ah! Luck's with us, Mort. It's padlocked—but we can force it open."

He looked around swiftly for a lever to pry the staples off without too much noise, but nothing suitable was to be seen.

"I'll use the gun," he told Crabb. He was wedging it under the padlock when the squeal of a car's brakes sounded from up in the alley.

"More luck," he told Crabb exultantly. "With a car for a getaway we're all set."

The staples started to come loose. He had the padlock half-way off when the voice of the senior stagehand rose from the top of the stairs.

"Come on up here—you're wanted—"

Footsteps thudded on the iron stairs.

"I'll find them," said a tart voice. "I'm in a hurry—I just want to ask them a question or two."

Trent spun around, pushed Crabb behind the nearest pile of boxes. "Hold everything!" he whispered. "It's Meat-Face!"

CHAPTER IV

Juggernaut Joust

"**W**HERE in *der Teufel*—" Sturmme swore irritably as he reached the bottom of the steps. Trent stepped out from behind the boxes, his head tilted so that the silk hat threw a shadow over his face.

"May I be of service?" he said in a ponderous voice.

"I want to know if you saw that those pilots actually trapped in the plane." Sturmme strode across the floor, cane in hand. Then he jerked to a halt with an utterly stunned expression. *"Ach, du Lieber Gott!"*

"Fancy our meeting here," Trent said, pleasantly. "No, I wouldn't try to yell if I were—" the hidden gun flashed out between the folds of his cape as Sturmme's mouth flew open for a shout. The Nazi spy-pilot whirled desperately to flee. Mortimer Crabb's lanky figure lunged from behind a box, and a bony leg sent Sturmme crashing to the floor.

"Now we're even, Mr. Heinie," grated Crabb, forgetting for the moment to be pessimistic.

Trent hastily bent over the fallen man. There was a bruise at Sturmme's temple, and his face had turned gray.

"Out cold," said Trent, cheerfully. "Now pry that lock off while I search him for Whittington-Leeds' tracing."

The staples jerked free just as he finished going over the unconscious Nazi clothing. He spoke up: "Nothing there! Only one other—"

"Where is that *Dumpkopf* of a magician?" snapped a voice from the top of the stairway. Trent leaped to his feet as he heard two or three men start down the steps.

"The door's stuck!" muttered Crabb. "I'll have to bust it open."

"No time, now," Trent said swiftly. He stooped, rolled the unconscious Sturmme back of a box, kicked the cane out of sight.

"Auf Wiedersehen, Herr Sturmme," he said in a loud voice, and kicked the door to make it sound as though it had closed. Just as he turned back toward the stairway, a dour-faced Nazi major stalked toward him from the stairwell with one of the military police and the senior stage-hand behind him.

"Do you realize you are keeping General Brucke waiting?" demanded the major.

"My deepest apologies," said Trent. *"Herr* Sturmme delayed me—we came down to inspect the trap-door apparatus, and he interrupted—"

"That is what I was trying to tell you, *Herr* Major," said the bald-headed stage-hand. "*Herr* Sturmme came here to ask these men if they saw the plane crash. He was in a hurry and would not wait—"

The major looked sourly toward the door to the alley.

"These smart secret agents!" he sneered. "Always more important than anyone else! Well, there's no need for further delay. Get up there and start your performance."

"Gladly, *mein Herr Major.*" Trent stood aside to let the Nazis precede him and Crabb, then he followed. When he reached the top of the steps he purposely caught the edge of his cape on the door knob. He turned impatiently as though to release it. When he swung back, a second later, the door had been quietly locked and the key was inside his cape pocket.

"Are you ready for the curtain?" snapped the major.

"It will go up by the time you reach your seat," Trent said smoothly. He nodded to Crabb, and the inventor followed, stiff-legged, to the center of the stage.

"Where's that pistol?" Trent whispered.

"Under this bell-hop hat," moaned Crabb. "You and your bright ideas. I'm scared to move."

"Hang on a little longer—I'll fix it," Trent said in an undertone. He glanced around, saw that the stagehands were waiting in the wings. He motioned for Crabb to help him roll the accessory table in closer, then made a rapid selection of several objects. He clipped a smoke grenade inside his cape, slid a wadded swastika-flag into his sleeves. "Just follow my motions," he told Crabb. "I'll whisper to you for anything else."

"I can't do it," Crabb said hoarsely. "My knees are knocking together. They'll see it—they'll know—"

"Of course they won't. Besides, an audience likes to be fooled," he grinned. "Just hold tight a few minutes. We'll have to go through a couple of tricks—and then we'll make our exit."

"I can see the firing-squad right now," groaned Crabb, as Trent motioned him to his place beside the wheeled rack. The senior stage-hand then jerked around to his helpers and the curtain went up hastily, with the house lights fading out.

A SEA of faces, a mass of gray uniforms, stretched beyond the footlights. Down in front, in the center row, was the gorilla-like figure of General Brucke, surrounded by a dozen Staff officers. A hundred other Nazi officers sat directly behind, with non-coms ranging on both sides. The air was blue with the smoke of *ersatz* tobacco.

Trent stepped to the center of the stage, bowed, lifted his hand in a Nazi salute.

"Heil Hitler!" he said, adding under his breath: *"May he quickly get put back on his old job of paper hanging!"*

The assembled Nazis got to their feet, and a chorus of loud—if mechanical—"heils" echoed through the theater. As the crowd sat down again, Trent idly moved his left hand, and a lighted cigarette appeared between his fingers. He took a puff, exhaled, tossed the cigarette to the stage, then plucked another one from the air as he walked to the accessory table. Discarding it, he picked up the prop pistol and beckoned to Mortimer Crabb.

A snicker ran through the audience, swelled into a roar of laughter, as Crabb came forward with the round bell-hop hat topping his mournful face and the too-tight jacket threatening to burst at every step. Trent laughed with the crowd.

"Gentlemen, I beg you to overlook *Herr* Hoopenfinkle's unhappy visage. He is really quite pleased to be here."

He held up his hand, and Crabb halted, perspiration dripping down his face, his Adam's-apple bobbing wildly. Trent stepped back a few paces, made a whirling motion with his left hand, triggered the prop pistol in his right. The swastika-flag flipped into the air, seemingly from nowhere, and the pistol vanished.

Trent now stepped forward, made a quick pass around Crabb's head, pulled off the bell-hop hat, and revealed the gun precariously perched there. He removed the weapon and put it on the table. Crabb mopped his face, and the Nazis roared.

"For Lord's sake, Eric, let's get out of here," Crabb moaned under cover of the applause.

"Almost set, old bean. Now, roll one of those tall, wheeled cabinets over the trap-door—and make very sure it's centered."

As Crabb went across to the cabinet, Trent quickly distracted the Nazis' attention. Stepping to the footlights, he bent down toward the front row.

"And now, if his Excellency, Major General Brucke, will be so kind as to lend me his watch for a moment, I will show you my famous double-disappearance act."

Dubiously, the general handed his watch to the dour-faced major, who passed it up to Trent. Turning to the prop table, Trent picked up a magician's wand, at the same time loosening the smoke-grenade inside his cape. He crossed the stage, opened the door of the second cabinet, which stood at the left of the one above the trap.

"A plain, empty cabinet, gentlemen—just like this other."Trent poked the wand inside both cabinets, switched on the row of electric lights at the bottom of each one, intended to give the impression of added visibility while in reality blinding the spectators so that they could not see underneath. Then he beckoned to Crabb, motioned him toward the centered cabinet.

"There's a false bottom," he whispered rapidly. "Step into the left corner the second I shut the door. When the bottom springs up, hop onto the trap."

Crabb scrambled inside, knocking off his hat, bringing another howl from the crowd. Trent picked up the hat, handed it to him, whispered last instructions:

"Ram that basement door open and get out and start Sturmme's car. I'll be there in a few seconds."

He closed the cabinet door, picked up the prop pistol, and fired a blank, ostentatiously holding up Brucke's watch as though timing the act.

"One, two, three"—he heard a faint click as the false bottom in the cabinet fell back into place—"and gone!"With a sweep he whipped open the door, displayed the empty cabinet. "Gentlemen, this is the first part of my double-disappearance. I will now enter the cabinet—and cause *myself* to vanish in a cloud of smoke! Immediately, the stage hands will move this cabinet to the footlights, replace it with the other one—and both my assistant and myself will reappear in exactly one minute!"

An expectant silence fell over the audience. Trent then turned back from the footlights, moved unhurriedly toward the cabinet, the door of which still stood open.

HE WAS within two feet of it, when the false bottom suddenly started up—and there, glaring at him from the swiftly, rising trap, was Sturmme!

"General Brucke! This man is a spy!" Sturmme cried wildly.

The theater was instantly in an uproar as officers and men jumped to their feet. Trent sprang to one side, as though to race for the wings. Sturmme lunged out of the cabinet after him, his bruised face livid. Trent seized one edge of the accessory table, threw it into Sturmme's path. The spy fell half-way across it, and Trent dived back at the cabinet.

Stage-hands and military police were now dashing out on the stage, dodging around the props. Trent spun the cabinet with a lightning motion, sent it rolling at the nearest Nazi. Then he leaped onto the trap.

A bullet whistled past his head as the trap carried him down. Two more shots roared down through the aperture, and the silk hat flew from his head, riddled. He jumped the remaining distance to the basement floor, raced toward the rear.

"Mort!" he shouted. "Where are you?"

"Here—by the door—" came the hoarse answer. Crabb was dragging himself up, a welt across his cheek. He was gripping a jagged section of Sturmme's cane. The door to the alleyway was partly open.

Trent seized one of Crabb's arms, hustled him into the alley. Sturmme's car was still there, partly blocking the door. Trent tumbled the inventor into the machine, vaulted over and snapped the switch-key. A pistol blazed, back in the dimly lighted basement, splintered the door as the engine caught. Trent threw the car into reverse, sent it roaring backward just as a score of Nazis burst from the stage-door. Two bullets drilled the windshield, and a third whanged off the side of the car.

"That devil… I should have known his head was too thick to crack," Crabb said huskily. "I tried to stop him—"

"Never mind, Mort," Trent said swiftly. "We're not up against a wall yet."

The car whirled crazily backward out of the alley, twisted around into the street where Sturmme had landed. Trent turned on the lights, saw the Hotspur a block away, sent the car speeding toward it. They were within two hundred feet of it when he saw three Henschel fighters lined up beyond the Hotspur. A dozen Nazi mechanics were running out from a nearby garage.

"We've hit a hornet's nest!" Crabb yelled hopelessly. "They're using this street for a front-line air patrol base!"

"I've something that'll fix those boys," said Trent. He slammed on the brakes, sprang out with the smoke-grenade he had intended to release in the cabinet. The lights of the car fell on the man in the lead, and Trent recognized the spy-corporal who had fled with Sturmme.

"It's the *Amerikaners* who—*Ach Himmel*—a bomb!" The spy jumped back with a howl of dismay as the grenade struck, with a puff of white smoke, directly in front of him. The next second he and the Nazi mechanics dashed for shelter, and Trent boosted Crabb into the Hotspur, jumped for the front seat.

The starter whined, and the warm Rolls-Royce Merlin kicked over instantly. Trent let off the brake, pivoted, sent the ship rolling past the Henschels. Switching on the lights, he revved up the engine to take-off speed. The Hotspur roared between the darkened buildings, lifted, and Trent swiftly zoomed clear.

Lights flashed on below as he banked toward the Allied lines. He looked down, saw one of the Henschels race through the street, hurtle up after the two-seater.

"Mort!" he shouted back. "Warm up your pea-shooter! I've a feeling that's our friend Sturmme, and it's time he was getting that lesson I spoke about."

Crabb cut loose with a brief burst, warming the turret gun. A searchlight stabbed at them, and Trent renversed out of the beam, lost sight of the Henschel.

"Climb, you idiot!" howled Crabb. "He'll soon dive on us."

Trent backsticked, caught a flicker of tracers, kicked away as the Henschel streaked toward them. As he twisted back, all six of the Henschel's guns blazed. He rolled swiftly away from that furious barrage, cut in with a searchlight beam between them. But his swift burst lasted only a second. For simultaneously, the searchlight and the Henschel's tracers faded.

TRENT had a flitting glimpse of something huge, dark, passing swiftly above. He climbed, watching sharply to avoid collision with the Henschel. That thing above had looked like a giant bomber carrying two tiny planes under its wing. If his sudden guess was right....

Something, barely distinguishable, showed against the stars, heading on a long power glide toward the Maginot Line. Trent cut in swiftly, flicked on his landing-lights for a moment. A giant Ju.89 four-motored Junkers bomber, dead-black, swept squarely before the light-beams. Under each wing was what looked like a tiny plane, black like the Junkers, with eight-foot wings, small props whirling. The tiny ships were secured to the Junkers' wings by tripod frames, with remote-control release rods and cables running in to the pilot's cockpit.

"Leaping Lena!" ejaculated Crabb. "Aerial torpedoes! So that's what made the crater."

Trent snapped off the lights, twisted into a tight climbing turn, as the bow-gunner of the Junkers sent a blast flaming at them.

"Unless my guess is wrong, those pretty little toys are filled with liquid oxygen and carbon—that new combination the Nazis tried out in Norway. Get ready—it's going to be hot for a minute."

"It's too hot right now to suit me," groaned Crabb, as Trent whipped down toward the Junkers, only a faint blur beneath. "Look out—you'll crash that ship head-on!"

"Got to make them turn tail—or Ironside and the Allied Brass Hats are going to be mincemeat." Trent cut on the lights again, ripped a quick burst into the side of the giant ship. Tracers blazed venomously from three Nazi guns, raked the Hotspur's tilted wing as he hastily plunged under the Junkers. He held the dive, lights off, pulled up after a second or two.

"Got to stop them, Mort! They must have planted another gadget like the one in the gum-machine. Some sort of short-wave battery-type transmitter to guide those torpedoes to—"

"Watch out—the Henschel," bawled Crabb. His turret-gun pounded fiercely, and as Trent switched on the lights once more he saw the Nazi fighter charging in, with Sturmme's head just visible at the rim of the cockpit. The Junkers had veered, but now it twisted back, slanted down toward a blur of buildings half-hidden in the trees beyond the Maginot Line. Searchlights had flashed up somewhere beyond.

Trent hurtled down past the Junkers. Crabb's fire had forced Sturmme to twist aside for a second, but the Henschel was darting back. With a lightning turn, Trent sent the Hotspur screeching around and up at the onrushing Junkers. The bow-gunner instantly opened fire again. And at that sinister instant, Sturmme ringed them in his sights. Withering tracers flashed from his guns, clipped the turret over Crabb's head and grazed the hatch above Trent's cockpit.

The torpedoes under the Junkers' wings had now dropped away. Trent slammed a furious burst straight at the winged projectile on his left. There was a terrific explosion, a shattering detonation that hurled the two-seater over on its wingtip as though it were a toy. Half-blinded, Trent heard another blast, as the second torpedo went off. The Junkers was blown into fragments.

Crabb's turret-gun hammered suddenly, and Trent looked around in time to see Sturmme frantically bail out, with the tail of his Henschel shot clear off. More searchlights came on, down in the Allied lines, and one of them spotted the chute, followed the descending spy. Trent grinned back at Crabb.

"Leave the rest to the boys below, Mort. They'll do an efficient job in taking care of *Herr* Sturmme."

"What about us?" said Crabb, dubiously. "Maybe they'll still think *we're* spies."

"Not after knocking down the Junkers. We'll be little tin heroes, my friend—but I'll settle for a square meal. Perhaps we can wangle that long-delayed dinner invitation now."

"WELL, Trent," said Colonel Whittington-Leeds, "I must admit—harumph—you right well squared things for the previous little—ah—trouble. And we've got the line-up on those flying torpedoes, too. Apologies, and all that sort of thing—"

Trent put down his empty wine glass, looked pleasantly across the table of the British Staff's underground mess-room.

"My dear colonel, this excellent steak makes up for our trifling inconvenience. The past is buried. Long live the King."

Whittington-Leeds drank, but shook his head gloomily.

"I'm finished, though. Losing that tracing—they'll court-martial me for sure."

"That reminds me," said Mortimer Crabb, and he began fishing inside his coat. But then his jaw dropped.

"Looking for this?" said Trent. And he withdrew a folded tracing from his pocket.

"The map!" bellowed Whittington-Leeds. "Thank heavens! Where did you get it?"

"Mort here gets all the credit," said Trent. "He found it inside Sturmme's cane after they had a little tussle. The thing was hollow. I filched the map on the way in from the field, in case we had to make a deal for our liberty."

"You pickpocket," Crabb said with sepulchral indignation. "I suppose some morning I'll wake up and find my gold fillings gone."

"Gentlemen," beamed Whittington-Leeds, "I'll see you both get rewarded for this."

"You might put in a good word for Mort's magnetic gun," chuckled Trent. "And you could do me a favor, at that, if you'll have one of your pilots drop General Brucke's watch over there some day with a little note."

"A note—saying what?" queried Whittington-Leeds.

Trent smiled. "Oh, just saying I hope he wasn't bored too much with that cheap vaudeville act."

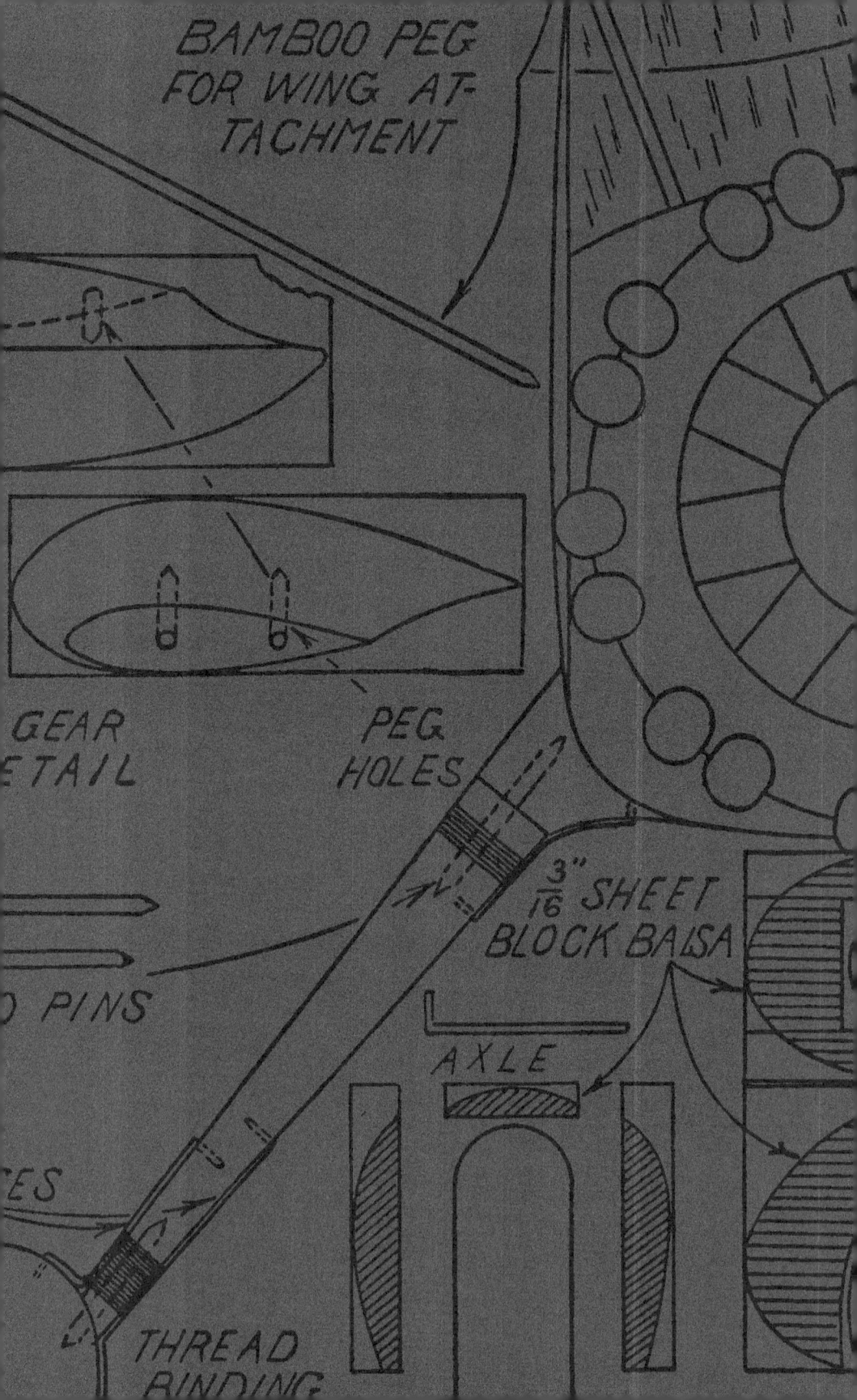

BAMBOO PEG
FOR WING AT-
TACHMENT

GEAR
ETAIL

PEG
HOLES

PINS

$\frac{3"}{16}$ SHEET
BLOCK BALSA

AXLE

ES

THREAD
BINDING

Swastika Scourge

CHAPTER I

False Colors

THE BIG Fokker seaplane was within fifty miles of the Canal Zone when Eric Trent saw the two Navy scout-bombers. It was almost dusk, but he recognized them as Vought-Sikorsky OS2U-1's. As they swung toward the Fokker, a rocket signal flared across the Dutch ship's path. Mortimer Crabb, Trent's sad-faced partner, sat up with an alarmed look on his gloomy countenance. But Trent only grinned at the approaching planes.

"Sorry, boys," he said amiably. "Mort and I have a date at Colon with a couple of steaks. See you later."

With a mock salute, he zoomed the T-4 into the clouds under which they had been cruising since they left the Colombian coast. A burst of tracer smoke passed one wing, then the clouds hid the pursuing craft.

"Now you've done it," Crabb said dismally. "Those ships were on Neutrality Patrol. They'll radio an alarm, and the whole Patrol will be on our tail."

An amused gleam came into Trent's dark eyes.

"At least, that'll be a change from Hitler's lads. Don't get me wrong, Mort—I wasn't snooting our Navy friends. But with the radio dead, we'd have had to fool around with a lot of wig-wag and red-tape, explaining why we're flying a Dutch military sea-plane over here in the Western Hemisphere. And the inner man is growling too loudly for one of those juicy steaks at the Strangers' Club."

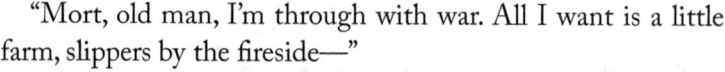

"We'll probably end up eating slum in a Navy brig," Crabb predicted mournfully. "I should think that fracas back in Brazil would've been enough to last you a few days, not to mention just getting out of Europe by the skin of our teeth."

A solemn look momentarily replaced Trent's habitual devil-may-care expression.

"Mort, old man, I'm through with war. All I want is a little farm, slippers by the fireside—"

"Don't try to be funny," Crabb said acidly. "You'll hop from one scrape into another until you get shot—or maybe hung. But you can bank on this—Mortimer Crabb won't be with you. I'm going back to my factory in Vermont. We'll split the money you phenagled out of the Nazis on those trick inventions of mine—and that ends our partnership. After all I've been through, it'll take a year to get my stomach back into shape."

Trent switched on the gyro-pilot, glanced at his partner. Crabb was dismally chewing gum, his protuberant Adam's-apple working up and down in time with his jaws. With his long, gloomy visage and the rusty black suit he always wore, he looked more like an undertaker than a shrewd if somewhat pessimistic inventor.

"Mort, you couldn't give up this free-and-easy life for a grubby old factory," Trent said reproachfully. "Think of the gay adventures we've had—"

"Dodging bullets," snorted Crabb.

"—all the countries we've seen together—"

"—one jump ahead of a firing-squad."

"And what about those magician tricks you wanted me to show you? It'll take a year to teach you all those—"

Trent broke off suddenly, as the Fokker came through the top of the cloud. Another plane was visible through the thinning cloud-mists, and for a moment he thought one of the Navy scout-bombers had trapped them. Then, as the wisps of cloud cleared completely, he saw that it was a foreign seaplane, with Colombian registry letters. The ship banked sharply as the T-4 appeared, and with a quick surprise Trent noted the cantilever high mid-wing and double-rudder. It was a German Blohm and Voss Ha.140, a type set on twin floats, powered with two 800-h.p. B.M.W. engines. And although it bore Colombian registry, it appeared to have been flying in from some point at sea, instead of along the coast.

"NOW what?" howled Crabb, as Trent abruptly chandelled and switched on the nose-turret guns.

"Get forward!" Trent said hurriedly. "There's something queer about that—"

"Look! The insignia's peeling off!" exclaimed Crabb. He dived from the co-pilot's seat, scrambled forward. Trent whipped into a right turn, staring across at the other ship. Long strips of dried paint were fluttering back in the slipstream, showing where the

Colombian registry letters had been placed to hide another marking—the Nazi swastika!

The German plane had started to dive into the clouds, but suddenly it pulled into a tight climbing turn. Two guns blazed from the aft turret and the already bullet-scarred T-4 quivered under a blast that riddled one wing. Before the gunner could jerk his weapons around to rake the cockpit, Trent plunged under the Nazi ship, came up in a furious zoom. Crabb loosed a barrage from the nose-turret guns and Trent saw the tracers hit the side of the other craft.

"Nice work, Mort!" Trent shouted. "Look out for that bow-gunner!"

The revolving turret in the nose of the Ha.140 whirled toward the Fokker and a vicious torrent flamed toward the T-4's tail. Trent snapped into a split-turn, hurdled the Nazi. His left pontoon was aimed directly at the mystery plane's double rudder and he had a flashing glimpse of the pilot's beak-nosed profile as the Nazi frantically nosed down. Then the Ha.140 disappeared, diving headlong into the clouds.

Trent swung off to one side, dived at full throttle.

"You idiot!" Crabb yelled. "You're liable to hit him in this stuff!"

"Get your trigger finger set, Daniel Boone!" Trent flung back. He chuckled as he saw Crabb shake his fist, hanging onto the gun with his other hand. Then the T-4 plunged into the clear beneath the clouds.

They had emerged not far from the headland at Point Manzanillo and Trent had a split-second glimpse of the San Blas Mountains and the dark jungle beyond. The Nazi ship had pulled out of its dive, was zooming back for the protection of the clouds, and heading toward shore. Trent backsticked, ruddered swiftly as the aft-turret m.g.'s of the Ha.140 spun toward the Fokker. Just as Crabb's guns flamed out in fierce answer to the Nazi's fusillade, something at one side caught Trent's eye. He flicked a glance to the left, soundlessly pursed his lips. The two Navy scout-bombers were charging into the fight, hastily warming their Brownings!

"If only they see that Nazi insignia," he said to himself. But without an instant's hesitation, the two Vought-Sikorskys darted toward the T-4. Trent held to the pursuit of the Nazi ship a moment longer, though the scout-bombers were almost in range. A burst of tracers from the German aft-turret guns grazed the top of his cockpit, ripping away the panels above his head. Crabb pitched a blast into the side of the Nazi, then with a yell of alarm swung his guns around as the first Vought-Sikorsky opened fire.

"Hold it, Mort!" shouted Trent. "That's our Navy friends."

"Friends?" bawled Crabb as Trent renversed and streaked for the clouds. "I'd hate to have—now what on earth's hit them?"

As suddenly as they had attacked, the two scout-bombers fled, zooming into the clouds after the Ha.140. Trent looked back and saw tracers smoking within a hundred feet of his left wing. Three Vought-Sikorskys were spreading out to intercept the Fokker. A flare-pistol was thrust from the rear pit of the leading ship and a crimson rocket flashed directly in front of Trent.

"Mort, I think they mean business," Trent said, as he nosed down. "Maybe we'd better postpone that date with the steaks."

"A jam like this and you can still think of food," Crabb said gloomily. He climbed back into the co-pilot's seat. "You idiot, do you realize they'll think we were firing on those other Navy ships? The German plane was in the clouds before they were close enough to see it."

"Doesn't it strike you as a bit odd, the way those two Vought-Sikorskys ran for it?" queried Trent.

"What's odd about it?" Crabb said morosely. "They saw these three had us cornered, so they dug after the Nazi."

"Maybe it's just my generally suspicious nature," observed Trent, "but I'd say there was a faint odor of the fish-market about that business."

The three scout-bombers had by this time closed in to within a hundred feet of the Fokker. While two of them rode the tail of the T-4, the third carefully drew alongside the right wing. The pilot pointed to his earphones, but Trent shook his head. After a glance at his compass, the Navy man motioned for them to fly parallel, then headed across Point Manzanillo toward the Atlantic end of the Canal.

With the Fokker leading, the two Vought-Sikorskys followed cautiously, close behind.

IT WAS almost twilight when Trent glided down inside the west breakwater at Limon Bay. The leader of the Vought-Sikorskys taxied ahead to a mooring buoy, after signaling Trent to approach one nearby. Two minutes later, Trent and Crabb climbed into a speedboat which drew alongside the battle-scarred Fokker. A middle-aged Navy commander, pompous and rather florid of face, curtly motioned them into the vessel. Two bluejackets with drawn .45s kept Trent and Crabb covered as the speedboat headed across to the first of the three seaplanes. The commander fixed a frosty eye on Trent.

"All right, let's have the story," he barked.

"All of it?" said Trent.

"Certainly!" snapped the Navy man.

"I was born in Cincinnati, of poor but honest parents," Trent began in a singsong voice. "At the age of three I had curly hair, which fortunately I outgrew—"

"You insolent beggar!" roared the commander. "I'll put you in irons—"

"I was merely following your orders," Trent said amiably. "Maybe we can shorten it. Suppose you play Professor Quiz and I'll bet you three to one I can get the answers."

The commander turned a violent purple and one of the bluejackets choked, trying to hide a snicker. Mortimer Crabb interposed before the officer could regain his breath.

"Don't pay any attention to this young lunatic," he said mournfully. "I'll tell you anything you want to know."

"Who are you—and what are you doing with that Dutch plane?" grated the commander.

"We're refugees from Europe," Crabb replied gloomily. "We're also American citizens. My name's Mortimer Crabb. You'll find me listed in Dun and Bradstreet's business directory."

"He's quite a reputable person, commander," Trent put in pleasantly. "A bit of a pessimist, given to looking on the sad side of life, but otherwise—"

"Shut up!" barked the Navy man. "I'll get the straight of this without your help. Coxswain, swing in and take off Lieutenant Jackson and his gunner."

The boat thumped against the Vought-Sikorsky's single float. The pilot, a chunky, red-headed man about twenty-eight years of age, stepped aboard, followed by his gunner-observer.

"I see you got my message, Commander Little," Jackson said quickly. "I knew it was a matter for Naval Intelligence."

"All I received was a garbled report," Little said tartly. "Something about this Dutch seaplane attacking Patrol planes. Just what happened?"

"We came on the Fokker as we were returning to the base," explained Jackson. "It was in a fight with two OS2U-1's. I think there was another ship, too, but it ducked into the clouds. The OS2U-1's climbed into the clouds, too, as though they were following another plane."

"They'll probably be in soon with a report," growled Commander Little. "What happened then?"

"We signaled the Fokker to head for Limon Bay, and that's all there is to it," said Jackson. "These birds didn't put up any fight. We had them cold."

"They're probably spies," Little said grimly. "That fellow in the black suit says he's an American business man named Crabb. The other one wouldn't talk."

Trent looked at him with mild reproach. "Now, Commander, I'd say that was departing somewhat from the truth. I attempted to hold up my end of the conversation, but you—"

"I'll give you one chance to answer straight questions," snapped Little. "What's your name? Where'd you get that plane? Why were you fighting with those OS2U-1's?"

"Answering in reverse order," Trent said airily, "they were fighting with us—we were proceeding peacefully when attacked. We borrowed the Fokker at Rotterdam, in making a hasty exit from Holland after a slight misunderstanding with Hitler's boy scouts. And the name is Eric Trent—*Mister* Trent to you."

"Eric Trent?" rasped the commander. "Now I know you're spies. Naval Intelligence got an official list of American casualties and Eric Trent was killed somewhere in Belgium."

"I wish you'd broken it more gently," Trent said with a pained look. "It's a shock, suddenly finding out you're dead. By the way, where am I buried?"

"I'll take the smartness out of you when we get ashore," Little promised savagely. He gave the coxswain an order and the speedboat curved in toward the Cristobal docks.

"You come along, too, Jackson," Little directed as the bluejackets marshaled Trent and Crabb from the boat. "I'm taking these men up to temporary O.N.I. headquarters. I want you to make out a full report of the affair, to include in my code to Washington."

"Then you don't think there's a chance they're telling the truth, Sir?" Jackson ventured. "Trent might have been falsely reported killed."

"If they're Americans, why would they fire on Navy planes?" Little said harshly.

"It might interest you," Trent said idly, "to know that those two 'Navy' ships were defending a Nazi seaplane."

"Now I'll tell one," snorted the commander. "There's a nice little cell at the O.N.I. building, and you can sit in there and think up another fairy story while—"

"Eric!" Mortimer Crabb suddenly exclaimed in an astonished tone. "Look over there—by that car."

They had reached the street which ran parallel with the docks. Trent halted, despite a jerk from the bluejacket who was holding him. Then he stared, unbelieving, as he glimpsed the beak-nosed profile of the man Crabb had pointed out.

"The Nazi pilot!" he exclaimed. "Hold everything, Mort—I'll nail him!"

CHAPTER II

Held For Murder

HIS QUICK lunge threw the bluejacket off balance. Before the sailor could recover, Trent sprang to the side of the waiting car. The beak-nosed man spun around with a frightened look, thrust one hand under his white linen coat. Then Commander Little and the bluejacket pounced on both of them.

"Trying a getaway, eh?" fumed Little.

"I'm breaking your case for you," Trent said coolly. "This man was the pilot of that German seaplane."

"You're crazy if you think I'll swallow—" Little broke off as he saw the half-drawn pistol in the hand of the beak-nosed man. "What's the idea of that gun? Who are you?"

"I'm N.D. Hunt, chief lock-operator at Gatun Lock," the man said shakily. His face was pale under a coat of tan. "You'd carry a gun, too, if somebody was trying to get you."

"Don't let him fool you, Commander," said Trent. "This man was in a Blohm and Voss Ha.140 seaplane forty-five minutes ago. I don't know how he got here so quickly, but I'd know that face anywhere."

The man who called himself Hunt gaped at Trent with a look of complete befuddlement.

"I've never been in a plane in my life. Commander, this man's insane."

Little reached over and took Hunt's pistol.

"A Luger? Where'd you get this'?"

"I've had it for years. Bought it at a Colon shop."

"You'll have to come up to Naval Intelligence until I check up on you," Little said gruffly.

"Can't I use my own car?" said Hunt. "You can send one of your men along with me. Otherwise, I'll have to come back here—"

"We'll all go in it," Little interrupted. "It'll save time getting a Navy car down here. But first, we'll see that this fake 'Trent' doesn't get loose again."

At the commander's order, one of the bluejackets produced a pair of handcuffs. He snapped one link on Trent's wrist and the other on his own.

"What were you doing at the docks?" Little fired at Hunt as the man started the car.

"I was canceling reservations for a trip to Honolulu," Hunt replied sullenly. "I was supposed to leave tomorrow, but with this emergency order—"

"Never mind that," snapped Little. He shot a sidewise look at Trent.

"Don't worry, Commander," said Trent. "Everybody probably knows all about it, anyway."

"I don't know what you're talking about," Little said angrily.

Trent chuckled. "Just because I'm not in Naval Intelligence doesn't mean I'm a moron. Also vice versa, if you get what I mean."

Mortimer Crabb groaned. "Here we are in bad already, and you go insulting people. How I ever was fool enough to team up with you, I can't understand."

Trent laughed. "Commander, don't pay any attention to my partner here. We're really the reincarnation of Damon and Pythias. By the way, will you have a cigarette—they're D'Artagnans, my personal blend."

Little's jaw dropped, as Trent offered him a lighted cigarette plucked out of thin air.

"Harker, I told you to handcuff this man!" he spluttered.

"But I did, Sir," protested the dazed bluejacket. "He slipped out of 'em like he was a Houdini."

THE COMMANDER stared from the empty handcuff to the gold cigarette case which Trent brought out so deftly that it seemed to materialize from nowhere.

"Nothing to be alarmed about," Trent said soothingly. "Just a couple of tricks I picked up when I was a magician's assistant."

"Keep him covered, Harker!" grated Little. "Shoot if he makes another move."

"Don't you think that's a bit melodramatic?" grinned Trent. "After all, I could have lifted Harker's gun and started some fireworks, if I'd been so inclined."

"You heard my order," Little grimly told the bluejacket. And then silence reigned until the car stopped before a trim white building not far from the line dividing Cristobal from the Panama town of Colon. Cheerful lights along the street and the softly waving palms made it a peaceful scene.

"A fine welcome home," Mortimer Crabb said lugubriously. "First time I set foot on American soil in months and then I get arrested."

"Cut out the chatter and get moving," grunted the sailor who guarded him. With Little and Jackson bringing up the rear, the group entered the Naval Intelligence building. Little ordered the three prisoners taken into a central room, opening off a short hall. There were no windows, and only the one door. Harker remained on guard in the hall, and the other sailor disappeared.

"Call the superintendent at Gatun," Little directed Jackson. "Find out if there's a chief lock-operator named N.D. Hunt. If so, get his description."

Jackson went out. The commander turned to Trent and Crabb.

"*Mein Herr*, the game is up!" he flung out suddenly in German. "You may as well tell the truth."

"For your benefit, Mort," Trent chuckled, "the commander is trying to trap us. He wants us to confess our sins."

"So! You do understand German!" roared Little.

"*Ja*," said Trent. "Also French, Spanish, and Dutch—and a smattering of others. Want to try me out?"

Little swore under his breath, sat down at a desk in one corner of the room, and scribbled out a message.

"Have this coded and sent to Washington by priority radio," he told Harker. When he turned back to the room, Trent was calmly holding the message pad up to the light, slanted so that the impression from Little's pencil was visible.

"Give that here!" thundered the commander. He snatched the pad from Trent's fingers.

"I could really save you the trouble of all that check-up," Trent offered agreeably. "You'll find our passports are in perfect order. We left the States before the European war broke out, in a DC-3 belonging to Mort—which unfortunately we had to leave behind after a little trouble in France. The passport photos you asked to have radioed aren't the best likenesses in the world—but you'll find that story of my death, like Mark Twain's, slightly exaggerated."

"Even if you are Trent, you've still a lot to explain," retorted Little. He jerked around as Lieutenant Jackson appeared.

"They gave Hunt a clean bill, sir," reported the junior officer. "Described him to a 'T,' and asked us to release him at once. Because of the emergency orders, he's needed at—"

Little stopped him with a quick gesture. "Hunt, I want to talk with you alone. You said something about the reason for carrying a gun...."

The rest was lost to Trent as Little motioned the lock-operator into the hall. Jackson took up a position near the door, facing the prisoners. There was a sound of another door closing not far off. And a few seconds later Trent heard a footstep in the hall. It ended, and there was a brief silence. Suddenly Jackson turned to the door, listening to something outside.

"Stay here," he said curtly to Trent and Crabb. Then he swung the door open. There was a stifled oath, and beyond the half-opened door Trent saw something flash in the light. Jackson staggered back with a groan, sagged to his knees, clutching at the knob. Trent leaped to the door, pushed it open, and caught the lieutenant's arm. There was a sound of swift-running feet in the main hall, but the connecting door was shut.

"Good Lord, he's been stabbed!" Crabb said hoarsely.

Trent knelt hastily beside the wounded man. A stiletto was buried almost to the hilt in Jackson's side.

"Get Commander Little! Have him call a doctor!" Trent called swiftly. As Crabb hurried to the hall door, Jackson collapsed to the floor. He looked up at Trent, his face ghastly white.

"Hunt… listening at door… must be… spy." A spasm shook him, and blood came to his lips in a reddish froth.

"Don't try to talk," Trent told him. "We'll have help in—"

"Get him, Harker!" came Little's furious voice from out in the main hall. Then the door burst open and Mortimer Crabb backed into the shorter hall, hands elevated.

"But I was only trying to find you," he protested.

"Don't try to bluff—" the commander's words ended in a gasp. "Jackson! Those devils have knifed him!"

Jackson's eyes were glazed, but he made a last desperate attempt to speak.

"Not—not—" he stopped, a wild, incredulous stare fixed on some one in the doorway. Trent turned, saw that it was Hunt. For a second longer, Jackson lay there, then the stunned look faded, and his eyes closed for the last time.

"YOU BUTCHERS!" rasped the commander. He motioned grimly to Harker. "Keep them covered. I'm holding them both for murder."

"We didn't kill him," Crabb said forlornly. "It was somebody out in the hall, just after you left."

"It won't do you any good to lie," retorted Little. "We caught you trying to sneak out."

"Just a moment, Commander," said Trent. He glanced at Hunt, saw the lock-keeper's frightened eyes rest on the corpse. "It may interest you to know that Jackson named the man who killed him."

Hunt stared at him, but he made no attempt to escape.

"You're only wasting your time," Little said harshly. But Trent interrupted: "When we came out, after Jackson heard a noise and stepped into the hall, we found him here, stabbed. I sent Mort for help. Just after that Jackson said: 'Hunt… listening at door… must be—spy.'"

Hunt's face was a picture of amazement. Commander Little, after an equally astonished look, turned an angry red.

"Why, you poor fool, Hunt was with me every second! Harker can testify to that, too."

"Certainly, Sir," said the bluejacket. "But—if the Commander will pardon me—I'm wondering about Seaman Morris. I told him to come back here and report to Lieutenant Jackson."

"Go look for him," ordered Little. "And phone the base hospital for a doctor and some men with a stretcher. Jackson's death will have to be certified as murder before he's moved."

Harker returned in a few moments, "No trace of Morris, Sir. I told your orderly to do sentry-guard at the door. They're sending an ambulance for the body."

"Cover him up," muttered Little. "Then we'll lock these two in a cell and send out an alarm for Morris."

Hunt was still looking, white-faced, at the dead man. "May I go now, Commander?" he said huskily. "This terrible thing—I'd like to get away. And I've a lot to do before midnight, as I told you."

"No reason why you should stay," answered Little. "You'll have to give evidence, later, at the trial."

Hunt hurried toward the front of the building. A few seconds later a Navy surgeon appeared, followed by two corpsmen with a stretcher. Little cut short Trent's attempt to explain to the surgeon, and after a brief examination of the body the medico ordered the corpse removed. Little and Seaman Harker marched the two prisoners back to a cell at the rear of the Intelligence building, and the steel door clanged shut on them.

"Stand guard out in the hall," the Commander directed Harker. "I've got to run over to Operations, and I want to get there before the blackout. I'll ask for a couple of men for special guard-duty. You'll be relieved in an hour or so."

The door to the brig closed, and for a moment the two prisoners looked at each other. Finally Trent shrugged.

"Well, Mort, you had it right—all but the Navy slum. Maybe that'll come later."

"This time we're sunk," Crabb said gloomily. "They'll hang us higher than a kite."

Trent sat down on the edge of an iron cot. "Don't let it worry you, Mort. We can prove we were searched and neither of us had that dagger on us."

"They'll say you hid it some way," Crabb replied morosely. "You and your magician's tricks—and why did you have to let them know about that, anyway?"

"I couldn't help deflating old Fuss-budget Little. If I'd dreamed it was this serious, I wouldn't have bothered."

"Oh, so you admit a murder charge is serious?" Crabb said sarcastically.

"I don't mean the murder charge. I mean whatever's back of this business. Mort, there's some big scheme afoot, and lock-keeper Hunt is at the center of it."

"You still think he killed Jackson?" demanded Crabb.

"No, that would mean Little and Harker were both in on it, and they're obviously loyal. And that strange look Jackson had when he saw Hunt, there at the last. It was as though he couldn't believe what he saw. He was about to clear us when he saw Hunt—then he stopped as though he'd been paralyzed."

"Poor devil," mumbled the inventor. "He seemed like a clean young chap. Terrible, to be struck down like that."

"The question is, *why* was he killed? I've a hunch whoever did it was trying to get at us. Afraid we'd upset some plan, maybe. Mort, we must have the key to this thing without knowing it."

"How could we have any key?" Crabb growled. "All we saw was that Nazi plane with the fake insignia—and Hunt. Maybe he didn't kill Jackson, but he must be a spy, or he wouldn't have been in that ship."

Trent sat up, snapped his fingers. "Mort, you've hit it! He wasn't in that ship, after all."

"But I saw him! So did you."

"You thought you saw—"Trent's words were drowned by the moan of a siren out on the reservation. The sound rose shrilly, with an eerie note that reminded Trent of the air-raid warnings he had heard with unhappy frequency, in Europe. The siren was still wailing, its volume increasing, when from somewhere beyond the door of the cell-room, there was a muffled report. Although it was barely audible above the siren, Trent knew it instantly for a pistol shot.

CHAPTER III
Jailbreak

SOMETHING like a strangled cry followed the shot, then the door of the cell-room was quickly flung open. Four men appeared, and beyond them on the floor Trent saw Harker doubled up with a red stain on the side of his uniform coat. The first of the four men was a big, massive figure in the uniform of a Navy two-striper. His head was set squattily on a thick neck and the glittering pupils of his pale blue eyes were like bits of black ice. In his hand was an automatic from which a wisp of smoke still curled. Behind him was the missing seaman, Morris, with a pinched-faced man in the garb of a chief petty officer beside him. And over the C.P.O.'s shoulder Trent saw the angular features and beak nose of lock-keeper Hunt.

"Krossen—come here!" said the big man. His voice was like the crack of a whip, and the beak-nosed man sprang forward.

"Ja, Herr Heimmler," he said hastily.

"Are these the ones?" demanded the big man.

"They are the men who flew the Fokker," said the one called Krossen. Mortimer Crabb glowered at him through the bars.

"So you *were* in on it, you lying traitor!"

Krossen's lips drew back in a mirthless laugh, exposing receding gums and long, almost pointed teeth. Crabb started.

"Eric, look at his teeth! It's not Hunt at all!"

"I had just figured that out—a little too late," Trent said regretfully.

"Unlock the door," Heimmler ordered Morris. Then he turned his pale eyes to Krossen. "For the last time, keep that shark grin off your face. One look at those teeth tonight, and they would know the deception. And it would be most unfortunate for you if you failed."

"I will remember, *Mein Herr,*" Krossen said in a subdued voice. "No one will know."

Morris opened the cell door and Heimmler grimly motioned with his gun.

"Come out, with your hands up. Morris, you and Schultz handcuff and gag them."

"The tall man, Trent, is a magician—" began Morris.

Heimmler jumped at the mention of Trent's name. *"Was ist?* You mean this is the Trent who caused all the trouble over the stolen bomb-sight last Fall?"

"He gave that name to Commander Little," Morris said nervously. "I would have told you sooner, but you kept me busy—"

"Lieber Gott, we have caught a real prize!" exclaimed Heimmler. "If I had known who these two were, I would not have waited for the blackout before breaking in. At that, it seems incredible they did not tell the Navy officer what they saw."

"Trent told him, but the commander wouldn't believe him," said Morris. He gave Krossen an ugly look. "If you show no more brains tonight than you did using a plane with a swastika—"

"The swastika was painted out, with Colombian registry letters over it," Krossen said defensively. "But the paint peeled off—there must have been a spy at the Azores base where we had it done. The paint contained something to make it dry too fast, but we did not notice until we were halfway across, and we could do nothing about it. If the pilots of the stolen scout-bombers had met us sooner, they could have kept the Fokker from getting close enough for these *Schweine* to notice."

"We've no time for petty squabbles," snapped Heimmler. "We have to get into Colon while the Zone is still blacked-out."

He gestured with his gun for Krossen to cover Crabb. In the split second that his pistol was turned away, Trent went into action. A lunge sent the steel cell-door thudding against Heimmler's arm, and the Nazi's gun clattered to the floor. Before Krossen could fire, Trent snatched the man's wrist, dropped to one knee. Krossen went headlong over his shoulder, pitched on top of Heimmler.

Mortimer Crabb leaped into the fray, his ham-like fists flying. The false C.P.O. went down with a howl and Crabb wheeled toward Morris. The psuedo-bluejacket took frantic aim, but before he could pull the trigger Trent dived in low and caught him with a flying tackle.

"Look out, Eric!" shouted Crabb as the two men toppled to the floor. There was a sound of a scuffle, then something hit Trent just above the ear. A roaring welled up inside his head, and then suddenly everything went dark....

WHEN Trent's senses returned, a steady vibration droned through his aching head. He groaned, opened his eyes, and found himself in the ill-smelling cabin of a fairly large motorboat. The hatch door was closed, but a faint light shone in through a nearby port.

"I think he's coming around," muttered a voice, which Trent recognized as Hunt's after a moment. He turned his head, painfully, saw the lock-keeper and Crabb bending over him. There was a bandage around Crabb's forehead, Hunt's face was bruised.

"Eric, are you all right?" whispered Crabb.

"I feel as though an elephant stepped on my head," Trent said thickly. "Aside from that, I guess I'm okay."

"The big fellow slugged you with a pistol butt," said Crabb. "I tried to block him, but Morris and that devil who looks like Hunt jumped me."

"Where are we?" Trent asked. "Feels like open water."

"We must be somewhere the other side of Point Manzanillo," Hunt put in. "They're hugging the coast and running without lights."

"How'd they get out?" queried Trent as he struggled to a sitting position.

"Two of them were in my car, waiting," Hunt answered glumly. "They grabbed me the second I climbed in, made me drive around in back. Then when the black-out came, they left me tied and gagged and went into the Intelligence office. When they brought you two out, they tumbled you into my car and drove from Cristobal into Colon. Heimmler's uniform got them past the sentry-post—they had the three of us on the floor so we couldn't be seen."

"Fine mess," Trent commented. "Little will think I worked the lock on that cell-door and killed Harker. But no use worrying about that angle now. Do you have any idea where we're heading?"

"I heard Heimmler say something about a river," answered Hunt. "No telling which one he meant—there are several along this coast which drain into the Atlantic."

"Probably they've fixed a hide-out back in the jungle," ventured Trent. "Just how much do you know about this thing, anyway?"

"Nothing," Hunt said helplessly. "That is, only what I've guessed. It's something about the Fleet—but I don't know what they're up to, or why they want me."

"The Fleet's coming through the Canal tonight, isn't it?" queried Trent.

"That's right. The first ship will reach Gatun Lock about midnight."

"And they've a man who can double for you," mused Trent. He leaned back, winced, rubbed the side of his head. "If I could only think straight. What was this story you told Little about having to carry a gun?"

"Several queer things happened to me," Hunt told him. "I begin to see now what was up—though it isn't all clear yet. I discovered I was being followed everywhere, but I couldn't find who was doing it. My house was ransacked one night. Another time some one slipped me a Mickey Finn at a bar, and when I came to, I was out on the edge of Colon with oil all over my face—"

"They were making a plaster mask of your face," hazarded Trent. "I'd say all that business was to get as much information as possible for somebody to impersonate you. They evidently searched until they found some one who could double for you."

"But why would things happen to my assistants, too?" said Hunt. "One of them had a smash-up in his car, and another got sick after eating at a restaurant in Colon. He's been in the hospital, poisoned—"

"That's not hard to guess," interrupted Trent. "They wanted to make sure you'd be on the job. You were set for a vacation, so they got two of your assistants out of the way to force you to stay here until the Fleet passed through. They're planning to have Krossen—"

your double—impersonate you tonight. Now what could he do out there at the locks?"

"Well, he could cause trouble, all right," Hunt said thoughtfully, "but I don't see how he could hurt the Fleet, though he might delay it temporarily by wrecking some of the lock mechanism."

"It must be something more than—"Trent stopped as the boat slackened speed. "We must be in the river—I don't feel the swells."

"Running in the dark, they'd have to slow down," said Hunt. "These rivers twist a lot."

There was silence in the cabin for a few minutes.

"Did Krossen come on the boat, too?"Trent asked suddenly.

"They left him back in Cristobal," Crabb replied. "I heard that big brute talking to him, but it was in German and I couldn't tell—"

"I understand German," said Hunt. "But I couldn't tell what they were up to. Heimmler told him to follow the directions on a sketch of some kind, and that he'd be taken to Gatun by Schultz—whoever he is."

"Schultz is the name of the spy in C.P.O. uniform," supplied Trent. "Mort, did he stay back there?"

"Yes, I forgot to mention that," said Crabb. He sighed gloomily. "What difference does it make? You can't laugh your way out of *this* jam."

"It's not a question of getting out of a jam,"Trent said grimly. "Unless I'm mistaken, most of the Fleet is in serious danger."

The boat's engines fell to idling speed, and a moment later the craft bumped against something. Then a key scraped in the lock of the cabin door.

"Pretend I'm still unconscious," Trent whispered swiftly. He let himself back on the deck. "No matter what they do, don't let on."

THE DOOR was flung open, and through half-slitted eyes Trent saw the glint of a gun in the starlight.

"Come out, you *Amerikaner* pigs," came Heimmler's curt voice.

"Speak English, you big ape," muttered Crabb.

Heimmler swore under his breath and a flashlight probed into the cabin. Trent closed his eyes as the beam twitched toward him. The big Nazi gave an order and Trent heard men hustling Crabb and Hunt out of the cabin. A boot tip thudded against his side, and he held back a groan with difficulty as another kick followed.

"Take him ashore," Heimmler directed. Trent was dragged across the deck, roughly hoisted up the hatchway. He kept his eyes closed until he felt the men reach solid ground, then he risked a glance through narrowed lids. The boat lay in a small inlet at the side of the river. Trees growing close along the banks merged their foliage to create a natural screen, and in this shaded lagoon he glimpsed the vague outlines of several planes. Beyond the crude landing where the boat lay, he saw the massive bulk of a large Navy patrol plane. It looked like a Consolidated flying-boat, but he could not be sure in the gloom.

The men carried him along a path toward a small group of native shacks at the end of the lagoon. There was a light showing from the opened door of one shack, and he saw a dozen men in the uniform of American bluejackets. Several others in the garb of Navy officers came forward as they saw the supposedly-unconscious prisoner.

"What's wrong?" one of them demanded in a tense voice.

"There's nothing wrong," Heimmler's clipped voice sounded from not far behind Trent. "This is one of the men who saw Krossen in the seaplane."

"Why bring them here?" said the other man gruffly. "Why couldn't you get rid of them back there—or dump them into the sea?"

"Because they may be useful to us later," snapped Heimmler. "The two who were in that Fokker happen to be the Americans Trent and Crabb. It means a decoration for capturing them. The other man is lock-keeper Hunt. His knowledge of the Canal will prove helpful later—when we are ready to put their Fleet back into operation."

"Then everything is ready?" said the other man in a relieved tone.

"Exactly as scheduled. Get the men aboard the patrol plane. Have the engines started, and also the other planes—"

Trent lost the rest of Heimmler's instructions as he was carried into the nearest shack and dumped down on the floor. "I'll watch him," growled one of the men, and Trent recognized Morris' voice. "Go get your parachute on."

Trent cautiously opened one eye, saw the other man leave. Morris stood near the doorway, hand on the butt of his .45, his face turned so he could look outside. The distance was too far to risk a leap for the spy's gun, and Trent lay motionless, making a quick survey of the shack. A cot stood in one corner, near a field desk on which was a map of the Canal Zone. Illumination came from a small electric lantern. At the foot of the cot was a box of grenades, and Trent's slitted eyes were puzzled as he translated the German label on the box. Tear-gas bombs. What purpose called for these relatively-harmless grenades?

He had no time to consider, for Heimmler appeared in the doorway, followed by the gruff-voiced man who had met him outside. Trent closed his eyes again.

CHAPTER IV
Panama Plot

"**I TELL** you there is nothing to worry about now," Heimmler said tartly. "Krossen works better under tension. Once he starts to play the role, he will carry through. As for the other act, they will never suspect a thing until it is too late."

"I hope not," mumbled the other man. "It is such a tremendous thing—it almost seems it is too great to succeed. Last night I had a dream that we had been tricked—that this Martensen had taken our money and lied to us about the controls."

"He wouldn't dare," rasped Heimmler. "The *Gestapo* would hunt him to the ends of the earth. Beside, there are the blueprints—the photographs—his detailed sketches."

"Photographs have been faked before," the other Nazi said sourly. "Remember the discrepancy between Martensen's sketch of the room itself and the blueprint? He could have taken the money, knowing we'd fail and be trapped, so the truth wouldn't come out until too late."

"I will soon make certain," growled Heimmler. "Morris, go get *Herr* Hunt—and have the other prisoner brought here, too. We'll put them under one guard."

"But you said to keep Trent separate from the others," objected Morris.

"I intended to question him alone—an adventurer of his type can always be bought, if the price is high enough. But there isn't time now."

Trent heard Morris go out. Then the gruff-voiced man spoke again.

"You still intend to fly one of the Vought-Sikorskys?"

"*Ja.* I mean to make that combat look real," Heimmler replied with a peculiar note.

"You don't mean—*Ach du Lieber,* you told the two men they would have a chance to escape if they volunteered to fly the Blohm and Voss."

"The lives of two men are not important with all we have at stake. Go ahead and order all engines started. Take off in the patrol plane as soon as your men are aboard. It is a tricky operation in this river, and you had better be clear before the other ships taxi out. Circle until I signal, then proceed according to plan."

Trent waited until the other man's footsteps had died, then he opened his eyes a fraction of an inch. Heimmler was at the field desk, taking a roll of blueprints and photographs from the drawer. Trent could see the bulge of an automatic under his left arm. The Nazi's back was partly turned, but it was almost fifteen feet to where he stood behind the desk. To jump up and reach him without giving the alarm would be almost an impossibility.

Trent's eyes shifted to the box at the foot of the cot. Swiftly, silently, he reached out to it, grasped one of the tear-gas grenades. Heimmler shoved the drawer of the desk closed. Trent had a freezing moment when he thought the big Nazi was going to turn around before he could snatch the grenade. Then Heimmler unrolled the blueprints and bent over one. The next moment Trent had the grenade hidden in his left hand, out of Heimmler's range of vision. He had the safety-pin almost withdrawn when voices sounded outside, and Morris and another Nazi spy appeared with Crabb and Hunt.

Heimmler wheeled, motioned for Hunt's guard to bring the man to the desk. Out in the lagoon, a motor thundered, and then another. As the first roar settled into the steady drone of the warming-up process, Trent heard Hunt give an exclamation of horror. Through slitted eyes, he saw the lock-keeper staring in consternation at the blueprints and sketches.

"Martensen! So that's why he kept asking me—"

The roar of another motor, close to the shack, drowned the rest of his words. There was a look of triumph on Heimmler's face.

"You understand quickly!" he jeered. "I see you can guess what will happen when the first vessel of your Fleet reaches the locks."

"You devils!" Hunt shouted. "You'll never get away with it. They'll stop him—" with a sudden fury, he hurled himself at the big Nazi.

HEIMMLER jumped back, hand thrust inside his coat, and Hunt's guard sprang forward with his gun lifted. Trent's hand flashed up from the floor, and the grenade struck the side of the shack, behind Heimmler. There was a spurt of whitish gas and the big spy staggered back, clawing at his eyes. Morris had whirled as Trent threw the grenade, but before he could fire, Crabb was upon him.

A huge fist sank deep in the traitor's solar plexus and he doubled up in agony. Crabb snatched his gun and Trent leaped after Hunt's now terrified guard. The German was halfway to the door, one hand before his eyes. Trent brought him down with a terrific left to the jaw. Scooping up the man's pistol, he grasped Hunt's arm and they stumbled out of the gas-filled shack with Crabb at their heels.

"*Hilfe!* The Americans are escaping!" Heimmler bellowed from inside, but the roar of the engines drowned his cry. Trent cast a swift glance around. Out on the river, the big Consolidated was taxiing into position for taking off, its landing-lights illuminating the surface. Silhouetted by the glow were the two Vought-Sikorskys with their waiting crews. The Ha. 140 was being turned around from where it had been beached.

"Come on!" Trent said hastily. "Mort, take that bird at the right pontoon—I'll get the other man."

He was within a few yards of the seaplane when Heimmler emerged from the shack, pawing his way blindly through the doorway. Just at that moment the Ha. 140's engines went to idling and the spy-leader's frantic yell cut through their rumble. A helmeted pilot in U.S. Navy uniform spun around, one hand at his hip.

"*Gott im Himmel!* The Americans!" he bawled.

He jerked his pistol from its holster. Trent fired a split-second before flame jetted from the Nazi's gun. The pilot stumbled, pitched across the pontoon, and fell into the water. Two more shots cut through the thrumming of the engines. Crabb grasped at his right arm, dropped his pistol. The Nazi gunner jumped back, aimed a hasty shot at Trent.

Trent's gun barked twice and the spy fell, shot through the heart. By now, the Vought-Sikorsky crews were running desperately toward the German plane.

"Get in!" Trent flung at Hunt. "Here—help Mort, quick!"

"I'm all right—just nicked my arm," Crabb said shakily. He tumbled into the Ha. 140 and Trent climbed up, threw himself down at the controls. Bullets drilled the starboard window panel as he shoved the throttles open. He bent low, sent the big seaplane thundering out of the lagoon. A machine-gun blazed from the rear cockpit of the second Vought-Sikorsky as he sent the German plane speeding past. The Consolidated was racing down the river and Trent saw it lift as he swung into the wind. Mortimer Crabb had crawled into the bow and Hunt was bent over him, bandaging his arm. The lock-keeper scrambled back as Trent took off, climbed into the radioman's seat, at Trent's left and slightly below his level.

"We've got to stop them!" he cried hoarsely. "They're going to open all three of the Gatun Locks and leave the Fleet stranded in the Canal!"

"So that's it!" Trent said tautly. "I knew it must be something tremendous—but how in Heaven's name can they work that? There must be safety devices—"

"There are—the three locks can't be opened at once by accident—but there's one way, and they've found it out!" Hunt's face was white in the reflected glow of the lights. "Those sketches were made by an engineer named Martensen—he was one of the anti-sabotage group that surveyed the canal three months ago. He kept asking if there was any way all three locks could be opened simultaneously, and I finally told him they could, by having someone hold or tie the circuit-breakers and remove a safety-block—"

"Never mind how they can do it," Trent cut in swiftly. "We've got to warn the men on duty at Gatun. Switch on that radio and try to raise the station at Cristobal."

Hunt bent over the set, despairingly shook his head.

"It's no good—it's been shot up."

"That's Fate for you," Trent said with a twisted grin. "We shot up this plane ourselves—Mort and I. Well, the only thing left is to beat them to Gatun."

"We're only about twenty-five miles from the locks, if you cut straight across the San Blas Mountains," Hunt said jerkily.

Trent switched off the lights as a stream of tracer flamed past the starboard wing.

"SO YOU want to play, *Herr* Heimmler? Well, I'll attend to you later."

The seaplane bored up into the darkness, straightened on a Southwest course.

"What about Mort's arm?" Trent said abruptly. "Was it badly hurt?"

"No. Luckily, the bullet went through the fleshy part of his forearm without cutting a vein."

"Thank Providence for that." Trent peered out into the gloom. "We ought to see the light of Colon as soon as we're over these hills—unless they're still blacked-out."

"The black-out was only a test," said Hunt. "The Canal lights have to be on for the Fleet to come through safely."

Trent shook his head. "Seems incredible, stranding a Fleet like that. Of course, they couldn't get all the ships—"

"They'll get almost half if this scheme works," Hunt said through tight lips. "They're making the transit in closer order than ever before, to see how fast it can be done. And every ship between Gatun and the Pedro Miguel locks—practically the entire length of the Canal—will be grounded when the three Gatun locks are opened. Gatun Lake is eighty-five feet above sea level. That water will start rushing out into the Atlantic, and any ship near the inner lock is sure to be smashed against it. The ones behind it will be whirled around, probably floated out of the channel. Even if these devils haven't found some way to keep Gatun Dam spillways shut, it won't do any good to try to fill up the lake again. The locks could never be closed against that flood, once it's going full force. And it will take six months for the lake and Canal to fill up with normal rainfall."

"Six months with half the Fleet grounded, at the mercy of Nazi bombers—the Atlantic coast unprotected," Trent said in a grim voice. "Hunt, no matter what happens to us—"

"There are the lights!" Hunt broke in. "Bear left a little—that's it. You're headed straight for the locks."

With engines full out, the Nazi plane roared across the thin range of mountains, tilted down at the great locks now only eight miles distant. Suddenly, a searchlight flicked across the intervening space, caught the seaplane's wing. Trent hurriedly ruddered out, dived, zigzagging to keep the light-crew from spotting them again.

"Get on a chute!" he flung at Hunt. "You'll have to bail out and warn them."

"No parachute here!" Hunt exclaimed, after a hasty search. "You'll have to land on Gatun Lake and—"

Br-r-r-r-t-t-t! The muffled pound of machine-guns cut through the engines' thunder, and a Vought-Sikorsky plunged through the searchlight beam at the Ha. 140. At the same moment two more searchlights stabbed up at the twisting ships, and still more blazed from vessels out on Gatun Lake. As Trent kicked out of the scout-bomber's fire, he saw the great hulk of a battle-ship slowly approaching the Western end of the Gatun Locks. Barely underway, some distance beyond, was an aircraft carrier, and at intervals across the Lake toward Culebra Cut he could see the lights of still other Navy ships. The gates of the first lock were starting to open, and a shiver ran through him as he thought of Krossen somewhere inside the control tower, ready to open those other locks.

"Hang on—fasten your belt!" he clipped at Hunt. "Mort—brace yourself up there—we're making a crack-up landing!"

"Never mind me!" Crabb howled back. "Watch out for that Consolidated!"

The big patrol plane suddenly swam into the glow of the lights, and at the same instant another Vought-Sikorsky joined the first in a furious charge at the Nazi ship. Trent's last doubts were swiftly erased as he saw Heimmler at the controls of the first scout-bomber.

"Get back on the rear guns!" Trent ordered Hunt. As the lock-keeper crawled aft, Crabb swung the nose-turret guns and sent a blasting fire into the cockpit of the patrol plane. The Consoli-dated dipped sharply, swung back over the locks. The next moment a figure went headlong into space, followed by a second, and a third. A parachute opened, tilted steeply as the spy beneath slipped it toward the locks. Trent pulled up in a tight chandelle, and two simultaneous bursts blazed from the nose and aft-turret guns. Smoke puffed from one of the patrol plane's engines, became a mantle of flame.

Anti-aircraft shells burst wildly around the Nazi seaplane. Trent kicked over onto one wing, slid out of one bracket, dived away from another. A spinning ship whirled past, and he saw it was one of the Vought-Sikorskys. Less than a hundred feet away, Heimmler appeared, swaying in a chute, his face set with a fierce purpose. Trent swore under his breath. The spy-leader, seeing his main group of parachutists lost, had bailed out to aid Krossen against any resistance that might develop.

Two of the descending chutists missed the locks, landed in the Canal, but the third came down on the center wall not far from the gate at the Atlantic-approach channel end. Trent saw him release himself from the chute, snatch up a sub-machine gun which he had cradled in his arms, and run toward the control tower.

SIX NAVY Grummans suddenly whirled out of the sky, hurling down at the Ha. 140. Trent snapped off the switch, dived at the center wall of the lock. As he backsticked, fishtailing madly to kill his speed, Crabb hauled himself up in the nose, pitched a fiery blast at the running parachutist. The Nazi sprawled on his face, made a last attempt to lift the machine-gun, then lay still. Heimmler was down to within two hundred feet of the locks as Trent leveled off above the center wall. There was a crash as the pontoons settled upon the track used by the electric "mules" in hauling ships through the locks. The seaplane, lurched violently to one side, skidded on its wrecked pontoons, then came to a jolting stop.

The flash of a pistol shot caught Trent's eye as he clawed out of the cockpit. Then he saw that two men were struggling furiously at the rail of the control tower. One was Krossen, the other obviously an assistant lock-keeper who had discovered the masquerade.

Trent was half-way to the tower when a bullet clanged against the base of the structure. As he dropped to the concrete, there was another shot and a slug scraped his shoulder, searing hot. He twisted around, saw Heimmler dashing along the wall, his collapsed chute back near the farther lock-gates.

"Krossen, you fool!" Heimmler screamed. "Open the other locks!"

Trent jumped up, raced to the body of the Nazi parachutist who had been felled by Crabb's burst. A wild cry-sounded from up in the tower and he saw Krossen's opponent topple limply over the rail. With a desperate effort, Trent snatched up the sub-machine gun, whirled it in an arc as his finger closed on the trigger. He had a flashing glimpse of Heimmler's terrified face as the hail of bullets cut across his chest, then the muzzle lifted to the tower. Krossen sprang back frantically, but too late.

"You got him!" gasped Hunt. "I'll run on up there, phone ashore, and tell them the truth—"

He vanished around the base of the tower and Trent turned to look for Mortimer Crabb. The inventor was only a few feet away, his bandaged arm dangling, a look of grim satisfaction on his face as he gazed back at Heimmler's motionless figure.

"Well, that's one less Nazi spy in the world. It's worth taking a bullet in the arm to see those devils finished off."

Trent laughed in spite of the ache in his stiffening shoulder. "Mort, you old war-horse, I'm going to miss you."

"What do you mean miss me?" demanded Crabb. "When those rats start working on the good old U.S.A., you can count me in any time!"

"Maybe I was right about that reincarnation stuff," chuckled Trent. "Come on, I want to go up in the tower and make a phone call—after Hunt gets us cleared with Commander Little and the rest of the Navy."

"What are you up to now?" said Crabb, suspiciously.

"Don't get alarmed," said Trent, with a grin. "I'm just going to order a couple of steaks for Damon and Pythias."

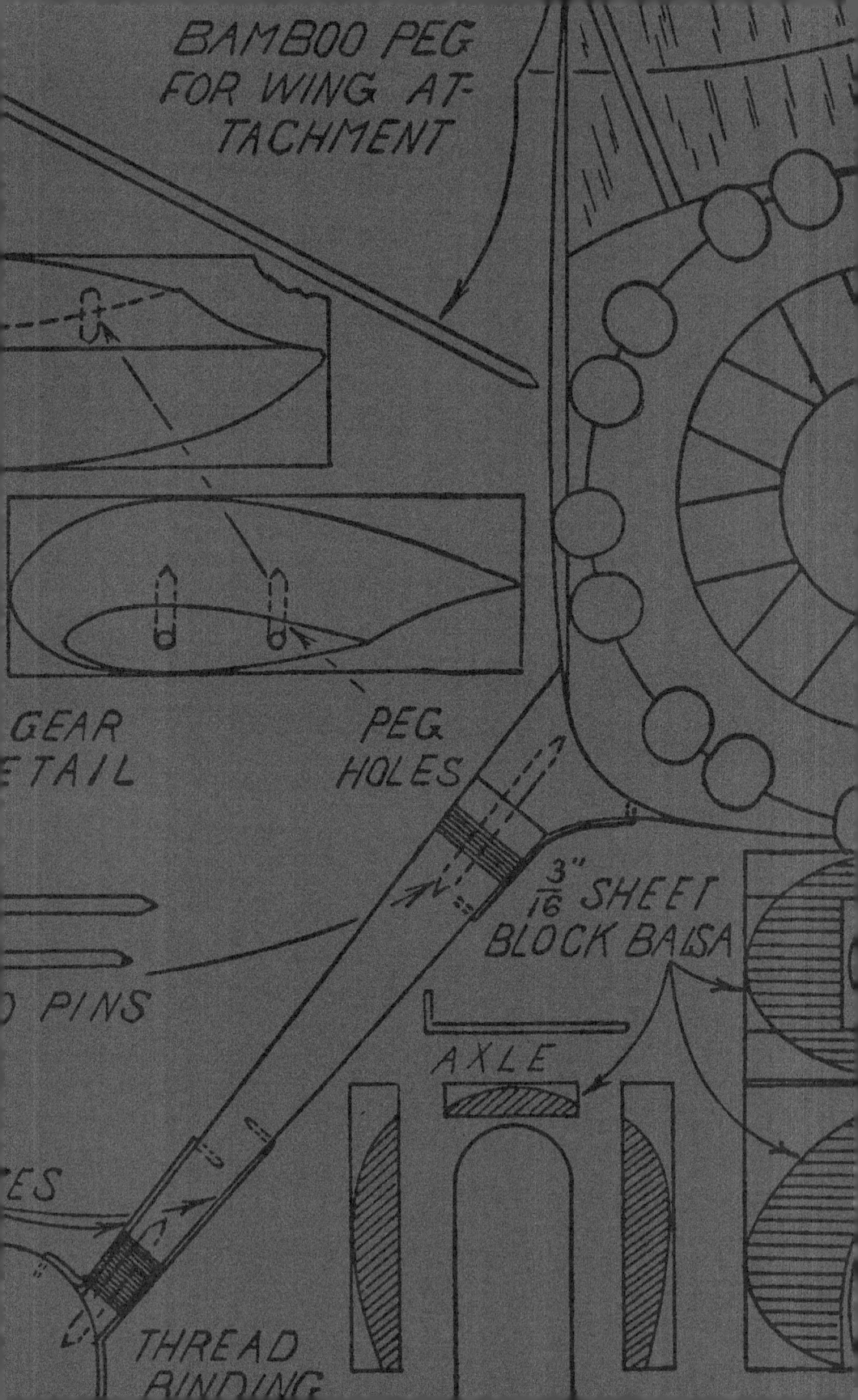

BAMBOO PEG
FOR WING AT-
TACHMENT

GEAR
ETAIL

PEG
HOLES

O PINS

$\frac{3"}{16}$ SHEET
BLOCK BALSA

AXLE

ES

THREAD
BINDING

The Ace From Hell

CHAPTER I

Murder Masquerade

"**I**S IT my fault that Atlanta police haven't a sense of humor?" asked Eric Trent. He grinned back at his sad-faced partner, Mortimer Crabb, as their borrowed Navy Corsair droned through a cold gray drizzle that hid ground and sky.

"You and your magician tricks," Crabb said bitterly. "It wasn't enough to pull fifty feet of ribbon out of that cop's nose. You had to lift his handcuffs and get us tossed into jail, just so you could stage a Houdini escape-act and win a bet."

"We got out, didn't we?" Trent chuckled. "I hope the turnkey finds his pants. Remind me to send back the chief's badge—and a bonus to that taxi driver for beating the scout cars to the airport."

"You can thank that Air Corps major for getting us cleared in time," retorted Crabb in a voice grating like a saw hitting a rusty nail.

"The gentleman had an axe to grind," answered Trent. "It seems General Busby, chief of Army Intelligence, would like to see us at Washington. From what I gathered in our hasty departure, a mysterious individual known as the 'Red Devil'—has the general's toupee standing on end. How, why, when, and where, the major didn't explain. It has an intriguing sound—"

"Not to me," Crabb said gloomily. "You go chase your red devils. I'm going into a sanitarium for a long rest."

"I've already declined," Trent said amiably. "Just because we spray a few Nazis away from the Canal on our return from the wars is no reason to think we're professional Hawkshaws, on call. Besides, we need a vacation. All work and no play makes Messieurs Crabb and Trent a couple of very dull lads."

"I wouldn't mind being dull," Crabb said in a dismal voice, "if I could do it sitting by a hot fire somewhere. Here it is November, and me freezing in this silly white suit!"

Trent looked back at his partner, who was dressed, like himself, in thin white tropical drill. When they left Panama, it had been their intention to buy warmer clothes on the way North, but that plan had not worked out.

"I'd have had you fitted from derby to spats at Atlanta, if the minions of the law hadn't interfered," Trent said. "Never mind, Mort, we'll be in Washington in a few minutes and I'll get you an Indian blanket."

"Very funny," Crabb said sourly. He huddled down in the rear seat, his hollow face a picture of woe, chattering teeth working on a wad of gum while his protruding Adam's-apple bobbed up and down in mournful accompaniment. Up forward, Trent indolently watched the instruments. His almost Latin darkness of hair and eyes, with the polished ease of his manner, was somehow reminiscent of the Riviera. But the audacious humor which was his chief trait was pure Yankee. A century before he would have been another D'Artagnan living by his sword, a price on his head—as there was now, put there by Nazi and Fascist governments.

"If that Air Corps thing is out, what're we going to Washington for?" Crabb suddenly demanded.

"Just a fuel stop," Trent answered airily. "We're headed for the Gay White Way. First, a haberdashers. Then the pleasure-spots— popping corks, music, shows, *femmes fatale*—"

"That settles it," Crabb grated. "I get out at Washington. And don't wire me for bail, either."

Trent laughed, reached for his earphones, intending to pick up the Washington airport beam. He listened a moment, changed course slightly. He was about to cut in his transmitter to call the airport tower when a blurred shape flashed out of the murk. It whipped to one side, revealed briefly as a Beechcraft 18-S twin-motored light transport.

In the same instant a gray Curtiss P-40 emerged like a wraith from the mists. Four streaks of fire shot from its cowl and wing-root guns as the Beechcraft frantically twisted into a vertical turn. As Trent swiftly banked, the P-40 pilot flung a lightning glance at the Corsair. Trent stared in amazement.

A red Satan's mask completely covered the pilot's face!

THE P-40 whirled to follow the fleeing Beechcraft, and Trent saw its wings and tail carried no insignia. He rammed his throttle full open, hurtled the Corsair after the gray fighter. The Beechcraft made another wild turn and Trent glimpsed the pilot's desperate countenance. Apparently there was no one else in the ship; no one appeared at the windows.

As Trent cut in his gun circuit with a quick warming burst, the masked pilot pitched another furious blast at the Beechcraft. Then Trent saw him snatch up a hand-mike, with a taut look toward the Navy two-seater. Trent twirled the dial of his receiver, and his earphones abruptly flooded with a squall of German:

"*Zwei... zwei! Eine Amerikaner Corsair... hilfe!*"

"So you want help?" Trent said with a gleam in his eye. "Have a little of this, *Herr Teufel!*"

He triggered a fiery blast at the P-40. The gray fighter renversed madly, and a fusillade ripped away the Corsair's cockpit enclosure. Trent raked the P-40's wing as the two ships screamed in a circle. The two blasts of tracer crossed like flaming swords—then, abruptly, the Corsair's engine went dead.

Trent nosed down steeply, as though to dive into the mists. Behind him Crabb was hastily swinging the rear-pit guns, but there was no time for that. The P-40 was plunging straight for the kill. Trent slammed the stick back, every bit of his speed thrown into a zoom for the gray ship. The masked pilot kicked hurriedly to the left. Trent stood on the rudder, and the Corsair's nose crashed through the P-40's wing-tip with a solidly satisfying roar.

The Corsair started a whipstall. Trent caught it, eased into a dive, with the crippled P-40 howling down beside them.

"You lunatic!" bawled Crabb. "You might've hit him head-on."

"And we might have had a dose of lead poisoning." Trent sheered away from the P-40, pulled up to a flat glide. "Over the side, old bean—unless you've a personal fondness for funerals."

Crabb scrambled out of the pit, dived awkwardly into space, and his chute blossomed dimly in the mists below. As Trent started to unfasten his belt to follow, a weird bluish light flashed up through the murk. A hole opened, mistily, some distance below, and he saw a ball of bluish-yellow flame whirling earthward. Almost directly above it was the Beechcraft, and wobbling in crookedly at the cabin ship was the crippled gray fighter. Before the 18-S could twist away, a terrific torrent of gunfire crashed into the tail.

The Beechcraft nosed over, streaked headlong down into the foggy dusk, and vanished. The Corsair was now within two hundred feet of the swaying P-40, and Trent saw the man with the Satan mask stare off to where Crabb's chute was revealed by the eerie blue light. German words again rattled into Trent's ears, and he realized he had forgotten to take off the phones. He listened a moment longer, then threw off the phones and took to his chute, for the ship was now down to two thousand feet.

As the chute opened he saw the P-40 pitch down steeply, barely visible in the gloom. Apparently the pilot had jumped, but he did not see him. He slipped his chute as the Corsair moaned earthward in its last dive. When he let up on the shrouds he saw another white spread not far below. For a moment he thought it was the mystery pilot, then he saw Mortimer Crabb swinging dolefully under the silk.

"Well, fancy meeting you here!" he yelled. "By the way, better unbuckle part of your harness and make a swing with the leg-straps—just in case we land in the Potomac."

"Why didn't we stick with the ship?" Crabb boomed back. "You could've floated her in."

"*If* we didn't meet up with a smokestack, one of some twenty radio towers, St. Elizabeth's hill, or some other trifling obstacle. And in case we're over settled country, it would be worse on the innocent bystanders to come tearing in at an angle than straight down—wider damage area. But I think we're still a bit south of the city."

"This world gets crazier every day," Crabb said with deep gloom. "That fellow in the red mask, what do you make of it?"

"I can understand Busby's toupee doing a tonga. Seems silly, on the face of it, flying around wearing a red devil mask—no pun, by the way. But that attack—and that queer blue flame—puts a different angle on it. Look out—there's terra firma!"

SCRUBBY trees bordering a plowed field became visible. Trent deftly slipped to miss a tree-top, landed, freed himself. Crabb climbed out of a ditch, a symphony in mud.

"Never mind your clothes," Trent told him. "We've got to make a quick change, anyway. They'd spot us in these outfits."

"Spot us? Who?"

"Whoever our 'Red Devil' friend was warning by radio. The gentleman, it appears, is a Nazi. He was very much concerned that some pals of his should look us up—quickly."

"Where you going to find any clothing store out here?" Crabb asked morosely.

"The store comes later. Right now, anything will do. There's a farm house over there. A judicious digging into the exchequer should get us the necessary—and I see a flivver we might charter."

Crabb sighed, plodded after him. Thirty minutes later, startlingly transformed, they sat in the front seat of the flivver as it rattled along No. 1 highway, into Alexandria, Virginia. Trent wore a pair of muchly patched overalls, a fur cap, and a sheepskin jacket. Beside him, Mortimer Crabb sat dejectedly, attired in the farmer's wife's second-best dress and coat. A heavily beflowered hat drooped over one eye, and his hamlike hands were folded over a worn shopping-bag.

"Too bad the farmer didn't have an extra suit, Mort," Trent said with a grin, "but that's really becoming. I'd no idea you had such a stunning figure."

"A hundred dollars for these rags," Crabb said bitterly. "Beside two hundred to use this jalopy. The robbers—they thought we were crooks and they soaked us."

"Your hide's worth a few hundred, isn't it? For your information, there was a big sedan parked off the road back at that spot where we came into the highway. The occupants were as tough-looking a mob as I've seen since we tangled with the *Gestapo* in Belgium. If we'd been wearing those white suits we'd be a couple of neatly punctured cadavers by now."

"I was a fool ever to join up with you," Crabb said unhappily. "You get me to buy a plane and fly to Europe to sell some inventions. And what happens? War breaks out. Do you come home, like any smart guy? No, you've got to stick your nose into Hitler's affairs and almost get me killed."

"Worth it, wasn't it?" Trent queried. "We nicked the Nazis plenty for that fake bomb-sight—not to mention the other little tricks we put over."

"A dead man can't spend money," his partner said. "If we were smart, we'd get out of Washington and forget all about this business. But no, you've got to hook up with Busby—"

"Only a temporary delay, my dear Mort. I phoned the general to meet us at an F Street clothing shop. We'll give him the story, then do a fade-out. Broadway calls me. In fact, after a few days' rest we might do a professional turn to maintain the financial status quo. We might do a magic act—that disappearing stunt we worked on the Nazi colonel. I'll get you a monkey-suit with brass buttons—"

"No magic," snorted Crabb. "Every time you start that we land in jail or have to make a getaway."

Trent laughed, but no more was said until they reached F Street, in Washington. It was almost six when Trent pulled up by a fireplug and climbed out.

"Come on, Mirandy. Never mind the car. The police will drag it off, and our farmer chap can get it back for a fine."

A SUPERCILIOUS clerk barred their way as they entered a nearby clothier's. "Sorry, we're just closing," he said.

"Show him the exchequer, Mirandy," said Trent. And Crabb gloomily hiked up one side of his dress, pulled a huge wad of bills from a trousers pocket. The clerk gaped at the muddy trousers, which were rolled to Crabb's bony knees.

"Masquerade party," ventured Trent. "We want complete outfits—"

"Eric Trent!" gasped a voice. A pompous, elderly man with a neatly-parted toupee pushed the clerk aside. "What's the idea of that crazy get-up?"

"Protective camouflage. Come on back, while we do another chameleon act, and I'll explain."

The flustered clerk led the way to the rear of the store, summoned another to assist him. Trent selected a neat tweed, quickly told General Busby what had happened as he tried on the suit in a dressing-booth.

"The 'Red-Devil'—in a P-40?" Busby said, stunned. "Are you sure?"

"If you search South of Alexandria you'll find the pieces—unless it fell into the river," replied Trent. "Just who is this Satanic squarehead?"

"We haven't the least idea. The thing began back in September. Unexplained crashes of Douglas B-18's. Then three P-40's, brand new ones, took off on a night test, and disappeared without a trace. The B-18's crashed at night, too. G-2 was busy on a series of factory fires, and we got the F.B.I. to help us on both problems. It was about then when these things began to come."

Busby fished out a card on which was printed the face of a mocking red Satan.

"At first, they were found near the scenes of the crashes, and the fires. Then factory owners began to get them in the mail—and their places would be burned. We doubled the guards, but no use. The queer part is that every fire or crash happened on a misty or rainy night.

"Then one day," he went on, "there was an exception. An F.B.I. man had just phoned me that he and another agent were flying out of here to follow a clue, and asked that I have a pursuit squadron standing by at Rantoul Field. The next thing I heard, the airliner they'd taken had crashed in Virginia—in a heavy rain. Everyone on board was killed. They still don't know what caused it, but I know it wasn't an accident."

Wasn't there a report of a peculiar ball of fire seen just before that airliner crashed?" queried Trent.

"Yes, but you know how things get twisted in crash stories. They think now it was a lightning flash."

"I don't. I was going to tell you, but I hadn't finished. There was a ball of bluish-yellow flame down in the rain this afternoon—just before that Beechcraft disappeared. Find who owned that Beechcraft, who was in it, and you'll have a lead to *Herr Teufel*."

"I'll phone the Civil Aeronautics Board—there may still be somebody in the office," exclaimed Busby. While he was making the call, Trent selected shoes, accessories, and a topcoat. Crabb had found a funeral black suit, was matching it with an equally somber-looking hat. Trent slipped the shoulder-harness of his .38 holster in place under his tweed coat, was idly practicing a coin disappearance trick when the general returned.

"No luck, Trent. Only a minor clerk there—the men who'd know the records are gone; and the inspection force is out chasing down those three crashes—yours and the other two ships. As nearly as they can tell, one ship burned and one fell in the river. May be days before they can find and identify that Beechcraft."

"Well, it's still your only lead," said Trent. "Mort, if you've finished assembling that undertaker's get-up, we'll be—"

He broke off as one of the clerks gave a startled cry. And as he whirled to follow the man's staring eyes, there was a sudden crash of broken glass at the rear of the building. Through the shattered window something red showed in the dim light from the alley.

It was the man with the Satan's mask!

CHAPTER II

Devil's Trap

WITH incredible swiftness, the killer's right arm flashed up, while his left hand held the mask in place. A grenade whizzed through the broken window, clattered to the floor. Trent thrust his hand inside his coat for his gun, leaped forward. He snatched up the bomb and hurled it back at the window. With a muffled oath, the masked man whirled and fled. There was a roar, a blinding flash. Fragments of brick and bits of window-frame and glass went flying through the air.

Trent had dived back of a show-case, with a shout of warning to the others. As the rain of debris ended, he jumped up and ran to the opening. Through the cloud of smoke and dust he could see a car without lights racing away. He sprang through the break in the wall, pumped two shots at the machine, but it did not swerve. When he came back into the store, the frightened clerks were emerging from behind show-cases. Busby was running for the phone, and Mortimer Crabb was picking himself up gingerly from the floor.

"You hurt, Mort?" asked Trent.

"I seem to be intact," Crabb said gloomily. "Better look at that fellow over there in the corner."

"That's a plaster dummy," grinned Trent. "General, you're wasting your energy calling the police. Our masked marvel didn't stand on the order of his going."

"Could you tell what kind of car it was?"

"Big sedan, that's all."

"The police will be up here, anyway," said Busby. "I'll phone the F.B.I. to help cover it, to keep the thing quiet. Then we can get out of here and discuss the next step in some private spot."

"We're not taking any next step," Crabb said with a sour note. "When they start heaving bombs through windows, Mortimer Crabb's going to find a nice quiet little cave somewhere."

"Don't pay any attention to him, General," said Trent, "I've a burning curiosity to see what's behind that red mask."

Busby turned to the store manager. The War Department will reimburse you for the damage done by that bomb, providing you don't talk to reporters. Above all, don't mention that devil mask."

As they left by the front door, pushing through a rapidly increasing crowd, the siren of a police car sounded.

"I hope we can keep the truth out of the papers," the general muttered. "There's enough hysteria in the country already. A few more of these 'Red Devil' cases and manufacturers will be so jittery they'll be bucking defense orders."

Trent looked carelessly back at the crowd. Apparently no one was trailing them. "Just how many people knew you were going to that store?" he queried.

"My secretary and maybe another clerk in my office. But I could easily have been followed—I came from the Department in a taxi."

"Where are we going now?"

"I was headed for the Willard Hotel—that is, I was intending to go there until I heard from you. One of the latest manufacturers to receive a threat from that masked scoundrel is here to see me. Man named Worton, head of a specialty plant out in Illinois. They've been converted for making machine-guns, and the plant's an important defense unit."

WHEN they reached the Willard, extras with garbled reports of the triple-crash story were on the stands. There was no mention of a masked pilot, Trent noted with satisfaction. General Busby led them into an elevator, and they found Worton's room on the eighth floor. At Busby's rap, a man about fifty, stout, once handsome but now heavy-jowled and soft-looking, cautiously opened the door. There was a look of fear at the back of his eyes, but it changed to relief as he saw the general.

"Thank the Lord you're here, General! This thing's getting worse every—" he stopped short as he saw Trent and Crabb. Behind him, Trent glimpsed a taller man, about thirty years old.

"Don't worry about these two," said Busby. "They're equal to a whole division of G-2—even if they are slightly offside when it comes to official practices."

"Make it 'screwy' while you're at it," Crabb said dismally. "But don't blame it on me."

Worton managed a sickly smile, motioned them into the room. Busby introduced the two partners, and Worton turned to his companion.

"This is Ed Hammond, my right-hand man at the plant. He's the one who urged me to see you personally. At first, I didn't take much stock in this 'Red Devil' business, but now—" the fearful look came back into his eyes.

"We'd like a military guard at the plant, General," said Hammond. His voice was firm, but Trent saw the veiled uneasiness at the back of his eyes, as in Worton's. "We know what happened at the Leffler factory and the others. We need more protection."

"An Army guard is out of the question," Busby answered. "We need every trained man to instruct the draftees. You've a factory guard unit—"

"It's not enough, unless you give us permission to set up machine guns covering the gates and vital points. State officials won't let us, unless you order it."

"I'll look into it. What about this latest threat?"

The haggard look on Worton's face deepened. "The card came in the mail yesterday morning, with 'Tomorrow at midnight' printed under that grinning red devil. That isn't all. Two of my most trusted officials have died in the last week. Hit-and-run victims, both of them. But I know it was murder. Three more have quit—scared out by this warning, and so have some of my oldest workmen. Hammond and I talked it over, decided to fly here and see you. My private plane wasn't in commission, so we took last night's train. The ship will be in here this evening—if you'll only send some men back with me—"

"One moment," said Eric Trent. "This plane of yours, it wouldn't by any chance be a Beechcraft 18-S?"

Worton stared. "Yes, it is. Why?"

"Good thing you took the train." Trent handed Worton the newspaper. "The story doesn't mention it, but one of those three planes was a Beechcraft. It was shot down—by this menace with the red mask."

The paper fell from Worton's shaking fingers. Hammond's face went deathly white.

"My ship—my pilot—shot down!" Worton gasped. "Wait— how do you know all this?"

"We had a front-row seat," said Trent. Without skipping a detail, he told what had happened from their sighting of the Beechcraft and the gray P-40 to the bombing at the clothier's. "Obviously, our Satanic friend intended to eliminate you. There must be something unusual linked with his scheme against your plant. General, I'd suggest we be on hand to greet him at the witching hour."

"How?" asked Busby. "It's almost seven—"

"The Air Corps still has *some* ships, hasn't it? A B-18 would get you and these gentlemen out there with time to spare."

"What about you and Crabb?"

"We'll be tagging along—in a two-seater, nicely armed, if you can wangle it. In fact, I'd suggest another two-seater, and a couple of Air Corps lads who can shoot fast and straight. Just to help force the boy in the red mask, in case he shows up."

"You can make sport of that fiend if you want to," Hammond said grimly, "I'd say he's as dangerous as a cobra."

"I still think the red mask is silly," replied Trent. "By the way, General, just how many people have actually seen this 'Red Devil'?"

"Only two—until today. At least, we've no other reports. Those two saw him at the Leffler Powder Works, the night of October 31st. One was a watchman who saw him just before it was blown up. The other was a villager who saw him run to a car after the explosion. Those devil cards have been left at a number of places, but no one's actually seen the man since then."

"I suppose I should consider myself favored, seeing him twice in one day," observed Trent. "You know, I've an odd hunch I'll see him again—before midnight."

AT FIVE thousand feet, the three ships cruised Westward in a dark and gloomy sky. In the front cockpit of the Northrop A-17 which had been provided at General Busby's order, Eric Trent made a quick estimate of their position.

"We're about seventy miles from the Worton plant field, Mort."

"Let's hope it's not some cow-pasture," Crabb said unhappily. "It'd be just my luck to get wrapped around a tree."

"Don't worry, my optimistic friend. According to Worton, it has all the latest gadgets—localizer beam, floodlights, two-way radio, and whatnot. Worton's a bug on aviation—was planning to build sport planes when the Government handed him the order to turn out machine guns."

A faint drizzle had intermittently pattered against the Plexiglas enclosure. It increased to a steady rain as the Northrop droned on through the night. Trent widened the gap between the other A-17 and their ship. Ahead, the Douglas B-18 bomber was distinguishable only by its white tail-light and the green and red riding lights on its wings.

"You've been acting mighty queer tonight," Crabb said suspiciously. "What's that pamphlet you've been looking at?"

"Just the Air Corps secret code," said Trent. "I borrowed this from the Communications Office at Bolling Field, while the officer on duty was talking to Busby. I've a feeling it might come in handy."

"You idiot," groaned Crabb. "You can get ten years for stealing that code. I knew things were too quiet, when you didn't pull any of those smart magic tricks on Worton and Hammond."

"There's a proper time for levity," Trent said with a grin. "The gentlemen weren't in the right mood to appreciate my skill at legerdemain. Maybe later I'll entertain them with a few choice numbers."

"I know they'll just love it," Crabb said dismally. "Maybe you can do some card tricks for the 'Red Devil,' too, if he comes around."

"No, I've something special arranged for him." Trent chuckled. "Don't ask what it is. I want it to be a surprise."

The three ships were approximately thirty miles from their destination when Crabb again spoke up from the rear cockpit. "Worton's calling his field. I hope he hasn't got us lost."

Trent put on his phones, heard the manufacturer's anxious voice.

"—and give us the localizer beam. We're at about five thousand feet, starting a glide... I think we're just about over Greenburg."

In another moment the localizer signals began to hum into Trent's phones. He banked to follow the B-18's lead, and in another few seconds they were riding the center of the beam, nosed down in a long power glide. Suddenly he flicked a glance up into the darkness, then whirled the Northrop in a violent turn. A faint glow he had seen abruptly became a ball of bluish-yellow fire, rolling down from the massed clouds at high speed.

The Northrop had barely whipped aside when the weird ball of fire burst into a score of smaller ones. Streaks of flame lanced down through the rain. The other A-17 banked wildly, but too late. The flaming streaks fell across its tail and right wing, writhing like serpents out of some pit of Hell. In another moment the ship was ablaze.

For an instant a huge dark shape was dimly visible in the bottom of the clouds, then it lifted up and vanished. At the same moment gray wings flashed in the glare of the burning Northrop, and tracers scorched down the sky at Trent and Crabb. Trent had already shoved the throttle full out, switched on his guns. The attacking ship veered hastily as the two-seater's forward guns hurled a furious blast across its path. It was a P-40, unmarked as the one which the masked pilot had flown.

With a swift renversement, the gray fighter dived beyond the blazing Northrop. The Air Corps pilots had jumped, and for a second Trent thought the P-40's guns would riddle the helpless men now swinging under their chutes. But the fighter raced past, pitched a burst at the B-18. The tracers went wide of their mark, and Trent charged in before the pilot could correct his aim.

The snake-like streaks of flame were twisting down the sky like fantastic fireworks. As Trent plunged in at the P-40, the gray fighter skidded madly to avoid the weird flames. The Northrop's guns raked the Curtiss' tilted wing. But before Trent could blast the cockpit another P-40 whirled out of the eerily lighted sky.

Tracer and cupro slugs hammered across the Northrop's tail. Trent hurled the ship into a lightning Immelmann, heard Crabb's tourelle-guns snarl into action. The first P-40 reeled, fell off apparently out of control. The other fighter banked hastily as Trent dived, guns thrashing. From off to the left, the nose-gunner of the B-18 flung a burst at the fleeing ship, but the range was too great. With a furious zoom, the gray P-40 shot into the clouds.

By now, the blazing Northrop was far below, and the mysterious streaks of fire likewise had settled too far to illuminate the scene clearly. The B-18 swung West, its running-lights turned off, and was quickly swallowed up in the dark. Trent cut off his lights, ruddered across to the right-hand side of the localizer beam, the signals of which were still ringing in his ears. He noted the course, took out the Air Corps code book, and switched on the transmitter.

"What are you doing?" demanded Crabb.

"Just reporting this little incident to Washington, so the record will be clear," said Trent. "Take over while I do a little key-pounding.

"If we had any sense, we'd drop this thing," said Crabb. "That flame business was enough for me."

"I've an idea that was meant for us," replied Trent. "Thank Heaven those Air Corps boys got clear."

He tapped out his message, took the controls again. A few minutes later floodlights came on at a point ahead. Circling warily, with an eye on the clouds, Trent watched the B-18 land. Three buildings showed vaguely in the misty light as he swiftly followed the bomber down. One was obviously the main factory. Near it was a hangar large enough for the lost Beechcraft. The other building, about half as large as the factory, was at the other end of the field.

General Busby and the others were already out of the B-18 when Trent taxied the Northrop toward the hangar. He pivoted the two-seater around parallel with the bomber, nosed out toward the field, then let the engine die. As he climbed out, Busby appeared alongside the ship.

"Are you two all right?" he asked.

"I think Mort swallowed his gum in the excitement," said Trent. "Otherwise no casualties. The B-18 wasn't hit, was it?"

"No, luckily." The general's face had a savage look. "I'm going to start a dragnet for that damned killer. This thing's gone far enough."

"There were two P-40's," said Trent.

"I know—obviously they're the ones that disappeared so mysteriously. But that masked butcher is the key to everything. I'll find him if it takes the whole Army. We've *got* to find him—if we're ever going to learn the secret of that fire-ball—"

Busby's words were cut off by a muffled yell that came from somewhere behind the floodlight unit. The next moment the light went out and the field was left in pitch darkness.

CHAPTER III
Unmasked

F *LAME* jetted from a pistol, not far from the radio shack. Then a car engine roared, and a machine sped away in the darkness.

"The gate! He's making for the gate!" Hammond's voice came frantically out of the blackness.

Trent heard some one scramble into the B-18, and in a few seconds the bomber's landing-lights came on. It was just in time to illuminate a section of the road that led to a gateway between a high woven-steel fence topped with barbed wire. The gates were open, and in the semi-gloom beyond the lighted area Trent saw a car take the turn on two wheels. It was lost to view before he could snatch out his gun.

"Who was it? What happened?" Worton asked tensely, as Hammond stumbled into the glow.

"He was in the radio shack," Hammond said thickly. He rubbed a bruised spot on the side of his face. "I didn't even get a look at him. He cut off the lights and shot at me—I tried to grab his gun. Either he hit me or there was another man—"

"Look! Over there by the shack!" exclaimed Worton.

Something red, crumpled, lay near the doorway. Trent picked it up, arched his brows. It was the Satan's mask!

"Our friend certainly gets around," he said with a trace of admiration.

"This is no time for humor, Trent," snapped General Busby. "We've got to flash word to the local police, State troopers, and district G-Men."

"What will you tell them to look for?" demanded Trent. "A man in a car? Your guess is as good as any—but the cops can't stop all the cars in—"

"All right," growled Busby. "What would *you* do?"

"Take a look around the premises, for one thing. Mr. Worton, you must have had a radio operator—"

"He was here ten minutes ago, when I last called him from the bomber," muttered the manufacturer. He started into the radio shack, halted abruptly. "Blood! There's blood on the floor—Peterson's gone!"

Busby wheeled to the pilot and two-man crew of the B-18. "Search the hangar—in back—around the plant. Have your guns ready."

The airmen snapped the safety catches off their .45's, hurried toward the hangar. Worton gingerly stepped into the radio shack, switched on the room-lights, then the floodlight unit. Trent glanced at the red pool on the floor, eyed the trail of drops which led outside.

"Peterson wasn't the assassin," Worton said quickly, following Trent's gaze. "He's been with me five years and is utterly loyal. He must have staggered out, wounded. They might have carried him away—maybe in that car."

"What about that open gate?" barked General Busby.

"That's another thing," Worton answered, staring around the lighted area. "Myers—the night watchman—has strict orders to admit no one after hours without a pass signed by me. The gates are always double-locked. Meyers would be armed—they'd have had to overpower him to get in."

"We'd better help those men search around the plant," Hammond said shakily.

"You and Crabb go ahead—you can work around this way and meet the others," said Busby. "The three of us will watch the ships."

As Crabb and Hammond left, the general looked uneasily into the murky sky. "I don't know about leaving that floodlight on. One of those P-40's is still on the loose. We'd be easy marks for a strafe."

"I'll cut off the floods," said Worton, "as soon as they finish the search. We could hear a plane coming, anyway."

"Twenty minutes to midnight," Busby said, half to himself, as he looked at his wrist-watch. "Well, the 'Red Devil' kept his date with you, Worton—though apparently he didn't damage your plant."

"Unless there's a bomb in there," Worton mumbled.

In a few minutes the searching parties returned.

"No windows broken—no signs of breaking in," reported Hammond. "But Myers is missing—looks as though there'd been a struggle, down in the guard-box at the gate. I closed the gate and locked it."

"I guess we're safe from a bomb, then," Worton said nervously. "We might as well go into my office—"

"Wait—I want to send a radio code to Washington," cut in Busby. "The crash of that P-40 is certain to be reported and Civil Aeronautics will get word as quickly as anyone. If the pilot's body wasn't burned, identiying him might be a short-cut to this riddle."

"A good idea," said Worton, "unless this 'Red Devil' group should happen to catch the message and get to that crash first."

"Not likely," said the general. "This is a new Air Corps code, carefully guarded."

"Humph!" put in Mortimer Crabb.

"What's that?" queried Busby.

"Just clearing my throat," Crabb said with a dismal look at Trent. "Don't mind me—nobody ever does."

"On second, thought, maybe I'd better put it through long distance," decided Busby. "We'll go into your office."

WORTON turned off the floodlight, as Busby detailed the Air Corps' pilot and his crew to remain at the ships. Trent lingered a moment for a second look at the red trail which led out of the radio shack. It ended a few yards away, still some distance from the road.

"What're you waiting for?" asked Crabb.

"Just meditating on the odd things of life. Peterson appears to have been snatched up to Heaven—or else he ran out of blood suddenly."

"You're the kind of guy that'd crack jokes in a morgue."

Trent sighed. "Sometimes, Mort, I wonder how your child-like simplicity remains unshaken."

Hammond had stopped for a word with the Air Corps pilot. As he caught up with them, Trent paused. "By the way, we didn't search around that building at the end of the field. Might be a bomb tucked away there."

"Then the joke would be on them," said Hammond. "Nothing but some old junk in there. The place hasn't been used in three years. Worton would be glad to see it go up; he'd collect insurance enough to build a tool-shop we really need."

They followed Worton and Busby into the offices, which were a series of rooms opening off a dim-lit hall. Worton led the way through an anteroom into a spacious office, turned on the lights. A photograph of the plant hung on one wall. Opposite it was a blueprint showing a proposed guard system, with machine gun locations, a system for electrifying an inner fence, and a special lighting and alarm circuit. On the wall facing the doorway was a standard airway map of the United States.

Busby sat down at the desk, put in his call to Washington. After a few moments he replaced the phone on the cradle. "They'll call back—I'm trying to get my aide, so we can have some personal action on it. May not lead to anything, but we've darned little else to go on."

Hammond's restless eyes lifted to the wall-clock. "Seven minutes to twelve. I'll be glad when midnight's past, even if the 'Red Devil' is already gone."

"He might be back," said Trent. "Especially since all his plans center around this place."

General Busby jerked around, and the others stared at him.

"What do you mean by that?" demanded Busby. "How could you know his plans?"

"All the other things linked with our Satanic squarehead have been near cases of sabotage—except the theft of the P-40's. That was evidently to secure an escort for whatever ship they're using. But look what happens when Worton decides to come to Washington to ask for an Okay on a special guard system—the one worked out on that chart. Things begin to pop. Something very special is hooked up with this place. It's not an attempt to destroy it. That could have been done tonight, either by one of those fireballs—which I'll wager set fire to those other factories—or by bombs planted after the radioman and watchman were eliminated."

"What are you driving at?" Worton said testily.

"Ever watch a magician?" asked Trent. "He always calls your attention away from what he's really up to. Like this—" he held up his right hand, watched their eyes shift, then calmly plucked a quarter out of the air with his left hand.

"Very clever," Busby growled with sarcasm. "What's that to do with the 'Red Devil'?"

Trent manipulated the coin with his left hand, then with a motion too swift for the eye to follow he flicked his right hand under his coat. The next instant, the muzzle of his .38 was trained squarely on Hammond.

"DON'T move, *Herr Rot Teufel,*" he said softly. "Don't even bat an eyelash—or it will be the last bat."

All the color went out of Hammond's face. "You fool! How could I be the—" he broke off, jaw clamped hard.

"So you do understand German," grinned Trent. "Worton, keep your hands above that desk, unless you'd like some permanent shut-eye on a marble slab."

"Trent, are you stark crazy?" gasped General Busby.

"A trifle eccentric perhaps, but otherwise quite sane," said Trent. "Mort, if you can pull yourself out of your stupor, put the bead on Worton while I watch our friend the 'Red Devil.'"

Crabb's mouth slowly closed. He took out his gun, aimed it at Worton's middle. The manufacturer turned an apoplectic purple.

"General Busby, call off these two madmen. A joke is a joke, but when it comes to—"

"The game's up, gentlemen," Trent said amiably. "You've left enough loopholes to drive a twenty-mule team through. *Herr* Hammond—or whatever your right name is—I'd advise thinking carefully before trying to draw that gun. General, maybe you'd better disarm him. You'll find a pistol in a holster clipped inside his belt."

Busby lifted the edge of Hammond's coat, removed a small but deadly-looking automatic. Hammond glared at him.

"I've a permit for that gun. After the threats made against us, I'd be a fool not to be armed."

"Trent, are you positive—" began the general.

"I wouldn't have come out here if I hadn't been. I suspected them the minute I found that the Beechcraft was their ship. Why would the 'Red Devil' want to destroy that plane and kill an unimportant pilot? Worton and Hammond weren't in the ship.

"It was fairly evident," Trent went on, "that the pilot had discovered something and had to be killed before he could tell some one in Washington. I thought he might have been bringing information to Worton—until I saw Hammond's shoes. There was clay on them, and you don't get fresh clay on Washington streets. It was the kind Mort wallowed in when he fell into that ditch. Then I remembered Hammond was breathing hard when we came in. I'd thought then he was just suffering from a case of nerves. But the answer is that he'd just made a fast trip from behind that clothing store, after dashing in from Virginia to meet Worton at the hotel. I checked up later and found Worton had called your office and your secretary had told him you would be at that store. Incidentally, General, you ought to know better than to tell a woman everything. She informed our plump friend here that you were meeting two men who'd discovered a new lead on the 'Red Devil' case. So when Hammond arrived, after bailing out of that P-40, he decided to get rid of us before we told too much."

"I tell you he's insane!" howled Worton. "If I were up to any crooked business, would I be asking Army Intelligence for help?"

"It was a clever move," Trent said, unperturbed. "I suspect your Nazi friend there worked it out. Between you, at least, you hatched out a beautiful scheme to sabotage the American defense program—and at the same time get ready for a Trojan Horse coup. It called for a landing-field and a place to hide some ships. That old building at the end of the field would make an excellent hangar. I imagine those stolen P-40's were slipped in there at night, without your regular staff knowing a thing—not to mention that big ship which carries the chemical bombs.

"What's more," Trent continued, "this place held possibilities as a Fifth Column base. With hundreds of machine-guns being turned out every week, you could hold back delivery at some prearranged time and sneak enough spies and Nazi sympathizers in here to create a small army overnight. You could deliver more guns to Nazi bund units and spy-groups around the country. And meantime, *Herr* Hammond could go ahead with his 'Red Devil' mummery and drop his fire-bombs on important munitions factories and aircraft plants."

"Good Lord!" whispered Busby. "If this is true—"

"It's true enough. We'll probably find enough evidence in that old building, and perhaps in Worton's secret files. The picture's clear enough now. They got away with their night-raiding for a while, with no one suspecting. Hammond seized on a smart idea to build up a bogeyman, the night they struck at the Leffler plant. That happened to be Halloween, in case you'd forgotten, and that was probably what suggested the devil-mask. My guess is that he had one of their spy-mob show himself deliberately in that Satan mask, to create the idea that the fires were started by some one on the ground—maybe they thought some fanatic pacifist would be suspected. After that, I suppose Hammond carried the mask to hide his face in case he ran into a tight spot where he might be recognized.

"The Beechcraft pilot must have stumbled onto the secret—the same as those men killed in fake hit-and-run accidents. He made a dash for Washington, and Hammond went after him with one of the. P-40's. There must have been another P-40 in the air, too, for I heard Hammond call 'Two' to help him. Worton had come ahead by himself to ask for 'protection.' He knew you couldn't spare an Army guard; what he really wanted was authority to set up machine guns and an electric-charged fence. Then when the Nazis moved in, they'd have a strong base to operate from. Probably they had some plan to add to their secret air defenses between now and *der Tag*."

"General, all this is crazy guess work!" Hammond burst out fiercely. "There's not a shred of truth to it. What about the attack here tonight? The 'Red Devil' tried to kill me—you saw that yourself. If I were the 'Red Devil,' or had any part in the plan, why would I be in danger? Busby, I tell you this man's mad!"

TRENT laughed. "That was a clumsy bit of stage work, *mein Freund.* At least you should have had your man Peterson dribble that red paint out to the road. The air attack was staged a little better—in fact, almost too well. Calling in your position and riding the localizer beam gave your fire-bomb pilot a perfect chance to spot the Northrops. It's lucky both ships weren't wiped out. But I noticed that first P-40 pilot took good care to miss the B-18 by a wide margin."

Worton sagged back in his chair, looked despairingly at Hammond. "It's no use, Munster—he's got us."

The man who had called himself Hammond nodded with an expression of glum resignation. "It is my fault," he muttered. "If I had shot straight—"

Trent's eyes narrowed a fraction of an inch. "General, get on that phone and call the State police. There's something phoney about this abject surrender."

Busby sprang to the desk. As he lifted the phone there was a sudden click from behind Trent and Crabb.

"Get 'em up!" a voice snarled. "Make a crooked move and I'll cut you to pieces."

Trent jerked his head around for a sidelong look, then slowly lifted his hands. The framed photograph of the Worton plant had swung outward on hinges, revealing a hole two feet square. Poked through the aperture from the adjoining room was the snout of a Tommy-gun, behind it a grim, shadowy face!

CHAPTER IV
Code Trick

B OTH Worton and Hammond had leaped aside, to give the gunman a clear range. As Trent and Crabb raised their hands, the two men reached out and jerked away their weapons.

Munster wheeled savagely toward Busby, and the general let the phone clatter back onto the cradle.

"Get over against that wall, the three of you!" Munster said harshly. "Damn you, Peterson, you took long enough."

The face behind the machine gun came closer to the aperture. Peterson's pale blue eyes shifted resentfully to the German. "I had to wait a good chance. Beside, I wanted to find out how much they knew. I'm risking my neck, the same as you are."

"He's right, Munster," Worton said shakily. "Now we know everything Trent learned."

"What about those men outside?" demanded Munster.

"Myers and the three *Gestapo* men got them," said Peterson. "They had to knock out the pilot and one mechanic. They gagged them and tied them up in the hangar."

Mortimer Crabb looked gloomily at Trent. "Let's see you get out of this, Mr. Fixit. If you knew all about them, why didn't you—"

"Keep that swine still!" Munster flung at Worton. He jerked his head at Peterson. "Meet us in the hall. We have them covered."

As the three captives were herded into the hall, a faint rumbling was audible from out on the field.

"There's the Junkers," Munster said with relief.

They went outside, and Trent saw a huge black ship trundling to a stop near the Air Corps planes. One of its landing-lights was on, and in the reflection Trent saw that the ship was a Junkers Ju. 86-K, painted dead black and devoid of markings. The remaining P-40 had already landed, and the pilot was coming toward a little group of men by the B-18. The Junkers swung around, its nose pointed toward the old building, then its engines went dead. In a few moments, the crew scrambled out. The pilot hurried to meet Munster, who had drawn apart from the captives, leaving Peterson to help Worton guard them. At the end of a hurried conversation which Trent could not hear the two men approached.

"*Gut!*" the Junkers pilot was saying. "Very good, *Herr* Munster. Now we can use those two planes and make up for the lost fighters."

"No, it is too dangerous," Munster said curtly. "This *verdammt Amerikaner* with the wig over one ear is the chief of their Army Intelligence. His disappearance would lead to an extensive search. We will get other planes—but those two must be sacrificed to cover the death of these men. Peterson, have Myers and his men bring the three from the hangar."

"What are you going to do?" Worton said uneasily.

"The General and the Air Corps men will be put in the B-18, with their parachutes on," said Munster. "One of our pilots will fly the ship back twenty or thirty miles. Another of our men will be aboard, and will tumble Busby and the two mechanics out through the bomb-bay doors. They will be unconscious when they are thrown out, so they will not open their parachutes. The Air Corps pilots will be left senseless at the controls when our men jump. A small flame-bomb will be set to go off a minute later. Then you and I show up at some house near the crash, with our parachutes spread somewhere nearby as evidence that we jumped from the plane. The Army will think Busby and the mechanics were stunned by the gyrations of the ship as they jumped, which will explain their chutes not opening."

"Excellent *mein Herr!*" said the Junkers pilot. He had a wolfish grin. "But what of these two?"

Munster hesitated then went on: "We'll drop Trent from the B-18 with the others, in the same way. Crabb will be put in the rear seat of the Northrop, unconscious or dead—it makes no difference. You can fly the ship and jump after you see the B-18 explode. Crabb will be found in the wreck of the Northrop, and it will look as though Trent jumped and left him to his fate. A gash in Trent's head will guarantee that he won't open his chute—and will make it seem he struck the stabilizer or something in getting out."

"Munster, you're a genius," said Worton. "The whole thing will be blamed on the 'Red Devil,' and we'll have stronger grounds for asking them to approve the electrified fence and machine gun defenses."

"At least we'll be done with this smart meddler," Munster said viciously. He turned to one of the Junkers crew, which had drawn near to listen. "Search these three to see if they're carrying anything important."

One of the Nazis produced a flashlight, for the Junkers landing-light had been switched off. Worton pursed his lips as he saw the roll of bills the man took from Mortimer Crabb.

"That will help our plans, eh, Munster? A good joke on these fools."

"The money was stolen from the Reich in the first place," Munster said angrily. "These two recovered the Air Corps bomb-sight we had obtained, and tricked an agent into paying a huge sum for some ridiculous device Crabb had invented, which they passed off for the bomb-sight."

"Here is a code book, *mein Herr!*" exclaimed one of the men searching Trent. *"Ach, Himmel*—it is the secret Air Corps code!"

GENERAL BUSBY stared dumbfounded at the book as Munster seized it. "I'm sorry, General," Trent said in a tone of deep regret. "I thought it would come in handy—didn't expect them to turn the tables like this."

Peterson had returned from the hangar. He bent over the book as Munster held it in the glow of the flashlight.

"I heard a strange code just before the B-18 landed," he said quickly. "I took down part of it, and it was a numeral and letter combination just like that."

Munster whirled on him furiously. Dolt! Why didn't you say so before? Get that message! Trent must have sent it after the attack."

Peterson sprinted for the radio shack. Worton wiped perspiration from his face. "If he reported that fight, then your plan's no good. We're in a fine mess."

"I'll think of a way out," snapped Munster. He motioned to the staring Nazis. "Tie the prisoner's hands. I'll decide what to do with them in a few minutes."

He disappeared inside the radio shack, and the Nazis hastily bound the captives' hands. Trent stiffened his arms, trying to twist his wrists as the rope was drawn tight. The hemp cut into his flesh, but he knew from his stage experience as a magician's assistant that he had maneuvered enough slack to free himself in a few minutes. But the Junkers pilot and another Nazi were behind him, and he dared not make the attempt.

Munster and Peterson suddenly appeared from the radio shack. Munster's voice was trembling with rage as he reached the group.

"Get the Junkers started!" he directed the pilot, then spun around to the other Nazis. "Start the Air Corps planes and the P-40."

"What's wrong?" Worton said. "A squadron's been ordered here from Rantoul! Trent's tricked us—he sent a message signed with Busby's name, ordering an armed squadron and the nearest motorized National Guard battalion to come here immediately!"

"Then we're lost!" groaned Worton.

"Stop your sniveling!" snarled Munster. "We can still carry through the plan. We'll drop these *Amerikaner* pigs just as I said—after the Junkers has sprayed those ships from Rantoul. That will break up the squadron and scatter them. We'll send out a message in this Air Corps code saying we're being attacked, and we'll sign Busby's name. We'll say it's all a scheme to destroy the Worton plant. Then we'll carry out our act; we'll actually jump from the B-18—and then rush back here and meet the National Guard and any pilots who land here."

"But if they find those chemical bombs in the old building we're trapped. This is your fault. If you'd had a proper guard, Johnson wouldn't has escaped after he broke in there this morning."

"I told you to let me take care of that nosey pilot," Munster said savagely. "I'd have seen that he met with an 'accident' like those others. But you had to fire him, even after he'd begun to get suspicious. And don't forget I was the one who stopped him from getting that chemical bomb to the Army."

The roar of the Junkers engines starting up broke in and drowned Worton's reply. Munster made an impatient gesture.

"Don't worry. Myers can have a time-bomb set in the old building after we take-off. If things get bad, one of the men can switch it on. It will look like an attempt to destroy the plant—but we'll do it as a last resort. We need a place to hide the Junkers."

The pilot of the Junkers ran up to Munster a moment later. "Ready to take-off, *mein Herr!* I've only two flame-bombs aboard."

"There's no time for loading any more," snapped the Nazi leader. "Take-off and get above the clouds. The Air Corps will probably be coming in above them. Peterson will relay any change in orders. But keep tuning to the Air Corps' frequency; they may be talking between ships, and you can take a bearing on them."

The Junkers pilot darted away, and in a moment the black ship thundered down the field and into the gloom. Worton put out his hand, looked anxiously into the dark sky.

"There's hardly more than a drizzle. What if there isn't enough moisture to set off the ferrous oxide and phosphorous?"

"It's enough," Munster said grimly. He motioned to Peterson and the Nazis who guarded the prisoners. "Get them aboard the B-18—except Crabb. Put him in the Northrop—and hurry!"

THE ENGINES of the two Air Corps ships were rumbling, and Trent saw the prop of the P-40 whirling dimly in the shadows as he and the others were shoved roughly toward the line. He twisted desperately at the bonds on his wrists. They were almost off, but another minute would be too late. He flicked a swift glance sidewise as a burly Nazi pushed him toward the B-18. The bomber was straining at the wheel-chocks, as the man at the controls revved up the engines. Trent purposely stumbled, sprawled head-long to the muddy ground. In a split second he had the end of the chock-rope in his teeth.

The Nazi guard lunged after him. Trent sank his teeth in the rope, rolled hastily to one side. The jerk almost dislocated his jaw, but the chock tumbled away from the B-18's right wheel. The bomber pivoted with a thunderous roar before the pilot could ram on the brakes. Trent's guard let out a strangled cry that ended abruptly as a whirling propeller struck him. Trent gave a last furious pull at his bonds, and his hands were free.

The wing of the B-18 whipped past him, and he saw Peterson and Munster hurl themselves aside to escape the nearest propeller. Trent leaped to his feet, swung from the hip. Peterson went down in a heap and Trent snatched the Tommy-gun. A pistol blazed from beside the Northrup, and Crabb's guard triggered a second shot as Trent swung the machine gun. There was a muffled roar and the Tommy-gun went into action. The Nazi fell, riddled.

Trent whirled the gun, dropped two more Germans. Munster dived frantically past the B-18's tail, just as a Nazi in the Air Corps ship swung the rear turret gun. Trent stopped the gunner with a quick burst, raced across to Crabb. Except for the men in the Douglas, the remaining Nazis had hurriedly sought cover. Trent dropped the Tommy-gun, swiftly loosened the knot at Crabb's wrists.

"Pile into the Northrop!" he said. "We've got to stop that Junkers!"

A pistol blazed twice from the shadows. Trent saw Munster's face by the stabbing flame of the second shot. He scooped up the Tommy-gun, emptied it toward the spy-leader, who was now only a blur in the darkness. Then with a leap he made the Northrop's front pit and flung off the hand-brake. The two-seater roared away, the target of three or four wild shots from back at the hangar.

"Get on that rear gun, Mort!" Trent flung back at his partner. "They'll be after us with those two ships."

"Not the B-18," Crabb said hoarsely. "That Nazi wrecked the prop when it hit him. I can't see the P-40."

Trent lifted the ship from the field, climbed as fast as he dared. "Switch on the transmitter," he told Crabb. "If we can raise that squadron from Rantoul—"

"Not a chance," Crabb broke in. "That last shot got the lead to the wing antenna."

"Try to splice it!" Trent jammed the headphones over his ears. As he bored up into the dank mass of cloud, he heard a scratching, as Crabb made momentary contact with the broken wires. The switch was on for receiving, and words suddenly filtered over the air.

"*—coming down through… give… beam and lights… ceiling….*"

Trent swiftly nosed down. The Air Corps squadron was already headed down through the clouds, calling Worton's field caretaker for the localizer and floodlights. The Junkers crew would hear that message, too… would be ready for a flaming barrage.

The dark mists thinned and something flickered, eerily, off to the left. Trent stiffened, for an instant fearing it was the beginning of that dreadful rain of fire. Then he recognized the dangerously close flash of a ship's exhaust. With a shove at the rudder, he swung alongside and snapped on his landing-lights.

A GIANT black wing tilted wildly as the lights cut through the drizzle. Simultaneously, tracers scorched from the nose and rear turrets of the raider. Trent kicked out of the blast, raked the tail as the Northrop whirled past. Above the din he heard Crabb yell something, then a string of red, green, and white lights loomed mistily ahead and below.

The Junkers twisted in a vertical bank, plunged toward the Air Corps formation. Trent hurled a furious burst from the forward guns and the Junkers' three turrets answered with a terrific cross-fire. The Northrop trembled as a fusillade hammered the wings. Trent crouched behind the stick, caught the rear gunner, then the midway turret in a murderous raking blast.

The Junkers swerved, lurched back toward the now scattering Air Corps ships. Something gray flashed into sight on Trent's right and the P-40 drilled in, tracers smoking in the Northrop's wing-lights. Trent saw Munster, his face ashen-white in the glare, as the spy rocketed in to save the black raider.

The Northrop screamed in a breathtaking turn, and for one fateful instant it seemed that the two ships would collide head-on. Then Munster's nerve broke. The P-40 zoomed wildly and its tail crumpled under Trent's battering fire. Without letting up on the stick-button, he whirled the bullet-torn two-seater back at the Junkers. Crabb's guns had finished the bow-gunner, and as the Northrop's lights swept across the black ship Trent saw the pilot fling up his hands in a wild plea for life. Without a qualm, Trent let the spouting guns rake across the pilot's cockpit and aft into the bomber.

Just as he struck the bomb-bay doors flipped open in a frenzied attempt by the crew to drop the deadly flame-bombs and save themselves from destruction. There was a blinding flash of bluish-yellow fire, and Trent backsticked away from the scorching heat. When he leveled out, he saw the Junkers plummeting down the sky, a mass of flame, the Air Corps ships circling safely half a mile distant.

A spread of white silk was billowed out beneath the Northrop. Munster had escaped from the crippled P-40. But writhing down the sky above him were ten or twelve of the serpentlike flames, hurled out from one of the chemical bombs. As Trent dived, he saw Munster twist around frantically, hands lifted. Then the Nazi spy-leader saw the falling flames A look of horror shot into his face and he clawed at the shrouds to slip his chute away. But it came too late.

A red tongue of fire licked across the white silk, then another, and suddenly the chute was ablaze. Trent had one last glimpse of Munster's terrified face, then the doomed man fell swiftly down the misty sky, the burning fragments of the chute like the tail of a meteor above him.

The field floodlight came on a few seconds later and the Air Corps ships began to land. Trent circled down, saw a line of khaki-colored trucks and cars moving through the gateway and into the Worton plant. Armed Guardsmen were hustling Munster's spy-mob into the hangar.

"I STILL can't see why you didn't let me in on that message business," complained Mortimer Crabb. He looked sourly across Worton's office at Eric Trent. "I'd have felt a lot better when they were getting ready to dump us out of the B-18, if I'd known the Army was coming."

"I didn't know whether they were coming or not," said Trent. "Besides, in case General Busby here decided to have somebody arrested for 'borrowing' that code book, I thought the less you knew the better."

"Well—er—now that it's turned out all right, we'll forget that little matter," said the general. "I'll tell Communications I took it. By the way, Mr. Crabb, here's your bankroll. We got it back from Worton when some Guardsmen caught him."

Crabb's mournful face brightened. "Well, that's fine. Eric, maybe we ought to give those Guardsmen a reward."

"No, no," put in Busby. "Matter of duty. Glad everything turned out all right. Worton confessed the whole thing, and we've a list of bundsmen and spies who were in on the scheme. G-2 will clean it up in short order."

"Naturally," said Trent. "It's been a pleasure to watch G-2 at work. The master touch and all that."

Busby reddened. "Now see here, Trent, I appreciate your—ah—assistance. Be glad to give you credit, at Washington—but we can't get around your making on; with that codebook, you know. Best way to cover it is to just let them assume I sent that message, don't you think?" Trent chuckled. "My dear General, I wouldn't rob you of the credit for the world. Come on, Mort, let's hop on to Chicago. The inner man is growling, and a thick steak is indicated."

But at the door he paused. "There's one thing that needs straightening. General. I believe you've overlooked it."

"What's that?" demanded Busby.

"Your toupee's on backward," said Trent. He was still grinning to himself when the Northrop roared up into the night.

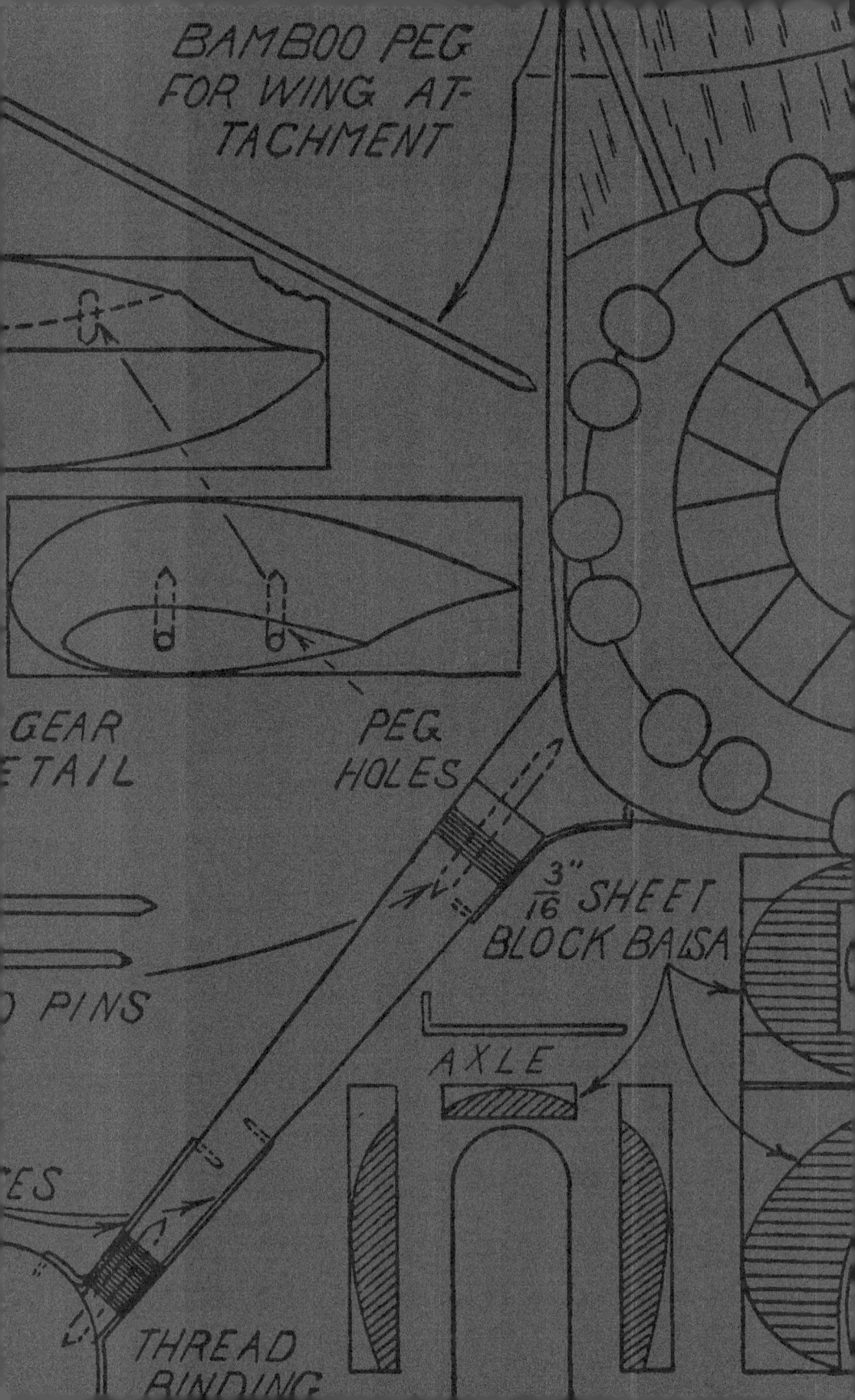

BAMBOO PEG
FOR WING AT-
TACHMENT

GEAR
ETAIL

PEG
HOLES

O PINS

$\frac{3}{16}$" SHEET
BLOCK BALSA

AXLE

ES

THREAD
BINDING

Television Tracers

CHAPTER I

The Green Skeleton

ERIC TRENT was half-way into the taxi when his hat gave a peculiar little jump and flipped over one ear. He climbed in beside Mortimer Crabb, gave his partner a whimsical grin.

"Very neat, Mort, but a trifle playful for one of your solemn demeanor."

Crabb's mournful countenance registered a gloomy suspicion. "What's this? What are you talking about?"

"That hat trick. My lessons in magic must be taking effect. I didn't see you make a move."

"I never touched your hat—" Crabb's long, sad face suddenly froze. "Hey, what's that up at the top?"

Trent took off his hat, a brand-new Homburg purchased late that afternoon on their arrival in Seattle. On the left side, an inch below the crown, was a small, neat hole.

"H-m-m," said Trent. "Hardly termites, that soon. Something tells me we have unsuspected friends in Seattle. Driver, it's worth five dollars if you put us somewhere else."

The driver had been staring back at the bullet-hole. The sound of the slug had been drowned by the passing cars.

"You said it!" he erupted. The cab shot forward, took the next corner on two wheels, roared ahead, and made another wild turn.

"That should be sufficient," Trent said drily, "unless it's Superman. Now suppose you zigzag to a spot known as 'Wing High,' if that happens to be on your general itinerary."

"Yeah, I know where it is," the driver said.

Trent sat back, his dark eyes faintly amused. He was a tall man, with something coolly audacious in his face. His almost black hair and close-clipped mustache gave him a slightly Latin appearance, a look that went well with his cosmopolitan air. But Eric Trent's blood was pure Yankee, and under that smoothly careless manner was a capacity for lightning action—a part of

which went back to his days as a magician's assistant, before he took up aerial globe-trotting as more suited to his devil-may-care existence.

"You may think it's funny, but I'm getting sick of it," grated Mortimer Crabb. He had a deep, rusty voice that sounded as though it came from the bottom of a well. "Isn't there any place in the world we can go without running into somebody who doesn't like you—or is that asking too much?"

Trent chuckled. "Mort, old bean, believe it or not but Seattle is one of the few places I've never been. I think that little token back there was meant for you."

CRABB'S over-sized Adam's-apple jumped up and down as the inventor gulped. "Me?" he said hoarsely. "Why should anybody want to take a pot-shot at me? I never did anything to—"

The taxi lurched to a stop, and the driver pointed to an areaway entrance to a basement-level taproom which had a flamboyant neon sign, "Wing High," flashing on and off.

"There she is. And if you ask me, it ain't the healthiest joint in town. But it's your funeral."

"Let's hope that's not too literally correct," Trent said amiably. He paid the man, waited until the cab had disappeared. "Just a second, Mort. Let's reconnoiter before we descend."

"What are we going in here for, anyway?" demanded Crabb.

"Because Captain Brennard left word at the hotel that he'd meet us here. Or at least the message was supposed to come from him. But I'm beginning to detect a piscatorial odor."

"I wish I'd never met you," Crabb said bitterly. "I haven't had a peaceful minute since then. Dragging me over to Europe just in time to get mixed up in a war. Getting chased out of every country we hit—"

"Better than getting hit before we were chased out. But this happens to be your affair. The Army Air Corps asked you to come out here and meet this Brennard chap from the Alaska experimental base. It seems somebody would prefer you didn't meet him."

"But why? It's purely a technical matter. Something went wrong with the television set I built for the Air Corps. They want me to check it over. Television's no secret, so why should anybody want to stop me from working on a set I built myself?"

"That," said Trent pleasantly, "is what I think we'll find out—very soon. Come on and if things start to get warm, let me handle the opening fireworks."

Crabb groaned, but followed him down the steps. The "Wing High" proved to be a second-rate cocktail lounge that more nearly deserved the name of bar-room. It was decorated, cheaply, with aeronautical effects—two or three old wooden propellers, an antiquated machine gun of World War days, and some panels ostensibly torn from captured German planes, but with suspiciously artificial bullet-holes. The waiters wore bell-hop type uniforms, with wings on the collars.

The lights were low and the air was filled with stale tobacco smoke. A squint-eyed head-waiter led Trent and Crabb past a row of booths, all filled, to a table at the end of the room, not far from a piano where a pimply-faced youth was rendering "Blueberry Hill" with the aid of a peroxide-blond violinist. A hulking waiter, with a seamy face and huge hands, came to take their order.

"One Manhattan," said Trent. "My friend doesn't drink, but you might bring him a couple of packs of gum. He's about worn out his present cargo."

As the waiter went to the bar, Trent saw him glance toward the semi-enclosed space near the kitchen door. Trent idly took a coin from his pocket. One side looked like an ordinary half-dollar; the other was a tiny mirror. He carelessly toyed with the coin a moment, then held it up as though inspecting it.

"Mort, are you acquainted with a small bald-headed gentleman about forty, with ears flat against his head and eyebrows that meet across the top of his nose?"

"Doesn't sound like anybody I know," Crabb said dismally. "Why, where is he?"

"Don't look around. He's back there near the side-entrance, to the right of the kitchen door, with a couple of gentry who look as though they'd cut each other's throats for the price of a beer. They seem quite interested in you—oh, oh! I think they're getting suspicious."

Trent flipped the coin into the air, caught it, put its mirror side down on the table. "Heads! You pay, old chap."

The squint-eyed man walked by, looked down at the table. Trent waited, pocketed the coin, and glanced toward the bar. The blond violinist stepped to one side of the piano, obstructing his view. She smiled at him, and Trent promptly got to his feet. The hulking waiter came by as he reached the piano, and Trent stopped him, took the Manhattan.

"Here, my friend," he said to the pimply youth, "you toss this one off while your fair virtuoso and I do a little close harmony. Waiter, another Manhattan."

He was on the piano stool before anyone could stop him. The waiter scowled, and the blond looked disconcerted. Trent ran his fingers over the keys, began to play "God Bless America." The blond violinist said curtly, "I don't know it well enough."

"How about this?" said Trent, gaily. He plunged suddenly into the Nazi "Horst Wessel" song. The blond stiffened, and he saw the bald-headed man near the kitchen jerk around, his mouth agape. He took his hands from the keys, but before he could get up there was an abrupt diversion. An Army Air Corps captain was striding toward Mortimer Crabb. The officer was a lean, middle-sized man with sandy hair and a determined jaw.

Trent could tell by Crabb's quick look of recognition that this was Captain Brennard. The Air Corps officer stopped at the table. After a hasty greeting he motioned for Crabb to come with him. The inventor looked at Trent, and Trent nodded carelessly, pointing to the second cocktail the waiter was bringing him.

FROM the corner of his eye, Trent saw the bald-headed man and the two shadowy figures near the door turn hurriedly to go out. He waited until Crabb and Brennard had reached the entrance, then briskly stood up, tossed a dollar bill onto the waiter's tray. "Here, Fritzy, that ought to cover the two Mickey Finns."

The waiter's jaw dropped. Trent turned swiftly to the rear. But before he could reach the side door the huge waiter came dashing after him, the squint-eyed man at his heels. Trent sidestepped the waiter's bear-like lunge. The kitchen door opened, and another waiter came out with a laden tray. With a lightning glance, Trent snatched a ketchup bottle and whacked it over the first waiter's head. The bottle broke, and ketchup flooded down over the man's face. The squint-eyed man leaped back, hand inside his coat.

Trent caught him neatly with a left hook to the chin, whirled, and was outside before the head-waiter had time to hit the floor. A black sedan was drawn up near an alley which ran back of the taproom. Trent raced up the steps to the street in time to see the bald-headed man and the two thugs trying to force Crabb and Brennard into the machine. He thrust his hand toward the .38 in his armpit holster, sprang toward the car. The Air Corps captain slumped inside the sedan, struck by a gun-butt, as Trent reached the machine. Mortimer Crabb had knocked the bald man off balance, was battling one of the gunmen. Trent triggered a swift shot as the other gunman spun around, pistol lifted.

The man sagged to his knees, and the other thugs scrambled into the car, where a third figure was crouched over the wheel. The sedan roared ahead, swung into the alley. Trent seized Crabb's arm.

"Come on—we've got to stop those devils!"

A taxi had pulled up across the street during the fight, with a coupe blocked behind it. But as Trent ran toward the coupe, the taxi driver threw his car into gear and sped away. The driver of the coupe was a timid-looking man with enormous tortoise shell glasses. As Trent wheeled, gun still in hand, he frantically dived from the car and ran down the street.

"The idiot!" said Trent. "I wasn't going to hurt him."

"How would he know?" panted Crabb, as he tumbled into the seat beside Trent. "You didn't look any too pleasant."

Trent hurled the coupe into the alley, accelerator jammed to the floor. The sedan was skidding into a cross-alley almost a block ahead. Trent took the same turn, with a wild screech of tires, raced two more blocks, scattering traffic as they charged through a downtown street. The fleeing car made another swift turn, into an alley Trent had not seen in time. He overshot, braked, and followed as quickly as he could.

Suddenly, out of the darkness ahead, something white loomed in the headlights. It was like a cloud of steam, but thicker, and it rolled and seethed furiously in the lights. Trent stood on the brake pedal, whipped the car aside. A fender grated against a brick wall, and they stopped.

"Go on through!" Crabb said tensely. "It's only a smoke-screen of some kind."

"It looks like gas," Trent muttered. "Close the windows and we'll make a dash through it."

The bumper was caught and it was several moments before Trent could pull it loose. As he stopped, shifting gears for a quick plunge, the swirling vapor thinned somewhat. A blurred shape appeared, ominously suggestive of a human form. It lay on the ground, twisted, motionless, with something horrible beginning to take shape as the lights penetrated that weird smoke.

"Good Lord!" Crabb said hoarsely. "It's—it's turning into a skeleton!"

THE GRIM lines of a skull began to emerge, with a frightful effect of something coming alive. Below it, Trent could see a bony arm and hand, then partially revealed ribs. The bones were a dull, mottled green in the lights, half obscured by the acrid smoke that still rolled upward. Sickened, Trent got out of the car and approached as close as he dared. Fragments of smoldering cloth and the man's shoes were all that remained when that strange dissolution was ended. Trent bent over, saw a tarnished, lumpy object on the skeleton's left hand.

"Class ring," he said, under his breath. "Mort, this was Captain Brennard!"

Crabb looked away, with a nauseated expression. "I knew—it must be. But how in Heaven's name Eric, could those fiends—"

"I don't know," Trent said thickly, as Crabb's words trailed off. "But we'll even the score, if it's humanly possible. Get in—we'll both be sick if we stay here another second."

"We can't leave him there," Crabb mumbled.

"There's nothing we can do for him now, poor devil," Trent said. "We'll go back to the hotel and I'll call G-2 at Washington. They'll have Army Intelligence in this area work with the Seattle police on it. I'll tell them to keep it as quiet as they can, while we go ahead on the other angle."

Crabb was silent a moment as Trent backed the car and turned. "What do you mean—other angle?"

"Fairbanks," Trent said. "The answer to this horrible thing lies, up there. I failed Brennard—I could have saved him if I'd moved faster. I'm going to follow this through."

"Count me in," the inventor said gruffly. "But I still don't see how my television set could be important enough to lead to—a thing like that."

"Did Brennard have time to tell you anything?"

"Only that he'd been delayed—he was on the liner *Alaska* that was grounded the day before yesterday on the shore of Elliott Bay, up in British Columbia. And when he got to the hotel he found that fake message—"

"The *Alaska*, eh?" Trent said thoughtfully. "Queer about that. Grounded on a clear, calm night—ran aground at full speed, and no explanation given."

"He said a seaman was reported to have seen a submarine almost in their path," Crabb told him. "Brennard said it might have been an attempt to sink the ship and destroy the set. He was bringing one of the two they had at the Fairbanks station. It was in the forward hold that was flooded, so the set was ruined."

A police-car siren moaned, somewhere nearby. Trent had turned into the first main street. He watched the cruiser go speeding by, toward the "Wing High" taproom.

"We'd better get rid of this car before we're picked up. We can lie low until we take-off, in case the driver describes us—but I think he was too scared for a good look."

Trent turned the machine into a dimly-lighted street and followed it until he found a suitable parking space. After the car had been backed in, they went on foot toward the hotel.

"How are you going to get a plane—through the Air Corps?" asked Crabb.

"No. Whoever's back of this might be watching the Army fields. We'll get G-2 to contact Navy, to give us a ship."

"We ought to tip off the police about that mob at the 'Wing High'," Crabb said grimly. "They'd round up those killers in short order."

"Maybe not," said Trent. "They'll expect that and keep out of sight for a while. Even if the police did nab them, they wouldn't talk. We'd still be in the dark about what's back of all this."

"I can't think of anything but Brennard. How did they do it? How could they turn a man into a skeleton in that short time?"

"Some powerful acid would do it— but they'd hardly risk carrying anything that deadly in a car. It must have been done some other way."

"I've got to stop thinking about it." Crabb was silent for a minute, then asked: "What was the idea of that act at the piano?"

"I had a hunch they were mixing me a knock-out. I wanted an excuse for turning it down without making it clear I suspected. And playing that Nazi song was a gag to find out if they were spies, as I thought. Don't worry, G-2 will have them covered after we flash word to Washington."

Crabb nodded slowly. "I know, Eric. Ordinarily, I'm not a vindictive person, but right now I'd like to get my own hands on the fiend back of that business."

"So would I," said Trent. "No death would be hard enough."

They were silent the rest of the way.

CHAPTER II

Blizzard Barrage

A**BOVE** and below the cruising Curtiss Navy SO3C-1 scout there was only a white world of snow, gradually thickening to a blizzard.

"All I hope," Mortimer Crabb said gloomily, "is that we haven't missed Alaska completely. Maybe we're headed for the North Pole."

"That's a fine compliment on my navigation," said Trent. "I flew you all over Europe and back, and never got you lost."

"You got me into plenty of spots worse than being lost," Crabb retorted. He peered out nervously into the snowy murk. "I haven't seen that other ship for ten minutes. Hope he's got enough sense to keep clear."

"I radioed him to fly at odd-number altitudes, if it got any worse," said Trent. "You were asleep—at least, I judge you were from the noise. I thought for a while the engine had burned out a bearing."

"All right, so I snore," Crabb said morosely. "I'm lucky to be able to do that, after a year and a half with you. It's a wonder I don't have perpetual insomnia."

"Forget the grouching," Trent said with a grin, "and give me the dope on that televisor. Is there any way I can pick up the radio part on this receiver?"

"No, it's a special wavelength. I called them Z-rays in my patent papers. They're higher than any frequency used in the States, except maybe in some experimental work."

Trent glanced at the clock, made an estimate of their position. "Why is the Air Corps using television up here at Fairbanks?"

"Well, that's the cold-weather testing station, and they wanted to try out a television-guide system, to bring pilots back to the field, even with snow blanking out the visibility. The idea was to hook it up with a radio-beacon, so they'd get a signal and also get a flash of conditions at the field—the ceiling and all. They hadn't got the transmitter finished, but two of my receivers were up there, and they were working on a special lightweight set to put in P-40's and Airacobras."

Trent shook his head. "I still don't see why anybody should get steamed up about it. But if it meant enough for some country to risk a war by sending a sub after the *Alaska*, it must be important."

"That might have been just a rumor," Crabb said.

"Maybe, but I'm inclined to believe it. Well, we're within sixty miles of Fairbanks, according to my figures. I'll call in and see what the ceiling is."

Trent switched on the transmitter. The message was half-completed when Crabb let out a yell.

A huge white eagle dived past above the ship, then turned and vanished in the blizzard.

"I thought birds didn't fly in snowstorms," ejaculated Crabb.

"I don't know about that," said Trent, "but I never saw an eagle that big before."

He stared out into the snow, then turned back to the transmitter. The operator at Fairbanks answered, and Trent gave their estimated position and time of arrival. Just as he switched the receiver off there was a blur of wings to the right and ahead. The next moment a trim fighter loomed up, a ship with the outlines of a Seversky P-35. On its wings was the rising-sun insignia of Japan.

The Seversky's guns blazed, and two more Japanese fighters whirled into sight. Trent backsticked, hurled the two-seater into a tight bank while he cut in his gun circuit. Over the Scout's blunt, smooth nose he saw the tilted wing of the first Nipponese ship. He pressed the gun-button, and the Brownings loosed a savage blast. The Seversky rolled wildly, almost collided with another fighter. Crabb flung a quick burst at the third ship from his rear cockpit guns, and the Jap's tracers twisted hurriedly aside.

The first Seversky came out of its roll nose down, went into a hasty zoom. Trent whipped the Scout onto its wingtips, poured a furious hail into the cowl of the Nipponese ship. There was a gush of oily smoke, then a spurt of flame which swiftly enveloped the fighter. As it plunged down through the snow, the two remaining Japs charged in fiercely. Tracers smoked into the turtleback, and bits of dural flew against Trent's shoulders as solid slugs went pounding through the metal section.

Crabb swung his guns dead-on as the nearest Seversky dived. The Japanese pilot sheered out at the last instant, and Crabb's fast-shifting guns raked the tail. The other fighter had pulled up after a burst that went into the deep belly of the Scout. Suddenly both the fighters banked, started to flee. Trent jerked around to see what had caused the swift change of course.

THE STRANGE eagle was swooping down toward the fight. As the Nipponese planes renversed, the mysterious white bird lurched around toward the SO3C-1. Trent rammed the stick forward, and the eagle whirled by overhead. As he pulled up, banking tightly, another plane appeared hazily through the blizzard. For a moment he thought it was one of the Seversky jobs, then he saw the SO3C-1 which the Navy had assigned as a special escort, at the request of G-2.

The white eagle was plummeting straight into the path of the escort plane. Trent saw the Scout skid madly, then a blinding flash hid everything for a moment. He circled, at half-throttle, saw the escort ship pitch down, with snow whirling eerily about it. It was an instant before he realized it was not snow, but a queer, whitish cloud....

"Eric!" Crabb shouted. "In Heaven's name—look!"

Some of the whitish vapor blew aside in the precipitous descent of the crippled ship. Trent had a glimpse of a shattered cockpit enclosure, of a face that was more like a skull. Then the escort plane pitched headlong into the blizzard—and was gone.

Trent looked back at his partner. Crabb was deathly pale.

"The same thing that happened to Brennard!" Crabb gasped.

Trent gazed down, shaken, at the spot where the Curtis had disappeared.

"You're right—it was the same thing. But there wasn't any white bird in that alley."

"You don't know. We didn't get there until it had happened—whatever it was."

Trent opened the throttle, set the Scout back on its course, his eyes tautly searching the whiteness about them.

"What do you think it was, Eric?" Crabb asked hoarsely.

"It couldn't be an eagle. No bird ever exploded like that. But how could it be—"Trent broke off, reached for the radio switch. Then he shook his head. The Japanese ships had appeared just after his call to Fairbanks, announcing their position. There was no use in risking another attack, though it seemed impossible now that anyone could, find them in this weather.

"I'll wait until we're a few miles from Fairbanks before calling in," he told Crabb. "Keep your guns ready, in case we happen to run into those Japs again."

But there was no sign of the Nipponese fighters, and after twenty minutes Trent called the Air Corps station. It took fifteen minutes more of careful maneuvering, with three attempted landings, before they came through under the ceiling and saw the field off to the left. Trent landed, taxied up to the hangar where a group of men in heavy coats and parka hoods waited.

Mechanics rolled the ship inside as soon as the engine went dead, and Trent and Crabb climbed out. One of the officers took a quick look at the bullet-scars on the ship. His swarthy face twitched back toward Trent.

"What happened? Where's your escort ship?" he asked with a tight-lipped precision.

Trent saw the group of staring mechanics beyond. "I'd rather explain inside. I'm Eric Trent, and this is Mortimer Crabb. I take it you're the C.O.?"

The other man nodded brusquely. "Major Palmer—glad to know you. Come along."

Three of the waiting men followed, from the hangar across to the office of the experimental laboratory. As they went into the warm hall, Major Palmer turned to the first of the trio, a big, genial-looking man.

"This is Mr. Christie—our chief civilian expert. And Captain McCabe, Engineer Officer—" nodding to a stocky, ruddy-faced officer who was taking off his parka. He gestured to the third man, a thin, wiry civilian, with a sallow face and intense dark eyes. "This is Mr. Howard—Christie's assistant."

The men shook hands. Palmer led the way into a nearby room, looked sharply at Trent. "All right, let's have it."

"It's not a pretty story," Trent said. "We ran into some Jap planes—but that's the least of it. I'd better start with—Seattle—I'm sorry to tell you that Captain Brennard has been murdered."

ALL FOUR men started. Trent went on, described what had occurred in Seattle. Palmer lost his brusque manner, sat down heavily at the desk.

"Poor Brennard," he muttered. "And to think I sent him to his death."

Trent eyed him a moment. "You don't seem surprised about the way he died."

The major slowly wagged his head. "It's already happened up here. One of our men died the same way. It was—ghastly."

"You said you were attacked by Japanese?" Christie asked. He had a slow, deliberate voice.

"Three Seversky fighters with Jap insignia," said Trent. "But here's something stranger than any air attack."

He told them about the mysterious white eagle, and the fate which had overtaken the escort plane crew. The four men looked at him, open-mouthed, then at each other.

"Preposterous!" Major Palmer said harshly. "How in hell could a bird—"

"I'm not saying how," Trent interrupted calmly. "I'm just telling you what I saw. Mort, you've a reputation with the Army. Maybe they'll believe you."

"It's just as Eric said," Crabb agreed, gloomily. "I know it sounds insane, but it's true."

McCabe turned to the major. "After all, we know what happened to Lowdray. Headquarters wouldn't believe us on that, either, till we sent the pictures."

The C.O. slowly nodded. "Lowdray was the man who was killed," he explained to Trent and Crabb. "It was the night when the first set went bad. Everyone else was at mess, and when we came back—we've been working at night—there was this green skeleton, out there in the hall. The door was open, and there was a charred spot on the floor. I thought at first it was somebody's idea of a joke—that it might be an old skeleton dug up from somewhere. Then the Medical Section checked the teeth, after we found Lowdray was missing. That's who it was—but how it happened, we've never had the slightest idea, until now."

"No clues at all?" asked Trent.

"Nothing. Sentries hadn't seen any strangers. But one of the television receivers was dead. Christie and McCabe and Howard worked on it three days without any luck. Then one night we found the other set had gone dead, too. That's when I sent word to Washington for you, Mr. Crabb. Headquarters thought we'd expedite things by having Captain Brennard take one set down to Seattle—maybe you'd have to take it back to your laboratory or something."

"I'd like to look at that other set now, if I may," said the inventor.

"It's almost time for mess," answered Palmer, "but that can wait. McCabe, telephone them to go ahead, that we'll be over later."

The captain made the call, and then they went out into the television-radio room. A motor was humming softly.

"What's that?" exclaimed Palmer. "Some one's left the television transmitter dynamo on."

"I guess I did that, major," said Howard. "I was running a test and then I heard the plane—"

"All right, shut it off so Mr. Crabb can check his receiver."

Mortimer Crabb went over to a workbench on which a compact television receiver had been set up. He peered at the cabinet.

"We transferred it from the original case," explained Christie, looking over the top of his glasses at Crabb. "Major Palmer wanted a small set capable of being used in a fighter—"

"I gathered that," Crabb said tartly. He looked in at the back of the set.

"If you ask me," offered Howard, bending to follow Crabb's gaze, "it's an inductive short."

"I didn't ask you, and keep your nose out of here until I can see what I'm doing." Crabb's mournful visage registered a growing resentment, and there was silence for a moment. Then Eric Trent chuckled.

"He's like a dog with a bone, gentlemen, when he starts tinkering with some gadget—especially one of his own pets. Best thing is to leave him alone."

"I'VE BEEN thinking about those Severskys," said Captain McCabe. His ruddy face had a serious look. "You know, Russia built some Severskys under license. They're our closest potential enemy—are you sure those ships had Jap insignia?"

"Positive," replied Trent. "But that could have been a fake. Judging from the Reds I've encountered, they wouldn't be averse to throwing the blame on Japan. Might even be glad to start a war between the Japs and us, so they'd have a freer hand in the East."

"There's been a lot of monkey-business up here in the Arctic," Major Palmer said in his thin, clipped voice. "We've had Intelligence reports of Jap and Red activity right across from the Aleutians—and plenty of evidence that the Nazis were behind the scenes."

"Not to mention losing a B-17," McCabe said grimly.

Palmer gave him a sharp look, then shrugged. "It's been a closely-guarded secret," he said to Trent and Crabb, "but you might as well know it—G-2 seems to have taken you into its confidence on everything else. We had two Flying Fortresses up here for tests—flying in sub-zero weather, testing instruments, new oxygen equipment, and so on at temperatures down to fifty below zero, along with some special surveys of the farther Aleutians. One day the Number One ship just didn't come back. No hint of trouble—radio communication okay up to an hour before they were due back—then silence. We sent planes over a wide area, but never a trace."

Trent took out a coin, absently juggled it. "The crews of those B-17's are hand-picked, aren't they?"

"Absolutely," said Palmer. "As it happened, there were some additional—"

"Humph!" growled Mortimer Crabb. "No wonder this thing didn't work. The rectifier circuit's been changed. Give me a soldering iron."

"But it couldn't be changed!" said Christie. "We took care not to break a single connection."

"Don't tell me you know my set better than I do," snapped Crabb. "I tell you it's been changed. Whoever did it made a clean job of it—even tarnished the solder so it wouldn't look fresh."

He set to work, and in fifteen minutes the circuit was changed back. As he switched on the receiver, the others crowded around the bench. Trent lit a cigarette, idly watching the ground-glass screen.

"Turn on that transmitter," ordered the inventor. "We'll make a reception check. One of you stand in front of the scanning beam."

Captain McCabe went over to the switchboard, but before he could turn on the transmitter there was a humming sound and then a flickering image came onto the receiver screen.

"What's that?" Palmer said, startled. "There's no other television transmitter in Alaska."

"That's what you think," Crabb said acidly. "Somebody's got one close enough to—" he stopped, and the C.O. gazed at the screen goggle-eyed.

"Impossible! Why, that's a televise of this base—taken from the air!"

CHAPTER III

Birds of Doom

*T*RENT whirled, snatched up a parka, and dashed for the hall, with the two Army officers at his heels. As he ran outside he heard a faint moaning sound somewhere up in the sky, but he could see nothing through the snow.

"The hangar!" he flung back at Palmer and McCabe. "The Scout's guns are still loaded."

A sentry helped them shove the SO3C-1 outside. Trent started to climb into the front pit, then he saw something sweep down through the snowy gloom. He scrambled into the rear cockpit, hastily swung the rear-guns. The blurred shape of an enormous white eagle showed for a moment. As the mysterious bird banked sharply, Trent's finger closed on the trigger and the twin fifties let go with a deafening roar. There was a bright flash, up in the snow, and a dull reverberation. Tiny fragments of something fell to the ground near the edge of the field, and a steamy vapor drifted down, spreading into a huge cloud, barely visible in the blizzard. Trent watched it settle beyond the hangar, sluggishly drift away, dissipating as the wind thinned it out.

"What in Hades was it?" Palmer said tensely, as Trent climbed out of the ship. McCabe spoke up before Trent could answer.

"It looked like a big white bird—I got a glimpse of it just before Trent hit it."

Men were running out of the barracks, and officers with hastily-donned parkas came out of the mess.

"Tell them what happened!" the C.O. ordered McCabe. "Have everyone stand by for emergency orders."

Trent stared up into the snow. "I don't hear any others, but you'd better have some gunners ready for action. The things make a humming noise—"

"I heard it," said Palmer. "It wasn't any bird. It's some kind of flying bomb."

He turned and dispatched the sentry to have gunners posted, then followed Trent back into the laboratory. Mortimer Crabb was at the entrance, bare-headed, shivering.

"Get inside, man!" said Palmer. "You can freeze in a hurry up here."

Crabb looked at Trent when they were inside. "I saw it. Another of those white eagles, but bigger than the first. They must be aerial torpedoes disguised as birds."

"What's more important is that television business," said Trent. He turned to Christie, who had come out into the hall. The big man was listening with an incredulous expression.

"Did you say that explosion was an aerial torpedo?" Christie exclaimed.

"If it wasn't, that eagle must have had a bad case of indigestion," Trent said. "Did you see anything else on that television screen after I went out?"

"The outline of the field building showed for a few seconds after that explosion," said Christie. "Then everything faded out slowly."

"I didn't notice that," said Crabb. "I was getting ready to dive into a bomb-proof. But there must have been a ship up there with a televisor it could lower on a cable."

They went back into the workroom and Crabb switched on the television receiver.

"Nothing on it," Howard said quickly. "I tried through the whole range."

"It might come back on," grunted Crabb.

"Cigarette?" Trent asked Christie, reaching inside his coat.

"No, thanks. I don't—Howard, have you gone mad?"

Howard had lunged toward a small fire extinguisher secured at the end of the bench. He spun around toward Mortimer Crabb. Trent's hand snaked out of his coat, the .38 in his fingers. But Christie wrenched the fire extinguisher out of the other man's hands, struck him a furious blow.

"Ach, Gott!" Howard groaned. He crumpled to the floor, lay there with his eyes closed. Crabb gaped at him.

"German—did you hear him, Eric?"

Palmer and McCabe came in before Trent could reply. They looked at the scene in astonishment.

"Howard—he tried to attack Mr. Crabb," Christie said huskily. "I still can't believe it—but he must be a Nazi spy."

"A spy?" rasped Palmer.

"He let out a yelp in German, just after Mr. Christie beaned him," Trent said coolly. "I think you've found the answer to the sabotaged television sets—maybe some other things."

"Howard was working on that B-17," interjected McCabe. "He could have planted a time-bomb or fixed it some way so the ship would be forced down over the Bering Sea."

CHRISTIE turned a distressed face to the C.O. "I had no reason to suspect him. He was sent out here after Military Intelligence selected him from others at the plant."

"Nobody's blaming you, Christie," began Palmer. He stopped as a guttural voice suddenly came from the television receiver.

"*Herr Kommandant,* we cannot establish contact with the torpedo… Liedner began a message, but it was broken off almost at once."

A flickering image appeared on the ground-glass screen, a shifting glimpse from the cockpit of a large plane. The scene took in a maze of instruments and then turned to include a blocky, worried face.

"The missing B-17!" McCabe blurted out. "The Germans have got it!"

"*Herr Kommandant,* this is Number G-11 identifying for reply, on wavelength Two," said the televised figure. The shadowy background of a Flying Fortress navigator's compartment showed behind him. The message was repeated, then the image abruptly disappeared. Almost immediately another scene replaced it, with two men seated at a desk in a small, windowless room with concrete walls. One of the men was a Japanese in naval uniform, the other a gaunt German in the tunic of the Luftwaffe. Behind the two was a third figure in civilian clothes. He had a dark, Slavic face.

"*Der Kommandant,* to G-11," the gaunt Nazi said curtly. "The torpedo was destroyed by gunfire at the Fairbanks base. You will prepare to—" the German broke off, as the Japanese muttered something and touched his arm. "Stand by, I will give you orders in a minute or two."

The screen went blank. Trent slowly laid down his gun, turned to look at Howard's still unmoving form.

"Liedner, eh? Major Palmer, you've the secret in the palm of your hand." He explained what the Germans had said. "Put the pressure on that squarehead and you'll get the secret of that hidden television station—and whatever the Japs and Nazis are up to."

"Don't think we won't work on him," Palmer said savagely. He started toward the prostrate spy.

"Stay where you are!" Christie ordered in a suddenly hard voice. He had Trent's gun, and as he backed away, covering them, he smiled mirthlessly. "You should have thought twice, Mr. Trent, before disarming yourself."

Trent's mouth opened, with a foolish look. "You—a spy, too?"

"Let us say an agent of the Greater Reich," Christie answered coldly. "Don't move, Palmer! Get your hands up, McCabe!"

There was a frozen moment when no one moved, then Christie's left hand closed on the fire extinguisher he had snatched from Liedner. He backed toward the door, the gun still leveled. Tiny drops of perspiration came out on his forehead, and Trent saw him feel underneath the rear end of the device.

"I think this act has gone far enough," Trent said pleasantly. He dropped his hands, leaped at the big spy. Christie frantically pulled the trigger. There was a click—and nothing else. Trent's fist thudded into the spy's face, and the man staggered back. With a swift movement, Trent jerked the fire extinguisher from his hand. Then Mortimer Crabb and the C.O. sprang in, seizing the spy's arms.

"You see, I did think twice," Trent grinned. "Long enough to unload that gun before I set my little trap."

"*Verdammt Schwein!*" raged the prisoner. "Liedner, you fool, do something!"

The sallow-faced spy was trying to get up, but McCabe had him collared in an instant. Liedner glared at the other captive.

"If you hadn't been so smart, knocking me out, this wouldn't have happened!"

"Trent would have shot you—he had his gun halfway out," snarled Christie. His glasses had fallen off and his formerly genial face was twisted with fury.

"They're coming back on the air!" Mortimer Crabb said hurriedly. He turned up the volume, and the scene at the unknown station reappeared on the screen.

"K-11," said the gaunt *Kommandant*, "we have changed the plan. Return to Viskya, and be ready to refuel and carry out a full-demolition attack on Fairbanks. Keep tuned for any relay-messages from Liedner or Reudemann. We will give them three hours to report. If they have not accomplished it by then, we will proceed with Plan Three."

THERE was a brief interval, then the Nazi in the B-17 answered. "G-11 acknowledging, proceeding to Viskya."

As the screen blanked again, Trent looked at the big spy. "So it's *Herr Reudemann.* Just a great big friendly cutthroat of *der Fuehrer's.*" He told the others what the *Kommandant* had ordered. Major Palmer's eyes darted to the clock.

"Three hours. We'll have every ship in the air—we'll show those dirty rats!"

"You'll never block them that way," Trent said calmly. "You're up against some devilish chemical gas that'll kill everybody on this base. Besides that, it will be dark by then and with this snow you'd never have a chance fighting them off."

"Then we'll evacuate the base," rapped Palmer, tautly.

Trent saw a surreptitious look pass between Reudemann and Liedner.

"We've missed the point of something here," he told the C.O. swiftly. "What if that attack is meant for all of Fairbanks, not just the base? And that Plan Three—it sounds like some big-scale move—perhaps a blitzkrieg."

Palmer turned pale. "A blitzkrieg against the whole Territory? Good Heavens—we haven't enough ships to meet any sizable force, especially if they use that hellish chemical."

"Where's Viskya?" Trent asked crisply.

"It's a Russian weather reporting station, just across the Bering Straits, near Cape Deslmef."

"That means the Reds are in on it, too. Either bribed or forced to let the Nazis and Japs establish a base there. That televised scene looked like an underground room. They've probably built up a secret base, subterranean hangars and quarters, to keep the word from getting around. The only way we can block them is to hit that base or their runways with a full load of bombs. They've got to have space cleared for taking-off, though they might be catapulting those aerial torpedoes."

Palmer jerked his head toward Reudemann. "Watch this big butcher, Trent, while I phone the guardhouse."

Trent had slid the magazine back into his .38. He snapped a cartridge into the chamber, covered Reudemann.

"All right, Mort, you can let our Teutonic friend loose now." He handed Crabb the fire extinguisher. "Hold that until Major Palmer can lock it in his safe. Watch out for that safety catch near the end, or we'll all end up like poor Brennard."

Crabb looked at the device, horrified. "You mean it's filled with that stuff?"

"I think that's fairly certain. It isn't any ordinary extinguisher— probably lined with glass or porcelain so the chemical won't eat through. Liedner lost his nerve and intended to do away with us and run for it. Big Boy Reudemann there had the same idea—only he was going to let his spy-pal die along with us. He'd have blamed it on us, most likely—"

"A guard squad will be over for these two," Palmer cut in, turning from the phone. "I ordered the Number Two Flying Fortress made ready, with a full bomb load. It's a desperate chance—how we can ever find Viskya I don't know—"

"Why not make our two playmates find it for us?" queried Trent, "Mort, how long will it take you to transfer that television transmitter and your receiver to the B-17? You can hook it up while we're in the air."

"Maybe half an hour or less," Crabb said after a moment. "We'll have to cut the transmitter in on the ship's 110-volt line, with a special transformer—but we could do that after we took off."

"What good will all that do?" demanded Palmer.

"When we get in range of Viskya, we'll put Big Boy in front of the scanning-beam," explained Trent amiably. "Mort can blur it a little, so it won't show any slight disgruntled expression. I know German, and I think I can fake Reudemann's voice enough to get by. I'll report that it was necessary to cut loose from Fairbanks and ask for a guide-signal, if they haven't got a radio-beacon."

"You *Schweinhund,* you'll never succeed with that trick!" fumed Reudemann.

"Then what are you so worried about?" grinned Trent.

The guard squad came in, took charge of the prisoners.

"Tie them securely and put them aboard the B-17," ordered Palmer. "An armed guard will be kept on them every second. McCabe, go rush the bomb loading. We'll get the television sets aboard as fast as we can."

"How far to Viskya?" Trent asked, as the prisoners were taken out.

"About six hundred and fifty miles. It's going to be a close squeeze, if they stick to that three-hour limit," answered the C.O. "I'm going to cable Seattle and have the Corps Area Commander warned about this. I'd radio the Navy, at Sitka, but I'm afraid the Nazis would hear, and set off the attack."

"You're right," said Trent. "It's a lone-wolf job—or lone-bomber, if you're going to be technical. They'd get suspicious if they heard more than one ship coming."

It was thirty-two minutes later when the huge Flying Fortress roared into the murky darkness and headed West, toward Bering Strait. The prisoners had been put in the crews' quarters, under guard. Mortimer Crabb and Captain McCabe set to work hooking up the two television sets in the navigator's cubby and the space behind it. Trent sat in the co-pilot's seat, beside a stolid-mannered first lieutenant named Good. After setting the course, Palmer disappeared aft. Trent plugged in on the radio hook-up, intermittently checked the signals from Fairbanks and the Juneau station, for which Palmer had arranged, as a cross-bearing check on their course.

Fully an hour and a half had passed and Crabb was almost finished with the televisor adjustments when Major Palmer came forward. He touched Trent's shoulder.

"Come on aft." His voice had a tense note. "I've finally broken Liedner down and he's starting to talk."

CHAPTER IV

Plan Three

T **RENT** followed back to the crews' quarters. A dim light was on. He saw Liedner, haggard and perspiring, over in one corner. Reudemann, gagged as well as bound, lay on the floor, with an armed mechanic grimly watching him.

"I had to shut up the big German," Palmer said harshly. "I promised Liedner he'd get consideration as State's evidence, if he came clean. I won't tell you what I promised him if he didn't."

"I'll tell—everything," Liedner said in a shaken voice. "Only don't let—him—at me." His eyes rolled toward the other Nazi, and Reudemann gave him a savage glare.

"Never mind him—talk!" snapped Palmer. "Go on about Crabb's televisor."

"The *Gestapo* stole the blueprints of his set, while he was in Europe," Liedner mumbled. "Germany wanted a television set with wavelength no one else was using, to put in observation planes. We thought Crabb was killed in France, and we went ahead and put a special small set in a flying torpedo, disguised as a bird. It worked and we made more of them. Then the Reich laboratories discovered, the corrosive-acid gas from nitric and sulphuric acid, and they put it in one of the torpedoes. They were afraid to use it on England for fear of reprisals, but it was kept in reserve. Then Hitler made Russia agree to Plan Three, for a sudden attack on the United States by Japan, Russia and Germany if it became necessary. He made Stalin give us a base at Viskya, for a blitzkrieg on Alaska, so the three axis groups would be able to seize it for an air and sea base against the Pacific Coast and Hawaii."

Liedner stopped, shivering under the murderous look Reude-mann gave him.

"Might as well go whole hog, *mein Freund*," Trent said. "He can't hate you any worse than he does now."

"Everything was about ready, in case *der Fuehrer* gave the order," Liedner continued unwillingly, "when Reudemann and I came to Fairbanks. We were planted in America four years ago, as radio engineers. When we got to Fairbanks and saw the Crabb Z-ray sets, we knew they would pick up the Viskya telecasts as soon as regular operations began. We warned Viskya and then sabotaged the sets. One of our agents smuggled us a container of the acid-gas in the extinguisher you saw, to get rid of anybody who learned the secret. Lowdray caught Reudemann one evening—"

"Forget that part," Palmer broke in. "What about this case? How many ships there? How many of those torpedoes?"

"Most of it's underground, except a launching platform for the torpedoes. I don't know, how many planes—there were two hundred and fifty a month ago, half of them bombers."

"Lord help us, if they ever get into the air," the C.O. told Trent. "They'd wipe out our Alaskan defenses at one stroke."

"This is Plan Three," Liedner said. "They expect to take Alaska in six hours—follow up the bombing by landing troops from transport planes. They've a shuttle schedule worked out, to put an army in the Territory within three days. Some of the troops are already massed at Viskya. After they've seized Alaska, they'll use it as an air base for raiding the air and naval bases and aircraft plants on the Pacific Coast."

Trent looked at the Air Corps major. "It sounds fantastic, but so did the blitzkriegs in Europe. I've a hunch they'll have Japan ready to attack at other points if this first attempt succeeds. It puts us on the spot to save the bacon."

"This is no time to be joking!" grated Palmer.

"Pulling a long face won't get us to Viskya any sooner." Trent turned back to Liedner. "About those torpedoes: I get the flying-eye idea. They flash back scenes of whatever they're over, or glimpses of planes in the air, to the control point—whether it's the base or the B-17. But what sets off the stuff, contact or radio?"

"Either one," mumbled Liedner. "The engineers back at Viskya transfer control to the stolen B-17 and it follows within thirty or forty miles, to keep in television range. They guide the torpedoes by Z-rays. And when they're over a target they can dive the 'birds' straight down and let them detonate when they hit, or they can aim one at a target and set off the charge any time. They, use the last hundred kilocycles in the Z-ray spectrum to detonate the charge that releases the acid-gas."

"I saw an exhibition today," Trent said with dry humor. "Somebody tried to hit our ship, but they got the other one by mistake."

"That was a small test-torpedo," Liedner said dully. "The regular ones are three times that big. They let loose enough acid-gas to cover a space three or four hundred feet square. It will go through any gas-mask, and it will kill a man in less than a minute, even diffused. If it hits him full strength, it—well you saw what it does."

THE RADIOMAN came aft just then, a young chap with alert blue eyes. The plug-in wires of his earphone helmet were dangling over one shoulder.

"What do you want?" demanded Palmer.

"Lieutenant Good sent me, Sir, to tell you we're only about 105 miles from Viskya. We've been riding a strong tail wind."

"Thank God for that," said the C.O. "Trent, we'd better use Liedner for that fake telecast. He'll say what we tell him."

The mechanic-guard turned to take Liedner's arm. Without warning, the radioman leaped at him from behind. A .45 butt thudded onto the guard's head, and as he fell the radioman spun around, covering Trent and Crabb. His face was pale and frightened.

"Get your hands up, both of you! Liedner, untie Reudemann."

A sick terror came into Liedner's eyes. He went down on his knees beside Reudemann, then made a desperate lunge at the radioman's knees. The young spy jumped aside, kicked him fiercely in the stomach, and Liedner collapsed with a groan. Trent snatched at the zipper of his heavy flying-suit, but before he could reach his gun the radioman had him backed against the bulkhead.

Reudemann had been chewing madly at his gag. He suddenly got it loose. "Keep them covered, Hans, and untie my right hand. I can unfasten the rest."

Hans hurriedly obeyed, and in another minute Reudemann was free. He seized the unconscious guard's pistol.

"I'll watch these two *Amerikaner* swine. Tie up Liedner; I've a score to settle with him later."

The young spy bound Liedner, hastily gagged him, and started to tie the mechanic.

"Let him go," snapped Reudemann. "He's clear out and we haven't time to waste. What kept you so damned long?"

"Lieutenant Good had me checking our position every five minutes after Trent came back here," Hans said defensively. "Before that, they had me helping with the televisor. It would have made them suspicious if I'd sneaked out."

"Then that message was true?" Reudemann said brusquely.

Hans nodded, nervously watching the passage. "We must be within twenty minutes of the base by now. And it's stopped snowing. They'd have an easy time with their bombing."

Reudemann's eyes narrowed as he looked at Trent and Palmer. "We're taking you two forward. If you try to warn them, you'll be killed. Wait—Hans, you'd better search Trent. Palmer doesn't have a gun."

As Hans stepped toward Trent, the C.O. made a frantic attempt to jump behind him and seize his pistol. Reudemann drove a furious blow at the major's jaw, missed, but caught him squarely in the throat. Palmer made an agonized, strangling sound and slumped to the floor.

"Fasten his hands behind him—use his belt!" grated Reudemann. "You'll have to gag him—he might come around in time to yell for the gunners."

Trent made no move, coolly waiting a better opportunity.

"Why not tie Trent and leave him here, *Herr* Reudemann?" Hans asked anxiously.

"We may need a shield, the first few moments up there," the big spy said callously. He took Trent's gun, forced him into the passage.

"Remember, no shots if we can help it!" he muttered to Hans. "I'll take McCabe and Crabb. You go for the pilot—and make sure he doesn't use his microphone and warn the gunners."

CRABB and McCabe did not look up until the three men were inside the shadowy control compartment. Then the inventor's jaw sagged and McCabe stood paralyzed for a moment as he saw Reudemann. Hans sprang past them, rammed his gun into Good's back. The pilot jerked around, froze.

"Switch on that televisor!" Reudemann rasped at Crabb. The inventor hesitated, with a taut look at Trent.

"Do what he says, Mort," Trent told him. "I'm afraid the game's up."

Crabb swore, turned to the small panel switchboard which had been laid against the navigator's desk. A flexible cable ran from the unit to the nearest 110-volt socket.

"Face around, all of you!" barked Reudemann, as the tubes warmed up. "Watch that pilot, Hans!"

Trent heard the dynamo hum, then Reudemann said swiftly, "R-51 calling *der Kommandant* at Viskya... R-51 calling der *Kommandant*—"

He repeated the call three times, then from the corner of his eye, Trent saw him switch on the television receiver. The scene in the underground headquarters came onto the screen, with a uniformed Nazi captain hurriedly giving up his seat to the gaunt-faced *Kommandant*.

"*Der Kommandant* to R-51. Go ahead!"

"I am in the other Flying Fortress, within fifteen minutes of Viskya," Reudemann said. Trent stared down at the flexible cable as the big spy moved a little closer to the scanning-beam unit. "The Americans intended to bomb Viskya, but we have seized the plane. Be ready to guide us in, and have men to take the prisoners when we land."

"*Lieber Gott!*" came the voice of the gaunt Nazi on the screen. "Are you sure you have them safely under control?"

"Absolutely," snapped Reudemann. "But Plan Three will have to go into operation at once. Get the entire force ready. I will explain when I land."

Trent's hands were raised, like the others. But as Reudemann reached out to cut off the televisor, he flicked his left hand down with a lightning motion and gripped the radioman's dangling head-set wires. Hans' gun roared as the sudden pull hauled him backward, and Reudemann whirled. Trent flung himself down, jerking the flexible cable up from the floor, as the big spy sprang at him. Reudemann tripped, and the .45 in his hand blasted deafeningly as he fell. The shot drilled the right cockpit window, and splintered glass gashed Trent's cheek. He brought down his stiffened hand on Reudemann's biceps in a swift jiu-jitsu blow.

Reudemann's numbed fingers contracted and he dropped the gun. Trent seized it and jumped up, but Hans was already on the floor, with Mortimer Crabb's ham-like fist smashing into his face.

"*Kommandant!*" Reudemann bawled wildly. "The Americans—we are captured!"

McCabe frantically cut off the televisor, but the damage had been done. As Trent switched on the receiver a scene of panic in the Viskya base became visible. The gaunt *Kommandant* was trying to call Reudemann back.

"R-51… R-51! What course—what altitude are you?" Then, as though realizing it was useless, he whirled to a small knot of Nazis and Japanese showing as blurred figures on the screen. "Get all planes ready for take-off! Have all torpedoes hoisted to platform level for—" one of the Germans sprang forward, obviously to reach the televisor controls, and the screen went blank.

One of the B-17 gunners came dashing into the forward compartment.

"What happened, sir?" he asked McCabe. "We heard shots—"

"Two spies!" McCabe said tensely. "We've got them—get back to your post. We're going in at Viskya—be ready for their pursuit!"

The ship nosed down, crookedly, and Good slid sidewise from his seat.

"Lieutenant Good—he's been hit!" exclaimed the gunner.

"You'll have to fly the ship, Trent," McCabe said as he eased Good to the cockpit floor and hastily bandaged his shoulder. "I've got to climb out there and handle the bomb-sight."

The gunner raced back to his gun-turret. McCabe crawled out to the bombardier's post in the nose, and Trent sent the B-17 down in a long, full-power glide for the secret base, while Mortimer Crabb covered the two Nazis.

"Don't worry about these two," he told Trent. "Say, where's Palmer?"

"Reudemann knocked him out—no time to think about that now," Trent flung back. The B-17 was roaring down through the dark Arctic night, with the air-speed needle climbing past 300, to 310, 325....

ABRUPTLY, a searchlight blazed up, ten miles ahead. Two more joined it, swung toward the hurtling bomber. As the B-17 streaked closer, now down to eight thousand feet, Trent saw two fighters, then a third, climbing at desperate speed. One of the turret-guns pounded, and McCabe let go a fiery blast from the guns in the nose. The base seemed to leap up at them in that thundering approach, and Trent saw other planes rolling out of a black maw in the earth. Then something white whirled up from a catapult platform.

Three Severskys raced in, tracers lancing at the B-17. There was a drum-roll from McCabe's fifties, and the nearest fighter burst into flames. One of the turret-guns aft caught the second, and it plunged down, its tail shot cleanly off. A burst from the third Seversky tore through the top of the pilots' compartment, riddled another window.

Then a whitish shape whipped through one of the searchlight beams, charging straight for them.

"It's a torpedo!" screamed Reudemann. "We're doomed—we're doomed!"

"Mort—cut in the televisor!" Trent shouted. "Roll your rheostat to the last tap."

There was one more frightful instant, with the deadly eagle-torpedo plunging at them head-on, and Reudemann's frenzied shriek filling the cockpit. Then the televisor went on.

A bright flash lit the sky, and the torpedo disintegrated directly ahead of the Flying Fortress. Trent shoved the controls down, in a desperate dive under the lethal white vapor that spread in their path. The B-17 screeched as he pulled out, and then he saw a vast whitish cloud enveloping the base below.

Mortimer Crabb's televised relay-wave had set off every torpedo prepared for operation!

The B-17's bombs hurtled down as the ship swept past, and Trent zoomed with the bomb-flashes luridly yellow behind. When, a few minutes later, he banked over the spot at two thousand feet, there was only a scene of chaos and ruin, with not a sign of life.

Trent wiped the blood from his cheek, sat back, relaxing his taut nerves. McCabe crawled back into the cockpit, then Trent saw him stare down at the floor. He turned. Reudemann lay there in a crumpled heap, motionless. Frozen on his face was a look of indescribable horror.

"He's dead," said Mortimer Crabb. "His heart must have stopped when he thought that torpedo was going to hit us."

Trent slowly nodded. "Maybe there's justice after all. I've heard of men dying from sheer terror. He must have gone through hell in those few seconds."

"Let's hope so," Crabb said grimly.

"Take Hans back and tie him up," said Trent. "He'll get his later—maybe a little slower. But he'll get it."

IT WAS seven o'clock in the morning, but the Arctic sky was still dark as midnight. Captain McCabe came into the quarters which had been assigned to Trent and Crabb, a satisfied look on his tired face.

"Lieutenant Good will pull through, and the major's going to be all right in an hour or so. I notified Washington by code, but they said to keep it quiet. With this thing blowing up in their faces, the Axis will be held off a while from attacking us, and they'd only say we started the war if we went ahead now."

"It's better this way," agreed Trent. "You have that sample of the acid-gas and they won't risk using it again."

"The country owes you two a big debt," said McCabe. "Too bad it has to be kept under cover."

"That's all right," Trent answered. "But there's a little matter of financial compensation."

"I don't think there'll be any kick on that," the Air Corps captain said, but he looked a trifle surprised.

"Humph!" said Crabb. He glowered at Trent. "First time I ever heard of you trying to gouge your own country."

Trent chuckled. "Never mind, old bean. I guess Uncle Sam can afford the price."

"The price of what?" said Crabb.

"A new hat," said Eric Trent. "I like mine without bullet-holes."

Donald E. Keyhoe

Dec. 12, 1961

YOUR comments about the Philip Strange stories are very much appreciated, also what you said about Dick Knight. I had almost forgotten about Knight, but I remember the stories now, of course. It has been a long time since I did any fiction like that—or any fiction at all, for that matter—but I hope to get back to it before long. Not the action adventure type so much, but *some* action, and perhaps some humor.

I'm sorry that none of those stories ever were put into book from: I'd like to have a permanent record of them myself, though I might not read all the old yarns. I do have a few I saved for samples, when I had to get rid of a lot of material in my file cases, but they don't total more than a dozen stories. I must have thrown away at least 300 magazines. I don't have and before August, 1936, the date you mention, but I know I was writing for *Flying Aces* as far back as 1929.

Now that you brought back the memories, I think I'll look over two or three of those earlier stories, to see if I have improved or slipped.

Sincerely yours,
Maj. Donald E. Keyhoe,
USMC, Ret.